CUMBRIA LIBRARIES

D0333715

THE
STRANGLED
QUEEN

BY MAURICE DRUON

The Accursed Kings

The Iron King

The Strangled Queen

The Poisoned Crown

The Royal Succession

The She-Wolf

The Lily and the Lion

The King Without a Kingdom

THE
STRANGLED
QUEEN

Book Two of The Accursed Kings

MAURICE DRUON

Translated from French by
Humphrey Hare

HarperCollins*Publishers*

HarperCollins*Publishers*
77–85 Fulham Palace Road,
Hammersmith, London w6 8jb

www.harpercollins.co.uk

First published in Great Britain by Rupert Hart-Davis 1956
Century edition 1985
Arrow edition 1987

Published by Harper*Voyager*
An imprint of HarperCollins*Publishers* 2013

I

Copyright © Maurice Druon 1955

Maurice Druon asserts the moral right to
be identified as the author of this work

A catalogue record for this book
is available from the British Library

ISBN: 978-0-00-749127-8

This novel is entirely a work of fiction.
The names, characters and incidents portrayed in it are
the work of the author's imagination. Any resemblance to
actual persons, living or dead, events or localities is
entirely coincidental.

Printed and bound in Great Britain by
Clays Ltd, St Ives plc

All rights reserved. No part of this publication may be
reproduced, stored in a retrieval system, or transmitted,
in any form or by any means, electronic, mechanical,
photocopying, recording or otherwise, without the prior
permission of the publishers.

MIX
Paper from
responsible sources
FSC
www.fsc.org   **FSC® C007454**

FSC is a non-profit international organisation established
to promote the responsible management of the world's forests.
Products carrying the FSC label are independently certified
to assure consumers that they come from forests that are managed
to meet the social, economic and ecological needs
of present and future generations.

Find out more about HarperCollins and the environment at
www.harpercollins.co.uk/green

'History is a novel that has been lived'
E. & J. DE GONCOURT

Foreword

GEORGE R.R. MARTIN

Over the years, more than one reviewer has described my fantasy series, *A Song of Ice and Fire*, as historical fiction about history that never happened, flavoured with a dash of sorcery and spiced with dragons. I take that as a compliment. I have always regarded historical fiction and fantasy as sisters under the skin, two genres separated at birth. My own series draws on both traditions . . . and while I undoubtedly drew much of my inspiration from Tolkien, Vance, Howard, and the other fantasists who came before me, *A Game of Thrones* and its sequels were also influenced by the works of great historical novelists like Thomas B. Costain, Mika Waltari, Howard Pyle . . . and Maurice Druon, the amazing French writer who gave us the *The Accursed Kings*, seven splendid novels that chronicle the downfall of the Capetian kings and the beginnings of the Hundred Years War.

Druon's novels have not been easy to find, especially in English translation (and the seventh and final volume was never translated into English at all). The series has *twice* been made into a television series in France, and both versions are available on DVD ... but only in French, undubbed, and without English subtitles. Very frustrating for English-speaking Druon fans like me.

The Accursed Kings has it all. Iron kings and strangled queens, battles and betrayals, lies and lust, deception, family rivalries, the curse of the Templars, babies switched at birth, she-wolves, sin, and swords, the doom of a great dynasty ... and all of it (well, most of it) straight from the pages of history. And believe me, the Starks and the Lannisters have nothing on the Capets and Plantagenets.

Whether you're a history buff or a fantasy fan, Druon's epic will keep you turning pages. This was the original game of thrones. If you like *A Song of Ice and Fire*, you will love *The Accursed Kings*.

George R.R. Martin

Author's Acknowledgements

I am most grateful to Georges Kessel, José-André Lacour, Gilbert Sigaux and Pierre de Lacretelle for their assistance in gathering material for this book; to Christiane Grémillon for help in compiling it; and to the *Bibliothèque Nationale* for indispensable aid in research.

Contents

Contents

Part Two: Dog Eats Dog

Part Three: The Road to Montfaucon

The Characters in this Book

THE KING OF FRANCE AND NAVARRE:
LOUIS X, called The Hutin, son of Philip IV, the Fair, great-grandson of Saint Louis, aged 25.

HIS BROTHERS:
MONSEIGNEUR PHILIPPE, Count of Poitiers, a peer of France, aged 21.
MONSEIGNEUR CHARLES, Count of La Marche, aged 20.

HIS UNCLES:
MONSEIGNEUR CHARLES, Count of Valois, titular Emperor of Constantinople, Count of Romagna, peer of France, aged 44.
MONSEIGNEUR LOUIS, Count of Evreux, aged about 41.

HIS WIFE:
MARGUERITE, daughter of the Duke of Burgundy, grand-daughter of Saint Louis, aged 21.

HIS DAUGHTER:

JEANNE OF FRANCE AND NAVARRE, aged 3.

HIS SISTER-IN-LAW:

BLANCHE, wife of Charles of La Marche, daughter of the Count Palatine of Burgundy and of Mahaut, Countess of Artois, aged about 19.

THE ARTOIS BRANCH DESCENDED FROM

A BROTHER OF SAINT LOUIS:

ROBERT III OF ARTOIS, Lord of Conches, Count of Beaumont-le-Roger, aged 27.

THE BRANCH OF ANJOU-SICILY DESCENDED FROM

ANOTHER BROTHER OF SAINT LOUIS:

MARIE OF HUNGARY, Queen of Naples, widow of Charles II of Naples, mother of the Kings Robert of Naples and Charles of Hungary, aged about 70.

CLÉMENCE OF HUNGARY, her granddaughter, daughter of Charles Martel and sister of Charobert, King of Hungary, aged 22.

THE BROTHERS MARIGNY:

ENGUERRAND, Coadjutor of King Philip the Fair and Rector-General of the kingdom, aged 49.

JEAN, Archbishop of Sens and Paris, aged about 35.

THE LOMBARDS:

SPINELLO TOLOMEI, a Siennese banker living in Paris, Captain-General of the Lombard Companies, aged about 60.

GUCCIO BAGLIONI, his nephew, aged 18.

SIGNOR BOCCACCIO, traveller for the Bardi Company.

THE STRANGLED QUEEN

THE CRESSAY FAMILY:

DAME ELIABEL, widow of the Squire of Cressay, aged about 40.

PIERRE and JEAN, her sons, aged about 20 and 22.

MARIE, her daughter, aged 16.

AND THESE:

EUDELINE, Louis X's mistress, aged about 32.

HUGUES DE BOUVILLE, First Chamberlain to King Philip the Fair.

ALAIN DE PAREILLES, Captain-General of the Archers.

JACQUES DUÈZE, Bishop of Porto, Cardinal of the Curia, aged 70.

ROBERT BERSUMÉE, Captain of Château-Gaillard, aged 35.

ROBERTO ODERISI, a Neapolitan painter, pupil of Giotto.

All the above are historical names, as are those of the barons, justiciars, chamberlains, members of the Council, chancellors, the Abbot of Saint-Denis and the great officers of the Crown; all these people really existed. The only imaginary names are those of a few extras, of whom no trace can be found, such as Robert of Artois's servant and the Provost of Montfort-l'Amaury.

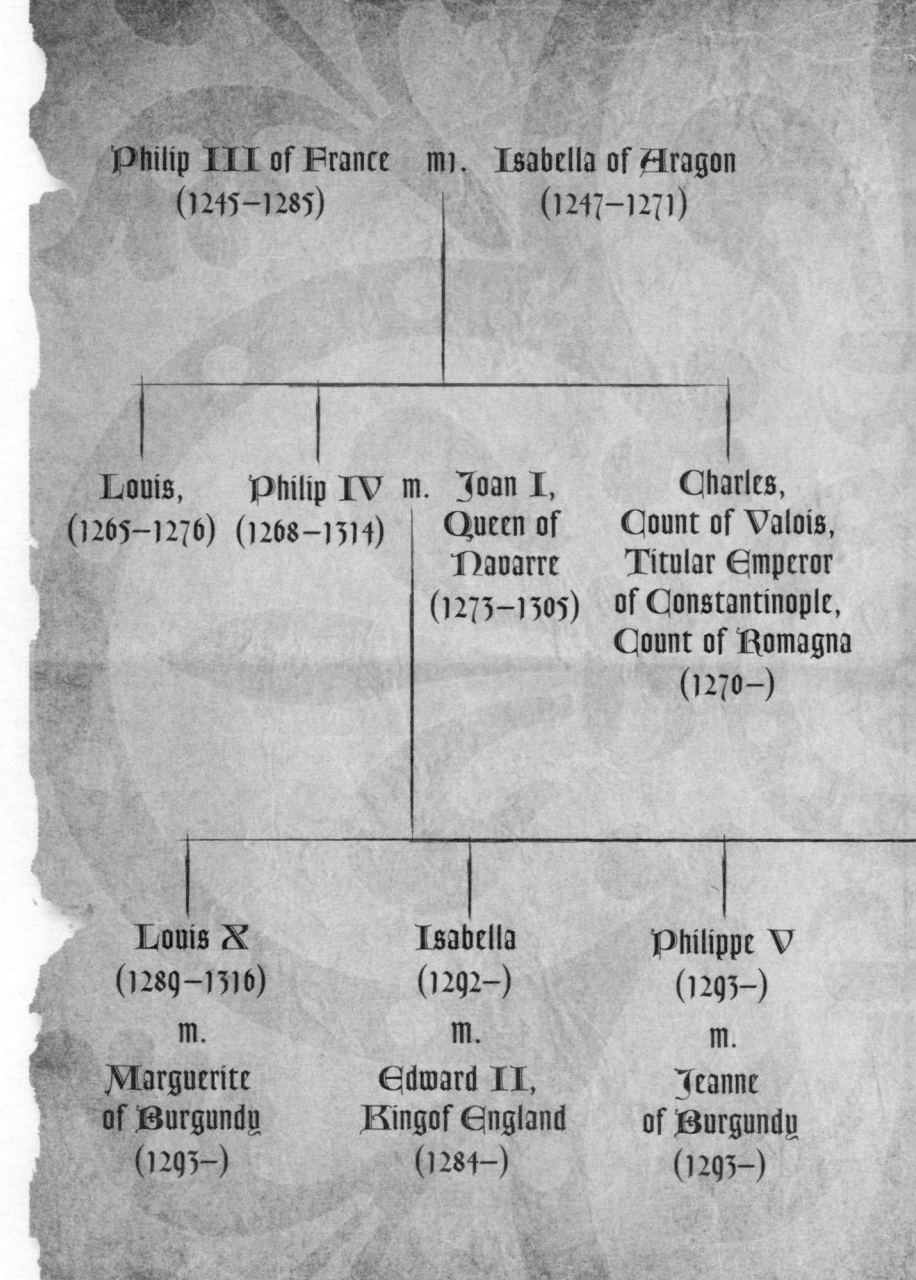

Philip III of France   m).   Isabella of Aragon
(1245–1285)   (1247–1271)

Louis,   Philip IV m. Joan I,   Charles,
(1265–1276) (1268–1314)   Queen of   Count of Valois,
                            Navarre   Titular Emperor
                            (1273–1305)   of Constantinople,
                                            Count of Romagna
                                            (1270–)

Louis X   Isabella   Philippe V
(1289–1316)   (1292–)   (1293–)

m.   m.   m.

Marguerite   Edward II,   Jeanne
of Burgundy   King of England   of Burgundy
(1293–)   (1284–)   (1293–)

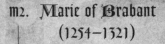

m2. Marie of Brabant
(1254–1321)

Louis Capet,
Count of Evereux
(1276–)

Blanche
(1278–1305)

Margaret
of France
(1282–)

Charles IV
(1294–)
m.
Blanche
of Burgundy
(1296–)

The
House of
Capet 1314

Prologue

On the 29th November 1314, two hours after vespers, twenty-four couriers, all dressed in black and wearing the emblems of France, passed out of the gate of the Château of Fontaylebleu at full gallop and disappeared into the forest. The roads were covered with snow; the sky was more sombre than the earth; darkness had fallen, or rather it had remained constant since the evening before.

The twenty-four couriers would have no rest before morning, and would gallop onwards all next day, all the following days, some towards Flanders, some towards Angoumois and Guyenne, some towards Dole in the Comté, some towards Rennes and Nantes, some towards Toulouse, some towards Lyons, Aigues-Mortes and Marseilles, awakening bailiffs, provosts and seneschals, to announce in town and village throughout the kingdom that King Philip IV, called the Fair, was dead.

All along the roads the knell tolled out in dark steeples, a wave of sonorous, sinister sound spreading ever further till it reached all the frontiers of the kingdom.

After twenty-nine years of stern rule, the Iron King was dead of a cerebral haemorrhage at the age of forty-six. It had occurred during an eclipse of the sun, which had spread a deep shadow over the land of France.

Thus, for the third time, the curse laid eight months earlier by the Grand Master of the Templars from the middle of a flaming pyre was fulfilled.*

King Philip, stern, haughty, intelligent and secretive, had reigned with such competence and so dominated his period that, upon this evening, it seemed that the heart of the kingdom had ceased to beat.

But nations never die of the death of a man, however great he may have been; their birth and their death derive from other causes.

The name of Philip the Fair would glow down the centuries only by the flicker of the faggots he had lighted beneath his enemies and the glitter of the gold he had seized. It would quickly be forgotten that he had curbed the powerful, maintained peace in so far as it was possible, reformed the law, constructed fortresses that the land might be cultivated in their shelter, united provinces, convoked assemblies of the middle class so that it might speak its mind, and watched unremittingly over the independence of France.

Hardly had his hands grown cold, hardly had the great power of his will become extinguished, than private interest, disappointed ambition, and the thirst for honours and wealth began to proclaim their presence.

---

* See *The Iron King*.

Two parties were in opposition, battling mercilessly for power: on the one hand, the clan of the reactionary Barons, at its head the Count of Valois, titular Emperor of Constantinople and brother of Philip the Fair; on the other, the clan of the high administration, at its head Enguerrand de Marigny, first Minister and Coadjutor of the dead king.

A strong king had been required to avoid or hold in balance the conflict which had been incubating for many months. And now the twenty-five-year-old prince, Monseigneur Louis, already King of Navarre, who was succeeding to the throne, seemed ill-endowed for sovereignty; his reputation was that, merely, of a cuckolded husband and whatever could be learned from his melancholy nickname of The Hutin, The Headstrong.

His wife, Marguerite of Burgundy, the eldest of the Princesses of the Tower of Nesle, had been imprisoned for adultery, and her life was, curiously enough, to be a stake in the interplay of the rival factions.

But the cost of faction, as always, was to be the misery of the poor, of those who lacked even the dreams of ambition. Moreover, the winter of 1314–15 was one of famine.

PART ONE

THE DAWN OF
A REIGN

The Prisoners of Château-Gaillard

BUILT SIX HUNDRED FEET up upon a chalky spur above the town of Petit-Andelys, Château-Gaillard both commanded and dominated the whole of Upper Normandy.

At this point the river Seine describes a large loop through rich pastures; Château-Gaillard held watch and ward above the river for twenty miles up and down stream.

Today the ruins of this formidable citadel can still startle the eye and defy the imagination. With the Krak des Chevaliers in the Lebanon, and the towers of Roumeli-Hissar on the Bosphorus, it remains one of the most imposing relics of the military architecture of the Middle Ages.

Before these monuments, constructed to make conquest good or threaten empire, the imagination is obsessed by the men, separated from us by no more than fifteen or twenty generations, who built them, used them, lived in them, and sacked them.

At the period of this story, Château-Gaillard was no more

than a hundred and twenty years old. Richard Cœur-de-Lion had built it in two years, in defiance of treaties, to defy the King of France. Seeing it finished, standing high upon its cliff, its freshly hewn stone white upon its two curtain walls, its outer works well advanced, its portcullises, battlements, thirteen towers, and huge, two-storied keep, he had cried: 'Oh, what a gallant [*gaillard*] castle!'

Ten years later Philip Augustus took it from him, together with the whole land of Normandy.

Since then Château-Gaillard had no longer served a military purpose and had become a royal prison.

Important state criminals were confined there, prisoners whom the King wished to preserve alive but incarcerate for life. Whoever crossed the drawbridge of Château-Gaillard had little chance of ever re-entering the world.

By day crows croaked upon its roofs; by night wolves howled beneath its walls. The only exercise permitted the prisoners was to walk to the chapel to hear Mass and return to their tower to await death.

Upon this last morning of November 1314, Château-Gaillard, its ramparts and its garrison of archers were employed merely in guarding two women, one of twenty-one years of age, the other of eighteen, Marguerite and Blanche of Burgundy, two cousins, both married to sons of Philip the Fair, convicted of adultery with two young equerries and condemned to life-imprisonment as the result of the most resounding scandal that had ever burst upon the Court of France.[1]*

---

* The numbers appearing in the text refer to the historical notes at the end of the book.

The chapel was inside the inner curtain wall. It was built against the natural rock; its interior was dark and cold; the walls had few openings and were unadorned.

Before the choir were placed three seats only: two on the left for the Princesses, one on the right for the Captain of the Fortress.

At the rear of the chapel the men-at-arms stood in their ranks, manifesting an air of boredom similar to the one they wore when engaged upon the fatigue of foraging.

'My brothers,' said the Chaplain, 'today we must pray with peculiar fervour and solemnity.'

He cleared his throat and hesitated a moment, as if concerned at the importance of what he had to announce.

'The Lord God has called to himself the soul of our much-beloved King Philip,' he went on. 'This is a profound tragedy for the whole kingdom.'

The two Princesses turned towards each other faces shrouded in hoods of coarse brown cloth.

'May those who have done him injury or wrong repent of it in their hearts,' continued the Chaplain. 'May those who had some grievance against him when he was alive, pray for that mercy for him of which every man, great or small, has equal need at his death before the tribunal of our Lord . . .'

The two Princesses had fallen on their knees, bending their heads to hide their joy. No longer did they feel the cold, no longer the pain and grief; a great surge of hope rose within them; and had the idea of praying to God crossed their minds, it would but have been to thank Him for delivering them from their terrible father-in-law. It was the first good news that had reached them from the outside world in all the seven months of their imprisonment in Château-Gaillard.

The men-at-arms, at the back of the chapel, whispered together, questioning each other in low voices, shuffling their feet, beginning to make too much noise.

'Shall we be given a silver penny each?'

'Why, because the King is dead?'

'It's usual, at least I'm told so.'

'No, you're wrong, not for his death; only, perhaps, for the coronation of the next one.'

'And what's the new king going to call himself?'

'Monsieur Saint Louis was the ninth; obviously this one will call himself Louis X.'

'Do you think he'll go to war so that we can move around a bit?'

The Captain of the Fortress turned about and shouted harshly, 'Silence!'

He too had his worries. The elder of the prisoners was the wife of Monseigneur Louis of Navarre, who was to become king today. 'So I am now in the position of being gaoler to the Queen of France,' he thought.

Being goaler to royal personages can never be a situation of much comfort; and Robert Bersumée owed some of the worst moments of his life to these two convicted criminals who had arrived, their heads shaven, towards the end of April, in black-draped wagons, escorted by a hundred archers under the command of Messire Alain de Pareilles. What anxiety and worry he had endured to set against the paltry satisfaction of his vanity! They were two young women, so young that he could not help pitying them despite their sin. They were too beautiful, even beneath their shapeless robes of rough serge,

6

for it to be possible to avoid some emotion at the sight of them day after day for seven months. Supposing they seduced some sergeant of the garrison, supposing they escaped, or one of them hanged herself, or they succumbed to some fatal disease, or again supposing their fortunes revived – for could one ever tell what might not happen in Court affairs? It would be he who was always in the wrong, culpable of being too harsh or too weak, and none of it would help him to promotion. Moreover, like the Chaplain, the prisoners and the men-at-arms themselves, he had no wish to finish his days and his career in a fortress battered by the winds, drenched by the mists, built to accommodate two thousand soldiers and which now held no more than one hundred and fifty, above a valley of the Seine from which war had long ago retreated.

'The Queen of France's gaoler,' the Captain of the Fortress repeated to himself; 'it needed but that.'

No one was praying; everyone pretended to follow the service while thinking only of himself.

'*Requiem æternam dona eis domine,*' the Chaplain intoned.

He was thinking with fierce jealousy of priests in rich chasubles at that moment singing the same notes beneath the vaults of Notre-Dame. A Dominican in disgrace, who had, upon taking orders, dreamed of being one day Grand Inquisitor, he had ended as a prison chaplain. He wondered whether the change of reign might bring him some renewal of favour.

'*Et lux perpetua luceat eis,*' responded the Captain of the Fortress, envying the lot of Alain de Pareilles, Captain-General of the Royal Archers, who marched at the head of every procession.

'*Requiem æternam* ... So they won't even issue us with an extra ration of wine?' murmured Private Gros-Guillaume to Sergeant Lalaine.

But the two prisoners dared not utter a word; they would have sung too loudly in their joy.

Certainly, upon that day, in many of the churches of France, there were people who sincerely mourned the death of King Philip, without perhaps being able to explain precisely the reasons for their emotion; it was simply because he was the King under whose rule they had lived, and his passing marked the passing of the years. But no such thoughts were to be found within the prison walls.

When Mass was over, Marguerite of Burgundy was the first to approach the Captain of the Fortress.

'Messire Bersumée,' she said, looking him straight in the eye, 'I wish to talk with you upon matters of importance which also concern yourself.'

The Captain of the Fortress was always embarrassed when Marguerite of Burgundy looked directly at him and on this occasion he felt even more uneasy than usual.

He lowered his eyes.

'I shall come to speak with you, Madam,' he replied, 'as soon as I have done my rounds and changed the guard.'

Then he ordered Sergeant Lalaine to accompany the Princesses, recommending him in a low voice to behave with particular correctness.

The tower in which Marguerite and Blanche were confined had but three high, identical, circular rooms, placed one above the other, each with hearth and overmantel and, for ceiling, an eight-arched vault; these rooms were connected by a spiral staircase constructed in the thickness of the wall. The ground-floor room was permanently occupied by a detachment of their guard – a guard which caused Captain Bersumée such anxiety that he had it relieved every six hours in continuous fear that it might be suborned, seduced or outwitted. Marguerite lived in the first-floor room and Blanche on the second floor. At night the two Princesses were separated by a heavy door closed halfway up the staircase; by day they were allowed to communicate with each other.

When the sergeant had accompanied them back, they waited till every hinge and lock had creaked into place at the bottom of the stairs.

Then they looked at each other and with a mutual impulse fell into each other's arms crying. 'He's dead, dead.'

They hugged each other, danced, laughed and cried all at once, repeating ceaselessly, 'He's dead!'

They tore off their hoods and freed their short hair, the growth of seven months.

Marguerite had little black curls all over her head, Blanche's hair had grown unequally, in thick locks like handfuls of straw. Blanche ran her hand from her forehead back to her neck and, looking at her cousin, cried, 'A looking-glass! The first thing I want is a looking-glass! Am I still beautiful, Marguerite?'

She behaved as if she were to be released within the hour and had now no concern but her appearance.

'If you ask me that, it must be because I look so much older myself,' said Marguerite.

'Oh no!' Blanche cried. 'You're as lovely as ever!'

She was sincere; in shared suffering change passes un-
noticed. But Marguerite shook her head; she knew very well
that it was not true.

And indeed the Princesses had suffered much since the
spring: the tragedy of Maubuisson coming upon them in the
midst of their happiness; their trial; the appalling death of
their lovers, executed in their presence in the Great Square
of Pontoise; the obscene shouts of the populace massed on
their route; and after that half a year spent in a fortress; the
wind howling among the eaves; the stifling heat of summer
reflected from the stone; the icy cold suffered since autumn
had begun; the black buckwheat gruel that formed their
meals; their shirts, rough as though made of hair, and which
they were allowed to change but once every two months; the
window narrow as a loophole through which, however you
placed your head, you could see no more than the helmet of
an invisible archer pacing up and down the battlements –
these things had so marked Marguerite's character, and she
knew it well, that they must also have left their mark upon
her face.

Perhaps Blanche with her eighteen years and curiously
volatile character, amounting almost to heedlessness, which
permitted her to pass instantaneously from despair to an
absurd optimism – Blanche, who could suddenly stop weeping because a bird was singing beyond the wall, and say
wonderingly, 'Marguerite! Do you hear the bird?' – Blanche,
who believed in signs, every kind of sign, and dreamed
unceasingly as other women stitch, Blanche, perhaps, if she
were freed from prison, might recover the complexion, the
manner and the heart of other days; Marguerite, never. There

was something broken in her that could never be mended.

Since the beginning of her imprisonment she had never shed so much as a single tear; but neither had she ever had a moment of remorse, of conscience or of regret.

The Chaplain, who confessed her every week, was shocked by her spiritual intransigence.

Not for an instant had Marguerite admitted her own responsibility for her misfortunes; not for an instant had she admitted that, when one is the granddaughter of Saint Louis, the daughter of the Duke of Burgundy, Queen of Navarre and destined to succeed to the most Christian throne of France, to take an equerry for lover, receive him in one's husband's house, and load him with gaudy presents, constituted a dangerous game which might cost one both honour and liberty. She felt that she was justified by the fact that she had been married to a prince whom she did not love, and whose nocturnal advances filled her with horror.

She did not reproach herself with having acted as she had; she merely hated those who had brought her disaster about; and it was upon others alone that she lavished her despairing anger: against her sister-in-law, the Queen of England, who had denounced her, against the royal family of France who had condemned her, against her own family of Burgundy who had failed to defend her, against the whole kingdom, against fate itself and against God. It was upon others that she wished so thirstily to be avenged when she thought that, on this very day, she should have been side by side with the new king, sharing in power and majesty, instead of being imprisoned, a derisory queen, behind walls twelve feet thick.

Blanche put her arm round her neck.

'It's all over now,' she said. 'I'm sure, my dear, that our misfortunes are over.'

'They are only over,' replied Marguerite, 'upon the condition that we are clever, and that quickly.'

She had a plan in mind, thought out during Mass, whose outcome she could not yet clearly envisage. Nevertheless she wished to turn the situation to her own advantage.

'You will let me speak alone with that great lout of a Bersumée, whose head I should prefer to see upon a pike than upon his shoulders,' she added.

A moment later the locks and hinges creaked at the base of the tower.

The two women put their hoods on again. Blanche went and stood in the embrasure of the narrow window; Marguerite, assuming a royal attitude, seated herself upon the bench which was the only seat in the room. The Captain of the Fortress came in.

'I have come, Madam, as you asked me to,' he said.

Marguerite took her time, looking him straight in the eye.

'Messire Bersumée,' she asked, 'do you realize whom you will be guarding from now on?'

Bersumée turned his eyes away, as if he were searching for something in the room.

'I know it well, Madam, I know it well,' he replied, 'and I have been thinking of it ever since this morning, when the courier woke me on his way to Criquebœuf and Rouen.'

'During the seven months of my imprisonment here I have had insufficient linen, no furniture or sheets; I have eaten the same gruel as your archers and I have but one hour's firing a day.'

'I have obeyed Messire de Nogaret's orders, Madam,' replied Bersumée.

'Messire de Nogaret is dead.'[2]

'He sent me the King's instructions.'

'King Philip is dead.'

Seeing where Marguerite was leading, Bersumée replied, 'But Monseigneur de Marigny is still alive, Madame, and he is in control of the judiciary and the prisons, as he controls all else in the kingdom, and I am responsible to him for everything.'

'Did this morning's courier give you no new orders concerning me?'

'None, Madam.'

'You will receive them shortly.'

'I await them, Madam.'

For a moment they looked at each other in silence. Robert Bersumée, Captain of Château-Gaillard, was thirty-five years old, at that epoch a ripe age. He had that precise, dutiful look professional soldiers assume so easily and which, from being continually assumed, eventually becomes natural to them. For ordinary everyday duty in the fortress he wore a wolfskin cap and a rather loose old coat of mail, black with grease, which hung in folds about his belt. His eyebrows made a single bar above his nose.

At the beginning of her imprisonment Marguerite had tried to seduce him, ready to offer herself to him in order to make him her ally. He had failed to respond for fear of the consequences. But he was always embarrassed in Marguerite's presence and felt a grudge against her for the part she had made him play. Today he was thinking, 'Well, there it is! I could have been the Queen of France's lover.' And he wondered whether his scrupulously soldierly conduct would turn out well or ill for his prospects of promotion.

'It has been no pleasure to me, Madam, to have had to inflict such treatment upon women, particularly of such high rank as yours,' he said.

'I can well believe it, Messire, I can well believe it,' replied Marguerite, 'because one can clearly see how knightly you are by nature and that you have felt great repugnance for your orders.'

As his father was a blacksmith and his mother the daughter of a sacristan, the Captain of the Fortress heard the word 'knightly' with considerable pleasure.

'Only, Messire Bersumée,' went on the prisoner, 'I am tired of chewing wood to keep my teeth white and of anointing my hands with the grease from my soup to prevent my skin chapping with the cold.'

'I can well understand it, Madam, I can well understand it.'

'I should be grateful to you if from now on you would see to it that I am protected from cold, vermin and hunger.'

Bersumée lowered his head.

'I have no orders, Madam,' he replied.

'I am only here because of the hatred of King Philip, and his death will change everything,' went on Marguerite with such assurance that she very nearly convinced herself. 'Do you intend to wait till you receive orders to open the prison doors before you show some consideration for the Queen of France? Don't you think you would be acting somewhat stupidly against your own interests?'

Soldiers are often indecisive by nature, which predisposes them towards obedience and causes them to lose many a battle. Bersumée was as slow in initiative as he was prompt in obedience. He was loud-mouthed and ready with his fists towards his subordinates, but he had very little ability to make up his mind when faced with an unexpected situation.

Between the resentment of a woman who, so she said, would be all-powerful tomorrow, and the anger of Monseigneur de Marigny who was all-powerful today, which risk was he to take?

'I also desire that Madame Blanche and myself,' continued Marguerite, 'may be allowed to go outside the fortifications for an hour or two a day, under your guardianship if you think proper, so that we may have a change of scene from battlements and your archers' pikes.'

She was going too fast and too far. Bersumée saw the trap. His prisoners were trying to slip through his fingers. They were therefore not so certain after all of their return to Court.

'Since you are Queen, Madam, you will understand that I owe loyalty to the service of the kingdom,' he said, 'and that I cannot infringe the orders I have received.'

Having said this, he went out so as to avoid further argument.

'He's a dog,' cried Marguerite when he had left, 'a guard-dog who is good for nothing but to bark and bite.'

She had made a false move and was beside herself to find some means of communicating with the outside world, receive news, and send letters which would be unread by

Marigny. She did not know that a messenger, selected from among the first lords of the kingdom, was already on his way to lay a strange proposal before her.

2

Robert of Artois

'You've got to be ready for anything when you're a Queen's gaoler,' said Bersumée to himself as he left the tower. He was seriously perturbed, filled with misgiving. So important an event as the King's death could not but result in a visitor to Château-Gaillard from Paris. So Bersumée, shouting at the top of his voice, made haste to make his garrison ready for inspection. On that count at least he intended to be blameless.

All day there was such commotion in the fortress as had not been seen since Richard Cœur-de-Lion. There was much sweeping and cleaning. Had an archer lost his quiver? Where could it have got to? And what of those coats of mail rusted under the armpits? Go on, take handfuls of sand, polish them till they shine!

'Should Messire de Pareilles appear suddenly, I don't want him to find a troop of ruffians!' shouted Bersumée. 'Make haste, get a move on there!'

The guard-house was cleaned; the chains of the drawbridge greased. The cauldrons for boiling pitch were brought out, as if the fortress were to be attacked within the hour. And bad luck to anyone who did not hurry! Private Gros-Guillaume, the same who had hoped for an extra ration of wine, got a kick on the backside. Sergeant Lalaine was worn out.

Doors were slamming everywhere; Château-Gaillard had an atmosphere of moving house. If the Princesses had wished to escape, this was the one day to choose among a hundred. Such was the chaos, no one would have seen them leave.

By evening Bersumée had lost his voice, and his archers slept upon the battlements. But the following day when, in the early hours of the morning, the look-outs reported a troop of horsemen, a banner at their head, advancing along the Seine from the direction of Paris, the Captain congratulated himself upon having taken the steps he had.

He rapidly donned his smartest coat of mail, his best boots, no more than five years old with spurs three inches long, and, putting on his helmet, went out into the courtyard. He had a few moments left in which to glance with anxious satisfaction at his still tired men, but their arms, well polished, shone in the pale winter light.

'Certainly no one can reprimand me for this turn-out,' he said to himself. 'And it will make it easier for me to complain of the meagreness of my salary, and the arrears of money due to me for the men's food.'

Already the horsemen's trumpets were sounding under the cliff, and the clatter of their horses' hooves could be heard upon the chalky soil.

'Raise the portcullis! Lower the drawbridge!'

The chains of the portcullis quivered in the guide-blocks and, a moment later, fifteen horsemen, bearing the royal arms and surrounding a red-clothed cavalier, who sat his mount as if impersonating his own equestrian statue, passed like a whirlwind beneath the vault of the guard-house and debouched into the courtyard of Château-Gaillard.

'Can it be the King?' thought Bersumée, rushing forward. 'Good God! Can the King have come to fetch his wife already?'

From emotion his breath came in short gasps, and it took him a moment to recognize the man in the blood-red cloak who, slipping from his horse, colossal in mantle, furs, leather and silver, was forcing a way towards him through the surrounding horsemen.

'On the King's service,' said the huge cavalier, fluttering a parchment with dependent seal under Bersumée's nose, but giving him no time to read it. 'I am Count Robert of Artois.'

The salutations were cut short, Monseigneur Robert of Artois slapped Bersumée on the shoulder to show that he was not haughty and made him wince; then asked for mulled wine for himself and his escort in a voice that made the watch-men turn about upon their towers. He created a hurricane about him as he paced to and fro.

Bersumée, the night before, had decided to shine who-ever his visitor might be, had determined not to be caught napping, to appear the perfect captain of an impeccable fortress, to make an impression that would not be forgotten. He had a speech ready; but it was never delivered.

Almost at once Bersumée found himself being invited to drink the wine he had been ordered to produce, heard himself stuttering servile flattery, saw the four rooms of his lodging, which was attached to the keep, reduced to absurd proportions by the immense size of his visitor, was aware of nervously spilling the contents of his goblet, and then of finding himself in the prisoners' tower, following in the wake of the Count of Artois, who was racing up the dark staircase at incredible speed. Until that day Bersumée had always considered himself a tall man; now he felt a dwarf.

Artois had only asked one question concerning the Princesses: 'How are they?'

And Bersumée, cursing himself for his stupidity, had replied, 'They are very well, thank you, Monseigneur.'

At a sign Sergeant Lalaine unlocked the door with trembling hands.

Marguerite and Blanche were waiting, standing in the middle of the round chamber. They were both pale and, with the opening of the door, with a single, instinctive impulse for mutual support, reached for each other's hands.

Artois looked them up and down. His eyes blinked. He had halted in the doorway, completely filling it.

'You, Cousin!' said Marguerite.

And, as he did not reply, gazing intently at these two women to whose distress he had so greatly contributed, she went on in a voice grown quickly firmer, 'Look at us, yes, look at us! See the misery to which we are reduced. It must offer a fine contrast to the spectacle presented by the Court, and to the memory you had of us. We have no linen. No dresses. No food. And no chair to offer so great a lord as you!'

'Do they know?' Artois wondered as he went slowly forward. Had they learnt the part he had played in their disaster, out of revenge, out of hate for Blanche's mother, that he had helped the Queen of England to lay the trap into which they had fallen?[3]

'Robert, are you bringing us our freedom?'

It was Blanche who said this and now went towards the Count, her hands extended before her, her eyes bright with hope.

'No, they know nothing,' he thought. 'It will make my mission the easier.'

He did not reply and turned upon his heel.

'Bersumée,' he said, 'is there no fire here?'

'No, Monseigneur; the orders I received . . .'

'Light one! And is there no furniture?'

'No, Monseigneur, but I . . .'

'Bring furniture! Take away this pallet! Bring a bed, chairs to sit on, hangings, torches. Don't tell me you haven't them! I saw everything necessary in your lodging. Fetch them at once!'

He took the Captain of the Fortress by the arm and pushed him out of the room as if he were a servant.

'And something to eat,' said Marguerite. 'You might also tell our good gaoler, who daily gives us food that pigs would leave at the bottom of their trough, to give us a proper meal for once.'

'And food, of course, Madam!' said Artois. 'Bring pastries and roasts. Fresh vegetables. Good winter pears and preserves. And wine, Bersumée, plenty of wine!'

'But, Monseigneur . . .' groaned the Captain.

'Don't you dare talk to me,' shouted Artois. 'Your breath stinks like a horse!'

He threw him out, and banged the door shut with a kick of his boot.

'My good Cousins,' went on Artois, 'I was expecting the worst indeed; but I see with relief that this sad time has not marked the two most beautiful faces in France.'

It was only now that he took off his hat and bowed low.

'We still manage to wash,' said Marguerite. 'Provided we break the ice on the basins they bring us, we have sufficient water.'

Artois sat down on the bench and continued to gaze at them. 'Well, my girls,' he murmured to himself, 'that's what comes of trying to carve yourselves the destinies of queens from the inheritance of Robert of Artois!' He tried to guess whether beneath the rough serge of their dresses, the two young women's bodies had lost the soft curves of the past. He was like a great cat making ready to play with caged mice.

'How is your hair, Marguerite?' he asked. 'Has it grown properly?'

Marguerite of Burgundy started as if she had been pricked with a needle. Her cheeks grew pale.

'Get up, Monseigneur of Artois!' she cried furiously. 'However reduced you may find me here, I will still not tolerate that a man should be seated in my presence when I am standing!'

He leapt to his feet, and for a moment their eyes confronted each other. She did not flinch.

In the pale light from the window he was better able to see this new face of Marguerite's, the face of a prisoner. The features had preserved their beauty, but all their sweetness had gone. The nose was sharper, the eyes more sunken. The dimples, which only last spring had shown at the corners of her amber cheeks, had become little wrinkles. 'So,' Artois said to himself, 'she can still defend herself. All the better, it will be the more amusing.' He liked a battle, having to fight to gain his ends.

'Cousin,' he said to Marguerite with feigned good-humour, 'I had no intention of insulting you; you have misunderstood me. I merely wanted to know if your hair had grown sufficiently to allow of your appearing in public.'

Distrustful as she was, Marguerite could not prevent herself giving a start of joy.

Appear in public? This must mean that she was to go free. Had she been pardoned? Was he bringing her a throne? No, it could not be that, he would have announced it at once.

Her thoughts raced on. She felt herself weakening. She could not prevent tears coming to her eyes.

'Robert,' she said, 'don't keep me in suspense. I know it's a characteristic of yours. But don't be cruel. What have you come to say to me?'

'Cousin, I have come to deliver you . . .'

Blanche uttered a cry and Robert thought that she was going to swoon. He had left his sentence suspended; he was playing the two women like a couple of fish at the end of a line.

'. . . a message,' he finished.

It pleased him to see their shoulders sag, to hear their sighs of disappointment.

'A message from whom?' asked Marguerite.

'From Louis, your husband, our King from now on. And

from our good cousin Monseigneur of Valois. But I may only speak to you alone. Perhaps Blanche would leave us?'

'Yes, yes,' said Blanche submissively, 'I will retire. But before I go, Cousin, tell me: what of Charles, my husband?'

'He has been much distressed by his father's death.'

'And what does he think of me? Does he speak of me?'

'I think he regrets you, in spite of the suffering you have caused him. Since Pontoise he has never been seen to show his old gaiety.'

Blanche burst into tears.

'Do you think,' she asked, 'that he has forgiven me?'

'That depends a great deal upon your cousin,' replied Artois mysteriously, indicating Marguerite.

And he led Blanche to the door, closing it behind her.

Then, returning to Marguerite, he said, 'To start with, my dear, there are a few things I must tell you. During these last days, when King Philip was dying, Louis your husband has seemed utterly confused. To wake up King, when one went to sleep a prince, is a matter for some surprise. He occupied his throne of Navarre only in name, and had no hand in governing. You will remember that he is twenty-five years old, and at that age one is able to reign; but you know as well as I do that, without being unkind, judgement is not his most outstanding quality. Thus, in these first days, Monseigneur of Valois, his uncle, stands behind him in everything, directing affairs with Monseigneur de Marigny. The trouble is that these two powerful minds dislike each other because they are too similar, hardly listening to what they say to each other. It is even thought that very soon they will no longer listen to each other at all, which, if it continued, would be most unfortunate, since a kingdom cannot be governed by two deaf men.'

Artois had completely changed his tone. He was speaking with sense and precision, giving the impression that his turbulent entrances were largely made for effect.

'As far as I am concerned, as you know very well,' he went on, 'I don't care at all for Messire de Marigny, who has so often stood in my way, and I hope with all my heart that my cousin Valois, whose friend and ally I am, will come out on top.'

Marguerite did her best to understand the intrigues which were everyday matters to Artois, and into which he was so abruptly plunging her once more. She was no longer in touch with affairs, and it seemed to her that she was awakening from a long slumber of the mind.

From the courtyard, blanketed to some extent by the walls, came the shouts of Bersumée, who was busy having his lodging emptied by the soldiers.

'Louis still hates me, doesn't he?' she said.

'Oh, as for that, I won't conceal from you that he hates you very well! You must admit that he has reason to,' replied Artois. 'To have decorated him with a cuckold's horns is an embarrassment when they must be worn above the crown of France! Had you done as much to me, Cousin, I should not have made such a clamour throughout the kingdom. I should have given you such a beating that you would never have desired to do the like again, or else . . .'

He looked so steadily at Marguerite that she was frightened.

'. . . or else I should have acted in such a way that I could feign the preservation of my honour. However, the late King, your father-in-law, clearly judged otherwise and things are as they are.'

He certainly possessed a fine assurance in deploring a scandal he had done everything in his power to set alight. He went on, 'Louis's first thought, after witnessing his father's death, indeed the only thought he has in mind at present, since I believe him incapable of entertaining more than one at a time, is to extricate himself from the embarrassment in which you have placed him and to live down the shame you have caused him.'

'What does Louis want?' asked Marguerite.

For a moment Artois swung his monumental leg backwards and forwards as if he were about to kick a stone.

'He intends asking for the annulment of your marriage,' he answered, 'and you can see, from the fact that he has sent me to you at once, that he wants to put it through as quickly as possible.'

'So I shall never be Queen of France,' thought Marguerite. The foolish dreams of the day before were already proved vain. A single day of dreaming to set against seven months of imprisonment, against the whole of time!

At this moment two men came in carrying wood and kindling. They lit the fire. Marguerite waited till they had gone again.

'Very well,' she said wearily, 'let him ask for an annulment. What can I do?'

She went over to the fireplace and held her hands out to the flames which were beginning to catch.

'Well, Cousin, there is much you can do, and indeed you can be the recipient of a certain gratitude if you will take a course that will cost you nothing. It happens that adultery is no ground for annulment; it's absurd, but so it is. You could have had a hundred lovers instead of one, pleasured every man in the kingdom, and you would be no less indissolubly married to the man to whom you were joined before God. Ask the chaplain or anyone else you like; so it is. I have taken the best advice upon it, because I know very little of church matters: a marriage cannot be broken, and if one wishes to break it, it must be proved that there was some impediment to its taking place, or that it has not been consummated, so that it might never have been. You're listening to me?'

'Yes, yes, I see what you mean,' said Marguerite.

It was no longer a question of the affairs of the kingdom, but of her own fate; and she was registering each word in her mind that she might not forget it.

'Well,' went on her visitor, 'this is what Monseigneur Valois has devised to get his nephew out of his difficulty.'

He paused and cleared his throat.

'You will admit that your daughter, the Princess Jeanne, is not Louis's child; you will admit that you have never slept with your husband and that there has therefore never been a true marriage. You will declare this voluntarily in the presence of myself and your chaplain as supporting witnesses. Among your previous servants and household there will be no difficulty in finding witnesses to testify that this is the truth. Thus the marriage will have no defence and the annulment will be automatic.'

'And what am I offered in exchange for this lie?' asked Marguerite.

'In exchange for your cooperation,' replied Artois, 'you are

27

offered safe passage to the Duchy of Burgundy, where you will be placed in a convent until the annulment has been pronounced, and thereafter to live as you please or as your family may desire.'

On first hearing, Marguerite very nearly answered, 'Yes, I accept; I declare all that is desired of me; I will sign no matter what, on condition that I may leave this place.' But she saw Artois watching her from under lowered lids, a gaze ill-matched with his good-natured air; and intuitively she knew that he was tricking her. 'I shall sign,' she thought, 'and then they will continue to keep me here.'

Duplicity in the heart is catching. But in fact Artois was for once telling the truth; he was the bearer of an honest proposal; he even had the order with him for Marguerite's removal, should she consent to the declaration required of her.

'It is asking me to commit a grave sin,' she said.

Artois burst out laughing.

'Good God, Marguerite,' he cried, 'it seems to me you have committed others with less scruple!'

'Perhaps I have altered and repented. I must think the matter over before deciding.'

The giant made a wry face, twisting his lips from side to side.

'Very well, Cousin, but think quickly,' he said, 'because I must be back in Paris tomorrow for the funeral mass at Notre-Dame. With fifty-eight miles in the saddle, even by the shortest way, and roads a couple of inches deep in mud, and daylight fading early and dawning late, and the delay for a relay of horses at Nantes, I have no time to dawdle and would much prefer not to have come all this way for nothing. Goodbye; I shall go and sleep an hour and come back to eat with you. It must not be said that I left you alone, Cousin, the first day upon which you fare well. I am sure you will have reached the right decision.'

He left like a whirlwind, as he had arrived, for he paid as much attention to his exits as his entrances, and nearly upset Private Gros-Guillaume in the staircase, as he came up bending and sweating under a huge coffer.

Then he disappeared into the Captain's denuded lodging and threw himself upon the one couch that still remained.

'Bersumée, my friend, see that dinner is ready in an hour's time,' he said. 'And call my valet Lormet, who must be with the horsemen. Tell him to come and watch over me while I sleep.'

For this Hercules feared nothing but to be found defence-less by his numerous enemies while he slept. And he preferred to any squire or equerry the guardianship of this short, squat, greying servant who followed him everywhere for the apparent purpose of handing him his coat or cloak.

Unusually vigorous for his fifty years, all the more dangerous for his mild appearance, capable of anything in the service of 'Monseigneur Robert', and above all of obliterating noiselessly in a few seconds people who were an embarrass-ment to his master, Lormet, purveyor of girls on occasion and a great recruiter of roughs, was a rogue less by nature than from devotion; a killer, he had the affection of a wet-nurse for his master.

Shy, and a clever deceiver of fools, he was an able spy. Not the least of his exploits was to have led the brothers Aunay into a trap, so that they might be taken by Robert of Artois almost *in flagrante delicto* at the foot of the Tower of Nesle.

When Lormet was asked why he was so attached to the Count of Artois, he shrugged his shoulders and replied grumblingly, 'Because from each of his old coats I can make two for myself.'

As soon as Lormet entered the Captain's lodging, Robert closed his eyes and fell asleep upon the instant, his arms and legs stretched wide, his chest rising and falling with the deep breathing of an ogre.

An hour later he awoke of his own accord, stretched himself like a huge tiger, stood upright, his muscles and his mind refreshed.

Lormet was sitting on a bench, his dagger on his knees. Round-headed and narrow-eyed, he looked tenderly upon his master's awakening.

'Now it's your turn to go and sleep, my good Lormet,' said Artois; 'but before you do, go and find me the Chaplain.'

3

Shall She be Queen?

THE DISGRACED DOMINICAN CAME at once, much agitated at being sent for personally by so important a lord.

'Brother,' Artois said to him, 'you must know Madame Marguerite well, since you are her confessor. In what lies the weakness of her character?'

'The flesh, Monseigneur,' replied the Chaplain, modestly lowering his eyes.

'We know that already! But in what else? Has her nature no emotional facet, no side upon which we can bring pressure to bear to force her to accept a certain course, which is not only to her own interest but to that of the kingdom?'

'I can see nothing, Monseigneur. I can see no weakness in her except upon the one point I have already mentioned. The Princess's spirit is as hard as a sword and even prison has not blunted its edge. Oh, believe me, she is no easy penitent!'

His hands in his sleeves, his broad brow bent, he was trying to appear both pious and clever at once. His tonsure had not been renewed for some time, and the skin of his skull showed blue above the thin circle of black hair.

Artois remained thoughtful for a moment, scratching his cheek because the Chaplain's skull made him think of his beard which was beginning to grow.

'As to the subject you have mentioned,' he went on, 'what has she found here in satisfaction of her particular weakness, since that appears to be the term you use for that form of vitality.'

'As far as I know, none, Monseigneur.'

'Bersumée? Does he ever visit her for rather over-long periods?'

'Never, Monseigneur, I can vouch for that.'

'And what about yourself?'

'Oh! Monseigneur!' cried the Chaplain, crossing himself.

'All right, all right!' said Artois. 'It would not be the first time that such things have been known to happen, one is acquainted with more than one member of your cloth who, his soutane removed, feels himself to be a man like another. For my part I see nothing wrong in it: indeed, to tell you the truth, I see in it matter for praise rather. What of her cousin? Do the two women console each other from time to time?'

'Oh! Monseigneur!' said the Chaplain, pretending to be more and more horrified. 'What you are asking me could only be a secret of the confessional.'

Artois gave the Chaplain's shoulder a little friendly slap which nearly sent him staggering to the wall for support.

'Now, now, Messire Chaplain, don't be ridiculous,' he cried. 'If you have been sent to a prison as officiating priest, it is not in order that you should keep such secrets, but that you should repeat them to those authorized to hear them.'

'Neither Madame Marguerite, nor Madame Blanche,' said the Chaplain in a low voice, 'have ever confessed to me of being culpable of anything of the kind, except in dreams.'

'Which does not prove that they are innocent, but merely that they are secretive. Can you write?'

'Certainly, Monseigneur.'

'Well, well!' said Artois with an air of astonishment. 'Apparently all monks are not so damned ignorant as is generally supposed! Very well, Messire Chaplain, you will take parchment, pens, and everything you need to scratch down words, and you will wait at the base of the Princesses' tower, ready to come up when I call you. You will make as much haste as you can.'

The Chaplain bowed; he seemed to have something more to say, but Artois had already donned his great scarlet cloak and was on his way out. The Chaplain hurried out behind him.

'Monseigneur! Monseigneur!' he said in a very obsequious voice. 'Would you have the very great kindness, if I am not offending you by making such a request, would you have the immense kindness to say to Brother Renaud, the Grand Inquisitor, if it should so happen that you should see him, that I am still his obedient son, and ask him not to forget me in this fortress for too long, where indeed I do my duty as best I may since God has placed me here, but I have certain capacities, Monseigneur, as you have seen, and I much desire that they should be found other employment.'

'I shall remember to do so, my good fellow, I shall remember,' replied Artois, who already knew that he would do nothing about it whatever.

When Robert entered Marguerite's room, the two Princesses had not quite finished dressing; they had washed lengthily before the fire with the warm water and the soapwort which had been brought them, making the restored pleasure last as long as possible; they had washed each other's short hair, now still pearly with drops of water, and had newly clothed themselves in long white shirts, closed at the neck by a running string, which had been provided. For a moment they were afflicted with modesty.

'Well, Cousins,' said Robert, 'you have no need to worry. Stay as you are. I am a member of the family; besides, those shirts you are wearing are more completely concealing than the dresses you used once to appear in. You look like a couple of little nuns. But you already look better than a while ago, and your complexions are beginning to revive. Admit that your living conditions have quickly altered with my coming.'

'Oh, yes indeed and thank you, Cousin!' cried Blanche.

The room was quite changed in appearance. A curtained bed had been brought, as well as two big chests which acted as benches, a chair with a back to it, and a trestle table upon which were already placed bowls, goblets and Bersumée's wine. A tapestry with a faded design had been hung over the dampest part of the curved wall. A thick taper, brought from the sacristy, was alight upon the table, for though the afternoon had barely begun, daylight was already waning; and upon the hearth under the cone-shaped overmantel huge logs were burning, the damp escaping from their ends with a singing noise of bursting bubbles.

Immediately behind Robert, Sergeant Lalaine entered with Private Gros-Guillaume and another soldier, bringing up a thick, smoking soup, a large white loaf, round as a pie, a five-pound pasty in a golden crust, a roast hare, a stuffed goose and some juicy pears of a late species, which Bersumée, upon threatening to sack the town, had been able to extract from a greengrocer of Andelys.

'What,' cried Artois, 'is that all you're giving us, when I asked for a decent dinner?'

'It's a wonder, Monseigneur, that we have been able to find as much as we have in this time of famine,' replied Lalaine.

'It's a time of famine, perhaps, for the poor, who are idle enough to expect the earth to produce without being tilled, but not for the wealthy,' replied Artois. 'I have never sat down to so poor a dinner since I was weaned!'

The prisoners gazed like young famished animals upon the food which Artois, the better to make the two women aware of their lamentable condition, affected to despise. There were tears in Blanche's eyes. And the three soldiers gazed at the table with a wondering covetousness.

Gros-Guillaume, who subsisted entirely on boiled rye, and normally served the Captain's dinner, went hesitatingly to the table to cut the bread.

'No, don't touch it with your filthy hands,' shouted Artois. 'We'll cut it ourselves. Go on, get out, before I lose my temper!'

He could have sent for Lormet, but his guard's slumber was one of the few things Robert respected. Or he could have sent for one of the horsemen, but he preferred to proceed without witnesses.

As soon as the archers had gone, he said in that facetious tone of voice still assumed by the rich today when by chance they have to carry a dish or wash a plate, 'I shall get accustomed to prison life myself. Who knows,' he added, 'perhaps one day, my dear Cousin, you will be putting me in prison?'

He made Marguerite sit on the chair with the back.

'Blanche and I will sit on this bench,' he said.

He poured out the wine, raised his goblet towards Marguerite, and cried, 'Long live the Queen!'

'Don't mock me, Cousin,' said Marguerite. 'It is lacking in charity.'

'I am not mocking you; you can take my words literally. As far as I know, you are still Queen this day, and I wish you a long life, that's all.'

Silence fell upon them, for they set about eating. Anyone but Robert might have been moved by the sight of the two women attacking their food like paupers.

At first they had tried to feign a dignified detachment, but hunger carried them away and they hardly gave themselves time to breathe between mouthfuls.

Artois spiked the hare upon his dagger and held it to the embers of the hearth to warm it. While doing so, he continued to watch his cousins, and had difficulty in controlling his laughter. 'I've a good mind to put their bowls on the ground and let them get down on all fours and lick the very grain of the wood clean,' he thought.

They drank too. They drank Bersumée's wine as if they needed to compensate all at once for seven months of cistern-water, and the colour came back to their cheeks. 'They'll make themselves sick,' thought Artois, 'and they'll finish this happy day spewing up their guts.'

He himself ate like a whole company of soldiers. His prodigious appetite was far from being a myth, and each mouthful would have needed dividing into four to suit an ordinary gullet. He devoured the stuffed goose as if it were a thrush, champing the bones. He modestly excused himself for not doing as much for the hare's carcass.

'Hare's bones,' he explained, 'break into splinters and tear the stomach.'

When they had all eaten enough, he caught Blanche's eye and indicated the door. She rose without being asked, though her legs were trembling under her; she felt giddy and badly wanted to go to bed. Then Robert had the first humanitarian impulse since his arrival. 'If she goes out into the cold in this state, she'll die of it,' he said to himself.

'Have they lighted a fire in your room?' he asked.

'Yes, thank you, Cousin,' replied Blanche. 'Our life . . .'

She was interrupted by a hiccough.

'. . . our life is really quite altered thanks to you. Oh, how fond I am of you, Cousin, really fond indeed. You'll tell Charles, won't you? You will tell him that I love him. Ask him to forgive me because I love him.'

At the moment she loved everyone. She went out, quite drunk, and tripped upon the staircase. 'If I were here merely for my own amusement,' thought Artois, 'I should meet with little resistance from that one. Give a princess enough wine, and you'll soon see that she turns into a whore. But the other one seems to me pretty tight too.'

He threw a big log on the fire, turned Marguerite's chair towards the hearth, and filled the goblets.

'Well, Cousin,' he asked, 'have you thought things over?'

'I have thought, Robert, I have thought. And I think I am going to refuse.'

She said this very softly. Apparently overcome as much by the warmth as by the wine, she was gently shaking her head.

'Cousin, you're not being sensible, you know!' cried Robert.

'But indeed, indeed, I think I shall refuse,' she replied in an ironic, sing-song voice.

The giant made a gesture of impatience. 'Listen to me, Marguerite,' he went on. 'It must be to your advantage to accept now. Louis is by nature an impatient man, ready to grant almost anything to get his own way at the moment. You will never again have the chance of doing so well for yourself. Merely agree to make the declaration asked of you. There is no need for the matter to go before the Holy See; we can get a judgement from the episcopal tribunal of Paris, which is under the jurisdiction of Monseigneur Jean de Marigny, Archbishop of Sens, who will be told to make haste. In three months' time you will have regained complete personal freedom.'

'And if I won't?'

She was leaning towards the fire, her hands extended before her. The running string which held together the collar of her long shirt had become unknotted and revealed most of her bosom to her cousin's wandering eye; but she did not seem to care. 'The bitch still has beautiful breasts,' thought Artois.

'And if I won't?' she repeated.

'If you won't, your marriage will be annulled anyway, my dear, because reasons can always be found for annulling a king's marriage,' replied Artois carelessly, intent upon the objects of his contemplation. 'As soon as there is a Pope . . .'

'Oh, is there still no Pope?' cried Marguerite.

Artois bit his lips. He had made a mistake. He ought to have remembered that she was ignorant, prisoner as she was, of what all the world knew, that since the death of Clement V the conclave had not succeeded in electing a new Pope. He had revealed a useful weapon to his adversary. And he realized by the quickness of Marguerite's reaction to the news that she was not as drunk as she pretended to be.

Having committed the blunder, he tried to turn it to his own advantage by playing that game of false frankness of which he was a master.

'But that is exactly where your good fortune lies!' he cried. 'That is precisely what I want you to understand. As soon as those rascally cardinals, who sell their promises as if they were at auction, have made enough out of their votes to consent to agree, Louis will no longer have need of you. You will merely have succeeded in making him hate you all the more, and he'll keep you shut up here for ever.'

'Yes, but so long as there is no Pope, nothing can be done without my agreement.'

'You're foolish to be so obstinate.'

He went and sat next to her, placed his huge hand as gently as he could about her neck and began to stroke her shoulder.

Marguerite seemed troubled by the contact of his huge

muscular hand. It was so long since she had felt a man's hand upon her skin!

'Why should you be so interested in my accepting?' she asked.

He bent low enough over her to brush her hair with his lips.

'I am very fond of you, Marguerite; I always have been very fond of you, as you know very well. And now our interests are bound up together. You must succeed in regaining your freedom. And I must give Louis cause for satisfaction, so that I may enjoy his favour. You can see very well that we must be allies.'

While speaking he had put his hand deep into the collar of the Queen of France's shirt and was stroking her bosom. She made no resistance. On the contrary, she leant her head against her cousin's heavy wrist and seemed to abandon herself to him.

'Is it not a pity,' went on Robert, 'that so beautiful a body, so soft and comely, should be deprived of the pleasures of the flesh? Accept, Marguerite, and I will take you far from this prison this very day; I shall lead you first to some well-endowed convent where I can visit you frequently and watch over you. What can it really matter to you to declare that your daughter is not Louis's, since you have never loved the child?'

She raised wary eyes to him and said these appalling words: 'If I don't love her, is not that certain proof that she is my husband's daughter?'

For a moment she seemed to be dreaming, her eyes gazing upwards. The logs shifted on the hearth, lighting up the room with a great fountain of sparks. And Marguerite suddenly began to laugh, revealing her little white teeth; her mouth was all pink inside like a cat's.

'Why are you laughing?' asked Robert.

'Because of the ceiling,' she replied, 'I have just noticed that it is like the ceiling of the Tower of Nesle.'

Artois rose in stupefaction. He couldn't help feeling a certain admiration for so much cynicism joined to so much cunning. 'My God, what a woman!' he thought.

She watched him as he stood enormous in front of the fire, planted on his legs solid as trunks of trees. The flames shone on his red boots, glinted on the gold of his spurs and the silver of his belt. If his capacity for desire were in proportion to the rest of him, there would be enough to atone for all the regrets of seven months' seclusion!

He raised her up and pulled her to him.

'Ah, Cousin,' he said, 'if only you had married me, or had chosen me as your lover instead of that young fool of an equerry, things would not have turned out for you as they have, and we would have been very happy.'

'Of course,' she murmured.

He held her by the waist, and he had the impression that the moment was near when she would cease to be able to think.

'It is not too late, Marguerite,' he said softly.

'Perhaps not,' she replied in a hoarse, consenting voice.

'Let's get rid of this letter now, so that we need have no concern but ourselves. Let's tell the Chaplain, who is waiting below, to come up.'

She started away from him.

'Waiting below, did you say?' she cried, her eyes bright

with anger. 'Oh, Cousin, do you think I am such a fool as all that? You have behaved towards me as whores normally do towards men, arousing their sensuality the better to bend them to their will. But you forget that in that line women are better than men, and you are no more than an apprentice.'

Angry, tensely upright, she defied him and re-knotted the collar of her shirt.

He tried to persuade her that she had misunderstood him, that he wanted nothing but her good, that their conversation had taken an unexpected turn, that he had suddenly remembered the poor priest freezing at the bottom of the staircase.

She looked at him with scorn and irony. He picked her up, though she did her best to defend herself, and carried her roughly to the bed.

'No, I shall not sign,' she cried, fighting against him. 'You can rape me if you like, because you are too strong for me to be able to resist you, but I shall tell the Chaplain, I shall tell Bersumée, I shall let Marigny know what sort of ambassador you are and how you have taken advantage of me.'

Furiously angry, he let her go, restraining himself from slapping her face as he felt inclined to do.

'Never, do you see,' she went on, 'will you get me to admit that my daughter is not Louis's, for should Louis die, which I hope he does with all my heart, my daughter would become Queen of France and then people would have to take some account of me as Queen Mother.'

For a moment Artois remained silent in astonishment. 'What she says makes sense, the clever bitch,' he said to himself, 'and if by chance fate should prove her right . . .' He was checkmated.

'It's an unlikely chance,' he replied all the same.

'I have no other, so I shall hang on to it.'

'As you will, Cousin,' he said, going to the door.

His double failure made him extremely angry. He went down the stairs, found the Chaplain waiting for him, chilled to the bone, a bunch of goose-quills in his hand.

'Monseigneur,' said the Priest, 'you won't forget to say to Brother Renaud . . .'

'Yes,' shouted Artois, 'I'll tell him that you're an ass, my fine fellow; I don't know where the hell you manage to find weaknesses in your penitents!'

Then he called, 'Escort! To horse!'

Bersumée arrived, still wearing the helmet which had not left his head since morning.

'What are my orders, Monseigneur?' he asked.

'What, your orders? Obey those you already have.'

'And my furniture?'

'I don't care a damn about your furniture.'

Artois's great Norman horse was already being led out to him, and Lormet held the stirrup ready.

'And who will pay for the food, Monseigneur?' asked Bersumée.

'You will get it from Messire de Marigny! Go and lower the drawbridge!'

Artois hoisted himself athletically into the saddle and set off at a mad gallop, followed by his whole escort.

Soon in the falling darkness nothing was to be seen upon the slopes of Château-Gaillard but the sparks struck by the horses' shoes.

4

Long Live the King!

THE FLAMES OF THOUSANDS of tapers, arranged in clusters against the pillars, threw their wavering light upon the effigies of the Kings of France; ever and again the long stone faces seemed to assume the mobile expressiveness of a dream world, and one might have thought that an army of knights was sleeping an enchanted sleep in the middle of a flaming forest.

In the basilica of Saint-Denis, the royal necropolis, the Court was attending the burial of Philip the Fair.

Drawn side by side in the central nave, facing the new tomb, the whole Capet tribe were present in sombre and sumptuous mourning: the princes of the blood, the lay peers, the ecclesiastical peers, the members of the Inner Council, the Grand Almoners, the High Constable, indeed all the principal dignitaries of the Crown.

The Lord Chamberlain, followed by five officers of the household,[4] advanced with solemn tread to the edge of the

44

open vault into which the body had already been lowered, threw into the cavity the carved wand which was the insignia of his office, and pronounced the formula which officially marked the change of reign: 'The King is dead! Long live the King!'

After him, all present repeated: 'The King is dead! Long live the King!'

And the cry from a hundred throats resounded from bay and arch and pillar and re-echoed among the high vaults.

The Prince with the lack-lustre eyes, narrow shoulders and hollow chest who, at this moment, had become Louis X, felt a curious sensation in the nape of his neck, as if stars were bursting there. His whole body was seized by an agonizing chill and he was afraid of falling down in a swoon. He began to pray for himself as he had never prayed for anyone in the world.

On his right hand his two brothers, Philippe, Count of Poitiers, and Prince Charles, who had not as yet acquired a territorial estate, gazed fixedly at the tomb, their hearts constricted by the emotion every man must feel, be he child of poverty or king's son, at the moment his father's body is lowered into the earth.

On the left of the new Sovereign were his two uncles, Monseigneur Charles of Valois and Monseigneur Louis of Evreux, both big men who had already passed their fortieth year.

The Count of Evreux was a prey to memories of the past. 'Twenty-nine years ago,' he thought, 'we too were three sons standing upon these same stones before our father's tomb. It seems such a little while ago; and now Philip has gone. Life is already over.'

His eyes turned to the nearest effigy, which was that of King Philip III. 'Father,' prayed Louis of Evreux with all his heart, 'receive my brother Philip kindly into the other kingdom, for he succeeded you well.'

Further along, near the altar, was the tomb of Saint Louis, and beyond again the stone effigies of the great ancestors. And then, on the other side of the nave, the empty spaces, bare flagstones which one day would open for this young man who was succeeding to the throne, and after him, reign upon reign, for all the kings of the future. 'There is still room for many centuries of them,' thought Louis of Evreux.

Monseigneur of Valois, his arms crossed, his chin held high, his eyes restless, observed all that was going on, watching to see that the ceremony was properly conducted.

'The King is dead! Long live the King!'

Five times more the cry sounded through the basilica as the chamberlains passed by. Then the last wand rebounded from the coffin and silence fell.

At that moment Louis X was seized with a violent fit of coughing that he was quite unable to control. A flux of blood mounted to his cheeks and for a long moment he was shaken by a paroxysm, as if he were about to spit his soul out before his father's grave.

All those present looked at each other, mitre bent towards mitre, crown towards crown; there were whispers of anxiety and pity. Everyone was thinking, 'Supposing he too were to die within a few weeks, what would happen then?'

Among the peers of France the redoubtable Countess Mahaut of Artois, her face red from the cold, watched her giant nephew Robert, and wondered why he had arrived at

Notre-Dame the day before only in the middle of the funeral mass, unshaven and muddied to the waist. Where had he come from, what had he been doing? As soon as Robert appeared, there was intrigue in the air. The favour in which he seemed to stand, since Philip the Fair had died a few days ago, did nothing to reassure the Countess. And she was thinking that if the new King should catch a bad chill while burying his father, her affairs would come to fruition all the quicker.

Surrounded by the justiciars of the Council, Monseigneur Enguerrand de Marigny, Coadjutor of the Sovereign they were burying, and Rector-General of the kingdom, wore a princely mourning. From time to time he exchanged glances with his younger brother, Jean de Marigny, Archbishop of Sens,[5] who had officiated the day before at Notre-Dame and now, mitre on head, crozier in hand, was surrounded by the high clergy of the capital.

For two middle-class Normans who, twenty years earlier, called themselves simply the brothers Le Portier, they had had prodigious careers and, the elder ever pushing the younger upwards, succeeded in sharing power successfully between them, one controlling the civil power, the other the ecclesiastical. Between them they had destroyed the Order of the Knights Templar.

Enguerrand de Marigny was one of those rare men who have the certainty of being part of history while still alive, because they have made it. And he needed to remember where he had started, and to what heights he had risen, in order at this moment to be able to bear the great sorrow which had come to him. 'Sire Philip, my King,' he thought as he gazed at the coffin, 'I served you as well as I knew

how, and you confided to me the highest tasks, as you con-
ferred upon me the greatest honours and innumerable gifts.
How many days did we work side by side? We thought alike
in everything; we made mistakes, and we corrected them. I
swear that I shall defend the work we accomplished together
and shall pursue it against those who are now making ready
to destroy it. But how lonely I shall feel!' For this great
politician had fervour, and he thought of the kingdom as
might a second king.

Egidius de Chambly, Abbot of Saint-Denis, on his knees at
the edge of the vault, made a last sign of the Cross. Then he
rose to his feet, signalled to the sextons, and the heavy flat
stone rolled into place above the tomb.

Never again would Louis X hear his father's terrible voice
saying, 'Be quiet, Louis!'

And far from being relieved, he was seized with panic. He
heard a voice beside him say, 'Come on, Louis!'

He started; it was Charles of Valois who had spoken, telling him to move forward. Louis X turned towards his uncle
and murmured, 'You saw him become King. What did he
say? What did he do?'

'He entered upon his responsibilities without hesitation,'
replied Charles of Valois.

'He was eighteen, seven years younger than I am,' thought
Louis X. Feeling everyone's eyes upon him, he did his best
to stand upright, and began to walk forward while the procession formed behind him, monks, their heads bent, hands
in sleeves, singing a psalm. Since they had been singing continuously for twenty-four hours, their voices were beginning
to grow hoarse.

Thus they went from the basilica to the chapter house of the Abbey, where was laid the traditional repast which closed the funeral ceremony.

'Sire,' said Abbot Egidius, leading Louis to his place, 'we shall say two prayers from now on, one for the King God has taken from us, the other for him whom He has given us.'

'Thank you, Father,' said Louis X in an uncertain voice.

Then he sat down with a tired sigh and at once asked for a cup of water which he swallowed at one gulp. During the whole meal he remained silent, eating nothing, drinking a great deal of water. He felt feverish, physically and mentally ill.

'One must be robust to be a king.' It was one of the maxims Philip the Fair used to his sons when, before they were knights, they used sometimes to grumble at the exercises of arms or at the quintain.[6] 'One must be robust to be a king,' Louis X repeated to himself during these first moments of his reign. He was one of those people whom fatigue makes irritable, and he thought irritably that when one is bequeathed a throne, one should also be bequeathed the necessary strength to sit upright on it. But who, unless he had the strength of an athlete, could have borne the past week without feeling exhausted?

That which precedent demanded of a new sovereign, as he assumed his post, was utterly inhuman. Louis had had to attend his father's deathbed, receive the transmission of the royal miraculous power,[7] countersign the last will and testament, and take his meals for two days beside the embalmed corpse. Then had followed the transportation of the body by water from Fontainebleu to Paris, a whole series of progresses and vigils, interminable religious services and processions, all in the most appalling winter weather, paddling in frozen mud, a sullen wind taking your breath away, sleet pricking your face.

But Louis X admired his uncle of Valois who, throughout these days, had been constantly at his side, making every decision, solving questions of precedent, indefatigably, helpfully, terribly present. 'Without him, what should I have done?' thought Louis.

It was Valois who seemed to have the sinews of a king. Already, talking to the Abbot of Saint-Denis, he was beginning to express concern about Louis's coronation, which could not take place till the following summer, for the Abbot of Saint-Denis had besides the guardianship of the royal tombs, the keeping of the banner of France, which was brought out when the King went to war, and the guardianship of the instruments and vestments of coronation. The Count of Valois wished to know whether all was in order: was the great mantle in need of repair? Were the caskets for transporting the sceptre, the spurs and the hand of justice to Rheims in good condition? And the gold crown? It was essential that the goldsmiths should measure Louis X's head as soon as possible in order to alter the crown to the right size.

How Monseigneur of Valois would have liked to wear that crown himself! And he fussed about like one of those old spinsters who busy themselves pinning the dresses of brides.

As he listened, Abbot Egidius watched the young King who, once again, was shaken by his cough, and he thought, 'Of course, every preparation must be made; but will he last till then?'

When the meal was over, Hugues de Bouville, First Chamberlain to Philip the Fair, rose to break his carved wand before Louis X, signifying that he had accomplished his ultimate office. Fat Bouville's eyes filled with tears, his hands trembled and he tried three times before he succeeded in breaking the wooden wand, the delegated counterpart of the great sceptre of gold. Then he sat down again next to young Mathieu de Trye, First Chamberlain to Louis who was to succeed him. He murmured, 'It's up to you now, Messire.'

Everyone went out, mounted their horses, and the procession re-formed for the last lap. Outside there was but a thin crowd to cry, 'Long live the King!' The populace had got cold enough the day before, watching the great procession whose head had already reached Saint-Denis when its tail had not yet passed the Porte de Paris; today's procession had nothing exciting to offer. Sleet was falling, soaking through everyone's clothes to the skin; only the most ardent spectators remained, or those who could shout from their own doorsteps without getting wet.

From the time when he had first known that he would one day be King, Louis had dreamed of entering his capital in glorious sunshine. And when the Iron King, rebuking him, said harshly, 'Louis, don't be so stubborn!' how often had he not wished that his father might die, thinking, 'When I can command, everything will be different, and people will see what kind of a man I am.'

But now he had been proclaimed King, and yet there seemed to be nothing to mark the fact that he had been suddenly transformed into a sovereign. If anything had altered, it was only that he felt himself weaker than yesterday,

ill-assured in his new-found majesty, and thinking at every
turn of his father whom he had so little loved.

With lowered head and shaking shoulders, he pressed his
horse on between empty fields where the stubbles showed
above a carpet of snow; he seemed to be leading the survivors
of a conquered army.

Thus they arrived at the outskirts and entered the gates.
The people of the capital seemed no more enthusiastic than
those of Saint-Denis. Besides, what reasons had they to
demonstrate happiness? The early winter hindered communi-
cations and increased the death-rate. The last harvest had
been extremely bad; food was scarce and its price continually
increasing. Famine was in the air. And the little that was
known about the new King contained nothing to awaken
hope.

He was considered stubborn and self-opinionated, from
whence derived his nickname of 'The Hutin', which from the
Court had spread across the town. No one knew of a single
great or generous action he had ever performed. He had only
the sad reputation of a prince deceived by his wife, and
who, once the scandal was discovered, had taken delight in
torturing and then drowning in the Seine those of his household servants whom he had believed to be accomplices of his
misfortune.

'That's why they feel contempt for me,' Louis X said to
himself. 'Because of that bitch who tricked me and made me
a laughing-stock before the world. But they will be made to
love me, and if they won't, I shall act so as to make them
tremble at sight of me and hail me, when they see me, as if
they loved me very much indeed. But the first thing I need

is to take another wife, to have a queen beside me, so that my dishonour may be effaced.'

Alas, the report his cousin of Artois had given him the day before, upon his return from Château-Gaillard, appeared to make this no easy matter. 'The bitch will give way; I shall bully her, torture her into yielding.'

Night had fallen and the archers of the escort held lighted torches. As it had been rumoured among the lower orders that pieces of silver would be thrown them, groups of the poor, their naked flesh showing through their rags, had gathered at street corners. But no coins fell.

Thus the melancholy torchlight procession, passing by the Châtelet and the Pont au Change, reached the Palace of the Cité.

With the support of an equerry's shoulder, Louis X dismounted, and the procession at once broke up. The Countess Mahaut gave the signal for dispersal, declaring that everyone needed warmth and rest, and that she was going to the Hôtel d'Artois.

The prelates and lords took advantage of this to go off to their own houses. Even the brothers of the new King departed. So, upon entering his Palace, Louis X found himself abandoned by everyone but his escort of equerries and servants, his two uncles, Valois and Evreux, Robert of Artois and Enguerrand de Marigny. They passed through the Mercers' Hall, immense and almost deserted at this hour. A few merchants,[8] padlocking their baskets after a bad day's business, removed their hats and gathered in a group to cry 'Long live the King!' Their voices sounded weak, lost among the vaults of the two enormous naves.

The Hutin moved slowly forward, his legs stiff in his too-heavy boots, his body hot with fever. He looked to right and left where, against the walls, were arranged awe-inspiring statues of the forty kings who, since Mérovée, had reigned over France. Philip the Fair had erected them at the entrance to the royal abode, so that the living sovereign might appear in a spectator's eye to be the continuation of a sacred race, designed by God for the exercise of power.

This colossal heritage in stone, white-eyed under the glow of the torches, dismayed still further the poor Prince of flesh and blood upon whom the succession had descended.

A merchant said to his wife, 'Our new King doesn't look much of a chap.' The merchant's wife, as she stopped blowing upon her fingers, replied with that peculiar sneer women so often adopt towards the victims of misfortune that can come from no one but themselves, 'He certainly looks a proper cuckold.'

She did not speak over-loud, but her shrill voice resounded in the silence. The Hutin turned about with a start, his face suddenly aglow, vainly trying to see who had dared pronounce that word as he passed. Everyone about him looked away, pretending not to have heard.

They reached the foot of the Grand Staircase. Dominating, framing the monumental doorway, rose the two statues of Philip the Fair and Enguerrand de Marigny, for the Rector-General of the kingdom had received the supreme honour of seeing his likeness placed in the gallery of history in his lifetime, a pair to his master's.

If there was anyone who hated the sight of that statue, it was Monseigneur of Valois. Whenever he had to pass by it, he raged with fury that a man of such mean birth should have been raised up so high. 'Cunning and intrigue have lent him such effrontery that he assumes all the airs of being of our blood,' thought Valois. 'But it's all very fine, Messire; we'll bring you down from that pedestal, I promise you. We'll show you pretty quick that the period of your meretricious greatness is over.'

'Messire Enguerrand,' he said, turning haughtily towards his enemy, 'I think the King desires only the company of his family.'

By the word 'family', he meant only Monseigneur of Evreux, Robert of Artois and himself.

Marigny pretended not to have understood and, addressing himself to the King, in order to avoid a scene and at the same time to signify clearly that he proposed taking no orders but his, said, 'Sire, there are many matters pending which require my attention. May I be permitted to withdraw?'

Louis was thinking of something else; the word uttered by the merchant's wife was still ringing in his head. He would have been incapable of repeating what Marigny had just said.

'Certainly, Messire, certainly,' he replied impatiently. And he mounted the stairs which led to his apartments.

5

The Princess in Naples

DURING THE LAST YEARS of his reign, Philip the Fair had entirely rebuilt the Palace of the Cité. This careful man, who was almost miserly in his personal spending, knew no limits when it was a matter of glorifying the idea of royalty. The Palace was huge, overawing, and a sort of pendant to Notre-Dame: on the one side was the House of God, on the other the House of the King. The interior still looked new; it was all very sumptuous and rather dull.

'My Palace,' Louis X said, to himself, looking about him. He had not stayed there since its rebuilding, living as he did in the Hôtel de Nesle which had come to him, as had the crown of Navarre, through his mother. He began surveying the apartments which he now saw with a new eye because they were his.

He opened doors, passed through huge rooms in which his footsteps echoed: the Throne Room, the Justice Room, the Council Room. Behind him Charles of Valois, Louis of

Evreux, Robert of Artois, and the Chamberlain, Mathieu de Trye walked in silence. Footmen passed silently through the corridors, secretaries disappeared into the staircases; but no voices were heard; everyone still behaved as at a death vigil. From the windows the glass of the Sainte-Chapelle could be seen glowing faintly through the night.

At last Louis X stopped in the room of modest proportions in which his father had normally worked. A fire, big enough to roast an ox, burnt there, but it was possible to keep warm while protected from the direct heat of the flames by damp-ened osier screens set around the hearth. Louis asked Mathieu de Trye to have dry clothes brought him; he took off his robe, placing it upon one of the screens. His uncles and his cousin Artois followed his example. Soon the heavy cloth, wet from the rain, the velvets, the furs, the embroideries, began to steam while the four men in their shirts and trunk-hose, like four peasants come home from the fields, stood there, turning about in the warmth.

The room was lit by a cluster of candles burning in a triangular stand of wrought-iron. The bell of the Sainte-Chapelle rang the evening angelus.

Suddenly a deep sigh, almost a groan, sounded from the darkest corner of the room; everyone started, and Louis X could not help crying out in a sharp voice, 'What's that?'

Mathieu de Trye entered, followed by a valet bringing Louis a dry robe. The valet went down on all fours and pulled from under a piece of furniture a big greyhound with a high curved backbone and a fierce eye.

'Come, Lombard, come here.'

It was Philip the Fair's favourite pet, present of the banker

Tolomei, the same dog that had been found near the King when he had fallen motionless during his last hunt.

'Four days ago this hound was at Fontainebleu, how has he managed to get here?' asked The Hutin furiously.

An equerry was called.

'He came with the rest of the pack, Sire,' explained the equerry, 'and he will not obey; he runs away at the sound of a voice and I have been wondering since yesterday where he had hidden himself.'

Louis ordered that Lombard should be taken away and shut up in the stables; and, as the big greyhound resisted, scraping the floor with its claws, he chased it out with kicks.

He had hated dogs since the day when, as a child, he had been bitten by one as he was amusing himself piercing its ear with a nail.

Voices were heard in a neighbouring room, a door opened and a little girl of three appeared, awkward in her mourning robe, pushed forward by her nurse who was saying, 'Go on, Madame Jeanne; go and kiss Messire the King, your father.'

Everyone turned towards the little figure with pale cheeks and too-big eyes, who had not yet reached the age of reasoning but was, for the moment, the heiress to the throne of France.

Jeanne had the round, protruding forehead of Marguerite of Burgundy, but her complexion and her hair were fair. She came forward looking about her at people and things with the anxious expression of an unloved child.

Louis X stopped her with a gesture.

'Why has she been brought here?' he cried. 'I don't want to see her. Take her back at once to the Hôtel de Nesle; that's where she must live, because it's there . . .'

He was going to say, '. . . that her mother conceived her in her illicit pleasures.' He stopped himself in time, and waited till the nurse had taken the child away.

'I don't want ever to see the bastard again!' he said.

'Are you really certain that she is one, Louis?' asked Monseigneur of Evreux, moving his clothes away from the fire to prevent their scorching.

'It's enough for me that there is a doubt,' replied The Hutin, 'and I refuse to recognize the progeny of a woman who has shamed me.'

'All the same, the child is fair-haired, as we all are.'

'Philippe d'Aunay was fair too,' replied The Hutin bitterly.

'Louis must have good reasons, Brother, to speak as he does,' said Charles of Valois.

'What's more,' Louis went on, shouting at the top of his voice, 'I don't ever again want to hear the word that was thrown at me as we passed through the hall; I don't want to go on imagining all the time that people are thinking it; I don't want ever again to give people the chance of thinking it.'

Monseigneur of Evreux was silent. He was thinking of the little girl who must live among a few servants in the deserted immensity of the Hôtel de Nesle. He heard Louis say, 'Oh, how lonely I shall be here!'

Louis of Evreux looked at him, surprised as always by this nephew of his who gave way to every impulse of his mood, who preserved resentments as a miser keeps his gold, chased dogs away because he had once been bitten, his daughter because he had once been deceived, and then complained of his solitude.

'If he had had a better nature and a kinder heart,' he thought, 'perhaps his wife would have loved him.'

'Every living man is alone, Louis,' he said gravely. 'Each one of us in his loneliness undergoes the moment of recognition of sin, and it is mere vanity to believe that there are not moments like this in life. Even the body of the wife with whom we sleep remains a stranger to us; even the children we have conceived are strangers. Doubtless the Creator has willed it thus so that we may each of us have no communion but with Him and with each other but through Him. There is no help but in compassion and in the knowledge that others suffer as we do.'

The Hutin shrugged his shoulders. Had Uncle Evreux never anything to offer as consolation but God, and as a remedy but charity?

'Yes, yes, you are doubtless right, Uncle,' he said. 'But that is no answer to the cares that oppress me.'

Then, turning to Artois who, his backside to the fire, was steaming like a soup-tureen, he said, 'So you're certain, Robert, that she will not yield?'

Artois shook his head.

'Sire, Cousin, as I told you last night, I pressed Madame Marguerite in every way in my power: I gave her the most convincing arguments,' replied Artois, with an irony which was valid only for himself. 'I ran up against such a hard core of refusal that I can assure you with certainty there is nothing to be got from her. Do you know what she's counting on?' he added perfidiously. 'She is hoping that you will die before her.'

Instinctively Louis X touched through his shirt the little reliquary he wore about his neck, and for a moment turned away, wild of eye, his hair in disorder. Then, speaking to the Count of Valois, he said, 'Well, Uncle, you see it's not all as simple as you promised, and it seems that my annulment is not to be had tomorrow!'

'I know, Nephew, I am thinking of nothing else,' replied Valois, his brow wrinkled in thought.

Artois, standing face to face with The Hutin, whose forehead came up only to his shoulder, said to him in a whisper that could have been heard twenty yards away, 'If you are afraid of a celibate life, Cousin, I can always furnish your bed with charming young females, whom the promise of a purse of gold and the vanity of pleasuring the King would render most agreeable to you.'

He spoke with a certain relish, as if of a fine roast or a dish with an exquisite sauce.

Monseigneur of Valois spread out his ring-laden hands.

'Of what use is an annulment to you, Louis,' he said, 'so long as you have not chosen the new woman you wish to marry? Don't be so anxious about your annulment; a Sovereign can always obtain one in the end. What you need to do at once is to set about finding the wife who will make a suitable figure as queen beside you and give you a fine posterity.'

Monseigneur of Valois had the habit, when an obstacle presented itself, of glancing at it contemptuously and of immediately leaping forward to the next step; in war he disregarded islands of resistance, by-passed them and went on to attack the next fortress.

'Brother,' said the prudent Count of Evreux, 'the matter is not as easy as all that, considering the position our nephew occupies, if he does not wish the wife he chooses to be of inferior rank.'

'Nonsense! I know ten princesses in Europe who would overlook a great many things to wear the crown of France. For instance, without having to look further, there's my niece Clémence of Hungary,' said Valois, as if the idea had only just occurred to him, when in fact he had been considering it for the last three days.

He waited for the effect of his suggestion. No one uttered a word. But The Hutin raised his head in interest.

'She is of our blood, since she is an Anjou,' went on Valois. 'Her father, Carlo-Martello, who renounced the throne of Naples-Sicily to lay claim to that of Hungary, is dead long ago; that, no doubt, is why she has not yet made a match. But her brother, Caroberto, is now reigning in Hungary and her uncle is King of Naples. Of course, she is a little past the age of marriage . . .'

'How old is she?' asked Louis X anxiously

'Twenty-two. But is not that better than these little girls who are brought to wed when they are still playing with their dolls, and when they grow up reveal themselves to be full of vice, lies and debauchery? Moreover, Nephew, it's not as if you were making a first marriage!'

'All this sounds too good to be true; there must be a fly in the ointment,' thought The Hutin. 'This Clémence must be one-eyed or hunchbacked.'

'And what is she like, good-looking?' he inquired.

'Nephew, I can tell you that she is the most beautiful woman in Naples and that the painters, so I am assured, try to reproduce her features when they paint images of the Virgin Mary in the churches. I remember that even in childhood she promised remarkable beauty, and from everything I hear she has fulfilled that promise.'

'It certainly seems that she is very beautiful indeed,' said Monsiegneur of Evreux.

'And virtuous,' added Charles of Valois. 'I feel sure that she has all those qualities which were her dear aunt's, who was my first wife, may God keep her. And do not forget that Louis of Anjou, her other uncle, my brother-in-law therefore, having relinquished the throne in order to take holy orders, was that saintly Bishop of Toulouse at whose tomb miracles are performed.'

'Thus we shall have a second Saint Louis,' remarked Robert of Artois.[9]

'Your idea seems to me a happy one, Uncle,' said Louis X. 'Daughter of a king, sister of a king, niece of a king and of a saint, beautiful and virtuous . . .'

He seemed to be dreaming for a moment, and then suddenly cried aloud, 'Oh, I hope at least that she is not dark like Marguerite, for then I could not do it!'

'No, no,' Valois replied quickly. 'Have no fear, Nephew; she is fair, of sound Frankish stock.'

'And do you think, Uncle Charles, that the proposal would be agreeable to her and her family.'

Monseigneur of Valois swelled up like a turkey cock.

'I have served my relations of Anjou well enough for them

to refuse me nothing,' he replied. 'Queen Marie, who in the past held it an honour to give me one of her daughters, will most certainly grant me her granddaughter for the dearest of my nephews, and that she may be queen of the finest kingdom in the world. I shall manage it.'

'Then don't waste time, Uncle,' said Louis. 'Send an embassy to Naples at once. What do you think of the idea, Robert? And you, Uncle Louis?'

Robert advanced a pace, his hands widespread as if he were proposing to leave at once for Italy. Louis of Evreux, who had sat down, replied that he approved the idea, but that the decision was as much a matter for the kingdom as for the family, and too important not to require consideration.

'It would seem to me wise,' he concluded, 'that you should take the advice of your Council.'

'So be it,' replied Louis excitedly. 'There will be a Council tomorrow therefore. I will send to Messire de Marigny telling him to convoke it.'

'Why Messire de Marigny?' said Valois, feigning surprise. 'I can very well take care of that myself. Marigny has too many duties and summons Councils in haste merely to approve his proceedings without looking into them too closely. But we shall change all that, and I shall convene a Council more worthy to serve you. Moreover, this was your father's wish. He told me this privately during his last days.'

By now their clothes were dry and they dressed.

Louis X gazed intently into the fire. 'Beautiful and virtuous,' he repeated to himself. 'Beautiful and virtuous . . .' Then he was attacked by a fit of coughing and barely heard the others taking their leave.

'I know someone who will lie feverishly between the sheets tonight,' said Artois, once they were outside in the corridor.

'Robert,' said Valois reproachfully, 'don't forget that from now on you are speaking of the King.'

'No, no, I don't forget it, and would never say anything like that before others. It doesn't alter the fact that you have put an idea into his head which is already exciting him physically. My God, you managed to sell him your niece Clémence all right!'

Monseigneur of Evreux was thinking of the beautiful princess living in a palace on the bay of Naples, whose fate had doubtless, all unknown to her, been decided that day. Monseigneur of Evreux always marvelled at the mysterious, unforeseen ways in which human destinies were forged.

Because a great sovereign had died before his time, because a young king disliked leading a celibate life, because his uncle was impatient to satisfy his needs, because a name had been mentioned and remembered, a young fair-haired girl who perhaps, this very day, a thousand miles away, was beset with melancholy beside an eternally blue sea, thinking that nothing would ever happen to her, was suddenly fated to become the central preoccupation of the Court of France.

Monseigneur of Evreux had a sudden attack of conscience.

'Brother,' he said to Valois, 'do you really think that little Jeanne is a bastard?'

'I am not certain of it today, Brother,' said Valois, placing a ringed hand upon his shoulder. 'But I can assure you that before long all the world will know that she is!'

By this answer Monseigneur of Valois thought that he was

momentarily serving his own interests; he did not know what the consequences of his attitude would be, that his own son would owe to it the fact that one day he would become King of France.

If Monseigneur of Evreux had been able to look into the future some fifteen years, he would have found further reason for reflection.

6

The Royal Bed

MONUMENTAL, SCULPTURED WITH heavy-winged symbolical figures, the royal bed filled a third of the room. The canopy, draped in dark blue samite embroidered with golden lilies, resembled a portion of the nocturnal firmament; and the curtains draped about the dais were like sails looped from their yards.

The room, overwhelming in its silent, dark and reverential atmosphere, was lit only by an oil-burning night-light, placed in a rose-red lamp suspended by three chains from the ceiling;[10] beneath the glow, the counterpane of gold brocade fell in stiff folds to the floor and seemed to shine with a strange phosphorescent light.

For the last two hours Louis X had vainly sought sleep in the enormous bed which had been his father's. He felt stifled beneath the double fur coverings, and shivered as soon as he dispensed with them. Extreme fatigue causes insomnia, and insomnia is the cause of unhappiness. Though Philip the

Fair had died at Fontainebleu, Louis felt as uneasy at finding himself in this bed as if he were aware of the presence of the corpse in it.

All the memories of the last few days, all the fears for the days to come, were mingled in his mind. Someone shouted 'Cuckold' from the crowd; Clémence of Hungary refused him, or perhaps was already affianced; the austere features of Abbot Egidius bent over the tomb; 'From now on we shall say two prayers . . .'; 'Do you know what she is counting on? She is hoping you will die before her!'

He suddenly got up, his heart beating like a crazy clock. The palace doctor, who had examined him before he went to bed, had assured him that his humours were not too heated and that he would have a good night. But Louis had not told him of the two moments of faintness he had felt at Saint-Denis, the chill which had seized upon his limbs, and the way the crowd about him had seemed to reel. Now the same disquiet, to which he could give no precise name, came upon him once more. Tortured by his fears, The Hutin, in a long white nightshirt, which seemed to float about a formless body, walked without respite round the room as if pursued by a *doppelgänger*, as if he must die at the least cessation of movement.

Was he to die like his father, smitten in the head by the Hand of God? 'I too,' he thought aghast, 'was present when they burnt the Templars before the Palace.' Can one ever know the night of one's death? Can one ever know the night one will go mad? And should he succeed in surviving this abominable night, should he see the lagging winter dawn, in what an appalling state of exhaustion he would have to preside at his first Council upon the morrow! He would say to them, 'Messires . . .' But indeed what words would he find to say to them? 'Each one of us in his loneliness undergoes the moment of recognition of sin, and it is mere vanity to believe that there are not moments like this in life.'

'Ah, Uncle,' said The Hutin aloud, 'why did you have to say that?'

His own voice seemed strange to him. He continued to hurry round the great bed of oak and gold, gasping like a fish out of water.

It was the bed that terrified him. It was the bed that was accursed; he would never be able to sleep in it. He had been conceived in it; it was therefore absurdly logical that he should die in it. 'Must I spend all the nights of my reign walking round and round so as not to die?' he wondered. But how could he go and sleep elsewhere, call servants to prepare him another room? Where could he find the courage to admit: I can no longer sleep here because I am afraid,' and appear before his equerries, chamberlains, and the masters of his household discomfited, trembling and fearful.

He was a king and knew not how to reign; he was a man and knew not how to live; he was married and had no wife. Even if Clémence of Hungary accepted him, how many weeks, how many months, must he wait before a human presence came to reassure his nights and help him sleep! 'And will this one love me? Or will she behave as the other did?'

Suddenly he went and opened the door, awoke the First Chamberlain who was sleeping fully clothed in the ante-chamber and asked him, 'Does Dame Eudeline still look after the Palace linen?'

'Yes, Sire. I think so, Sire,' replied Mathieu de Trye.

'Well, find out. And if she does, send for her at once.'

Surprised and half asleep – 'Anyway, he seems able to sleep!' thought The Hutin with hatred – the Chamberlain asked whether the King wished to have his sheets changed.

The Hutin made a gesture of impatience.

'Yes, that's what I want. Go and find her, I tell you!'

He went back into the bedroom and resumed his anxious pacing to and fro, wondering, 'Does she still live in the Palace? Will she be found?'

A few minutes later Dame Eudeline appeared, carrying a pile of sheets. And at once Louis X had the feeling that he was no longer cold.

'Monseigneur Louis, I mean to say, Sire!' she cried, 'I knew that I must not put new sheets on your bed. One always sleeps badly in them. It was Messire de Trye who ordered me to do it! He said that it was the precedent. Whereas I wanted to give you thin, well-washed sheets.'

She was a big fair merry woman, large-breasted, with the comfortable look of a wet-nurse about her, giving an impression of peace, warmth and repose. She was thirty-two years old and her face seemed to preserve naturally, a calm expression of youthful surprise which was pleasant and grateful to behold. From under her white nightcap flowed long tresses of golden hair which fell upon her shoulders. She had hastily put on a dressing-gown over her nightgown.

Louis looked at her a moment without speaking.

'It was not because of the sheets I sent for you,' he said at length.

A sweet, modest blush suffused the linen-maid's cheeks.

'Oh, Monseigneur! Sire, I mean to say! Has returning to the Palace made you remember me?'

She had been his first mistress and that was ten years ago. The day upon which he had learnt – he was then fifteen – that he was soon to be married to a Princess of Burgundy. The Hutin had been consumed with an extraordinary frenzy to discover what love was, and at the same time was panic-stricken at the idea that he would not know how to behave towards his wife. While the marriage was being negotiated, and Marigny was engaged with Philip the Fair in weighing the territorial and military benefits of the alliance, the young prince could think of nothing else. At night he imagined all the ladies of the Court succumbing to the ardour of his desires, while during the day he was nervous and shy in their presence.

And then one afternoon, in one of the Palace corridors, he had suddenly run into this handsome girl, walking calmly in front of him, her hands full of linen. He had thrown himself upon her with violence and anger as if he owed her a grudge for the fear that troubled him. It must be her or no one, now or never. However, he had not raped her; his agitation, his anxiety, his clumsiness would have rendered him incapable of doing so. He had demanded from Eudeline that she should teach him love. Lacking a man's assurance, he intended to use the prerogatives of a prince. He had been lucky; Eudeline had not laughed at him, and had indeed evinced a certain pride at surrendering to the desires of a king's son, even allowing him to believe that she had found a certain pleasure in it. She had been so successful in this that for ever after he had felt himself to be a man in her presence.

Louis always sent for her when he was dressing himself to hunt or for the exercise of arms, and Eudeline had quickly realized that he particularly needed love when he was frightened. For several months before Marguerite came to Court, and even for some time afterwards, she had helped him, by the mere presence of her calm and generous body, to overcome his fears. And if The Hutin was capable of any hidden capacity for tenderness, he owed it to this handsome woman.

'Where is your daughter?' he asked.

'She is with my mother, who is bringing her up. I didn't want her to stay here with me; she looks too like her father,' replied Eudeline with a half-smile.

'At least,' Louis said, 'I believe she is mine.'

'Oh, but of course, Monseigneur, she is certainly yours! Sire, I mean to say. Every day her looks became more like yours. And it could only embarrass you to let her be seen by the Palace people.'

Because, indeed, a child, who was to be baptized Eudeline like her mother, had resulted from his hasty love-making. Any woman with a gift for intrigue would have assured her fortune by her pregnancy, and founded a line of barons. But The Hutin was so afraid of revealing the event to his father, that Eudeline had taken pity on him once again and remained silent. Her husband, who was clerk to Messire de Nogaret, had had some difficulty in accepting the fact that her pregnancy was due to a miracle which had, curiously enough, taken place while he was accompanying the Justiciar along the roads of Provence. He had protested so much that Eudeline had at last admitted the facts. The same kind of men are always attracted to the same kind of women. The clerk was not very courageous, and as soon as he knew from whom the gift came, his fear overwhelmed his anger as rain allays the wind. He too kept silent and arranged matters so that he might be absent from Paris as much as possible. He had, moreover, died soon afterwards, less from sorrow than from dysentery.

And Dame Eudeline had continued to manage the Palace washing, at the rate of fivepence per hundred pieces washed. She had become first linen-maid, which in the royal household was a position of middling importance.

During all this period the little Eudeline was growing up in that peculiar insolence common to bastards, that they bear upon their features the characteristics of their illegitimacy. But very few people knew about it.

Dame Eudeline always said to herself that one day The Hutin would remember. He had made so many promises, so solemnly sworn that when he became king he would lavish wealth and titles upon her daughter, and that she had everything to gain by waiting till that day!

She now thought that she had been right to believe him, surprised that he was so promptly fulfilling his promises. 'He really has a certain kindness of heart,' she thought. 'He is eccentric, but not ill-natured.'

Moved by her memories, by the thought of times past, by the strangeness of fate, she gazed at this sovereign who had found in her arms the first expression of his anxious virility, and who was now there before her, clothed in a nightshirt and sitting in an armchair, his hair falling to the level of his chin, his hands clasped about his knees. 'Why did this happen to me?' she said to herself. 'Why should it have happened to me?'

'How old is my daughter now?' he asked. 'Nine, isn't she?'

'Just nine, Sire.'

'I will give her the precedence of a princess as soon as she is old enough to marry. I wish it. And what can I do for you?'

He needed her. It was now or never to ask for rewards. Discretion counts for nothing with the great ones of the earth, and one must quickly take advantage of their momentary disposition to satisfy one's ambition. Because, later on, they inevitably feel themselves freed of their gratitude simply by having made the offer, and they forget to give. The Hutin would happily have spent the whole night discussing the benefits he would lavish upon her, merely so that Eudeline should keep him company till dawn. But, surprised by his question, she was content to reply, 'What you will, Sire.'

And then, since he was never much inclined to consider other people, he began thinking only of himself again.

'Oh, Eudeline, Eudeline!' he cried. 'I should have sent for you earlier and got you to come to the Hôtel de Nesle where I have been very unhappy these many months.'

'I know, Monseigneur Louis, that you have been very badly treated by your wife. But I would not have dared to come to you; I did not know whether you would have been glad or ashamed to see me again.'

He was no longer listening to her. He, too, had his vivid memories. His huge blue eyes, turned upon her, gleamed in the glow of the night-light. Eudeline well knew what that look meant. He had had it at fifteen, and never would have other in a woman's presence.

'Lie down,' he said shortly.

'Do you mean there, Monseigneur, I mean to say, Sire?' she murmured, somewhat afraid, indicating Philip the Fair's bed.

'Yes, there, that's what I do mean,' replied The Hutin in a hoarse voice.

Between what seemed to her sacrilege on the one hand and disobedience on the other, what could she do? After all, he was now King, and the bed was his. She took off her night-cap, let her dressing-gown and nightdress fall, and her golden tresses flowed down her back. She was rather stouter than she had been, but still had a beautifully curved waist, a broad and reassuring back, a silken thigh upon which the light played. All her gestures were submissive, and it was pre-cisely this submissiveness that The Hutin was in need of. He watched her mount the little oaken steps to get into bed and thought that, as a warming-pan overcame its chill, so this beautiful body would overcome the demons that haunted it.

A little anxious and bewildered, but above all submitting to her destiny, Eudeline had slipped beneath the golden counterpane.

'He was right,' she thought immediately; 'these new sheets scratch! I knew it.'

Louis had feverishly taken off his nightshirt; narrow of chest, bony of shoulder, heavily clumsy, he threw himself upon her with a desperate haste, as if he could not risk deferring for one instant the opportunity that was now his.

A vain haste. In certain things kings are like other men; they cannot control everything. The Hutin's desires were largely cerebral. Clutching Eudeline's shoulders, as might a drowning man a lifebuoy, he strove with every feint to over-come an impotence which seemed beyond hope. 'Certainly, if he was unable to honour Madame Marguerite with more satisfactory attentions than these,' Eudeline said to herself, 'one can see why she deceived him.'

Every silent encouragement that she gave him, all the efforts he made, which certainly had none of the appearance of a prince marching to victory, remained unsuccessful. At last he sat up, trembling, defeated, ashamed, hesitating between rage and tears.

She tried to calm him. 'You have walked a long way today. And you got very cold,' she said. 'You must also be sad at heart, and it's quite natural upon the evening of the day you have buried your father; it can happen to anyone, you know.'

With staring eyes he looked at the beautiful fair woman, so available but so inaccessible, stretched out before him as if she were the incarnation of some mythological punishment.

She gazed at him with compassion.

'It's all due to that bitch!' he said. 'It's all her fault.'

Eudeline drew away from him, thinking that the insult was meant for her.

'I was thinking of Marguerite. I cannot help thinking of her, seeing her in my imagination. And this bed is accursed too!' he cried. 'To sleep in it is to sleep in misfortune!'

'No, Monseigneur Louis,' she replied gently, drawing him to her. 'No, it's a fine bed, but it is the bed of a king. I under-stand very well; to free yourself of your impotence, you must put a queen in it.'

She was moved, and being modest was not in the least put

out, since she was a good-natured creature. 'Do you really think so, Eudeline?' he asked, gazing at her.

'Of course, Monseigneur Louis; I am sure of it; in a king's bed there should be a queen,' she repeated.

'Perhaps I shall soon have one. It seems that she is fair like you.'

'That is a great compliment you are paying me,' replied Eudeline.

And she turned her face away to hide the wound that he had just dealt her heart.

'It seems that she is very beautiful,' went on The Hutin, 'and extremely virtuous. She lives in Naples.'

'Of course, Monseigneur Louis, of course. I am sure that she will make you happy. Now you must try to go to sleep.'

She had drawn his head down on to her warm, lavender-smelling shoulder. She listened maternally to his dreaming aloud of this unknown woman, of this distant princess whose place tonight she had so vainly taken. With the mirage of the future he consoled himself for the misfortunes of the past and the disappointments of the present.

'Of course, Monseigneur Louis, that is exactly the kind of wife you need. You will see how virile you will be with her.'

At last he grew silent. And Eudeline remained still, not daring to move, thinking, staring wide-eyed at the flickering glow of the night-light, waiting for dawn to release her.

The King of France slept.

PART TWO
DOG EATS DOG

The Hutin's First Council

EVERY DAY FOR THE last sixteen years Enguerrand de Marigny had known that when he went into the Council Chamber he would find friends there. But this morning he had hardly entered the room when he felt with certainty that everything had changed. He stood still for a moment, his left hand at the collar of his robe, his right hand gripping his file of documents.

There were more or less the same number of people as usual sitting on each side of the long table, while the fire on the hearth crackled and filled the room with the familiar odour of burning wood. It was the faces that were no longer the same.

Certainly, the members of the royal family, who by right and tradition attended the Inner Council, were present; the Counts of Valois and Evreux, the Count of Poitiers and the young Prince Charles; the Constable Gaudier de Châtillon; but they no longer sat in their accustomed places, and

Monseigneur of Valois had installed himself upon the right of the royal chair, where ordinarily Marigny sat.

Nor were Raoul de Presles, or Nicole le Loquetier, or Guillaume Dubois, eminent justiciars, faithful servants of Philip the Fair, present. New men had taken their places: Mathieu de Trye, Chamberlain to Louis X, Etienne de Mornay, Chancellor to the Count of Valois, and others besides, whom Marigny knew but with whom he had never worked.

It was not exactly a change of ministry, but rather, as one would say in the language of today, a remodelling of the cabinet. Of the former Councillors of the Iron King, only Hugues de Bouville and Béraud de Mercœur had been kept, doubtless because they both belonged to the great nobility. And indeed they too had been sent down to the bottom of the table. All the Councillors who had risen from the middle class had been eliminated. 'I might at least have been told!' thought Marigny angrily.

Speaking to Hugues de Bouville, he asked in a loud voice, so that he might be heard by all present, 'Is Messire de Presles ill? Have Messires de Bourdenai, de Briançon and Dubois been prevented from attending, since I see none of them here? Have they sent excuses for their absence?'

Fat Bouville hesitated for a moment and then replied, lowering his eyes as if he were to blame, 'I was not responsible for summoning the Council. Messire de Mornay attended to it.'

Marigny's expression hardened and those present awaited an outburst.

But Monseigneur of Valois quickly intervened, saying slowly and affably, 'You have not forgotten, my good Marigny, that the King calls whom he will to the Council in accordance with his own judgement. It is the sovereign's right.'

There was a certain contemptuous condescension in the phrase, 'My good Marigny,' which did not escape the Rector of the kingdom. Never would Valois have spoken to him in that manner during Philip the Fair's life. Marigny very nearly replied that, if it was in fact the King's right to summon to his Council whom he pleased, it was also his duty to choose its members from men who understood affairs of state, and that people did not become competent in these matters in twenty-four hours.

But he preferred to reserve his strength for some more important argument and sat down, apparently calm, opposite Monseigneur of Valois, upon the chair left empty on the left of the royal seat.

Enguerrand de Marigny was forty-nine years old, had red hair turning somewhat yellow with the years, a deep chest and wide shoulders. His chin was heavy and determined, his aspect rugged, his nose short with wide nostrils.

He held his head somewhat inclined forward and seemed always about to charge like a bull with his forehead. His eyes, under heavy lids, were restless, quick and authoritative, and his hands, in their nervous slenderness, were in contrast to the heaviness of his general appearance.

He opened his file of documents, took out papers, parchments and tablets, placing them in front of him. But failing to find beneath the table-top the hook upon which he normally hung his file, he sighed irritably and shrugged his shoulders.

Monseigneur of Valois had begun talking to his nephew Charles, whom he was telling that a happy surprise would shortly be announced and that he counted upon his support on all points. Monseigneur of Valois, in spite of Court mourning, or perhaps because of it, was more superbly dressed than ever. The black velvet of his robe had the richness of fur and was ornamented with silver embroidery and miniver which gave him an appearance of being caparisoned like a horse in a hearse. He had no papers before him, nor any materials for taking notes. His Chancellor, Etienne de Mornay, had the subaltern duty of reading and writing: as for himself, he contented himself with talking.

There were steps in the corridor.

'Here comes Monseigneur Louis,' said Hugues de Bouville.

Valois was the first to get to his feet, which he did with so majestic and obvious a deference for him who entered that his manner became of itself protective.

Louis X glanced round the standing gathering.

'Messires, forgive my being late . . .'

He fell silent, annoyed by what he had said.

He had forgotten that the King was never late, since he always entered the Council Room last.

He was seized with the same sort of anxiety that he had felt the day before at Saint-Denis and during the previous night.

Now was the time that he must show himself King. But it is not a state that is miraculously achieved, and Louis waited, his arms hanging loose, his eyes red from the insomnia for which his too-short sleep had not succeeded in making up. He forgot to ask the Council to sit down, or to sit down himself.

Seconds passed, the silence became painful, and everyone felt that the King was a prey to irresolution.

Marigny made the necessary gesture; he slightly moved

the royal chair as if to make it easy for Louis to sit down.

Louis took his seat and murmured, 'Be seated, Messires.'

In his mind he saw once more his father sitting in the same place and automatically assumed his usual pose: both hands flat upon the table, his glance fixed, apparently absent. This gave him sufficient assurance to turn to his two brothers and say to them in a natural voice, 'You should know, my dear Brothers, that my first commands this morning have been on your behalf. Philippe, your Countship of Poitiers is raised to a peerage of the realm, and from now on you are numbered among the peers so that you may stand by my side, as Uncle Valois stood beside a father whom God keep, to assist me in supporting the crown. Charles, you will receive in fief and apanage the County of la Marche, which our father bought back from the Lusignan, and which he had the intention, I know, of giving you.'

Philippe and Charles rose to their feet and went to kiss their brother's cheek as a sign of their gratitude. Monseigneur of Valois looked towards his nephew Charles with an expression that seemed to say, 'You see, I have done pretty well by you.'

The others present nodded their heads with satisfaction; as a start, it was not too bad.

But Louis X was displeased with himself, for he had forgotten to begin by rendering homage to the memory of his father and by speaking of the continuity of power.

Moreover, he had had a couple of admirable sentences prepared for him during the morning; but they had escaped his mind in the emotion caused by his entrance, and now he had nothing more to say.

The silence soon became unbearable again. There was obviously someone missing from this assembly: the dead man.

Enguerrand de Marigny gazed at the young King, obviously expecting him to say, 'Messire, I confirm you in your duties of Coadjutor and Rector-General of the kingdom, Chamberlain, Chancellor of the Exchequer and Minister of Works, Captain of the Louvre . . .'

Since nothing happened, Marigny behaved as if it had been said, and asked, 'Upon what matters does the King wish to be informed? Of the collecting of the subsidies and taxes, of the state of the Treasury, of the decisions of Parliament, of the growing famine in the provinces, of the dispositions of the garrisons, of the situation in Flanders, of the claims and demands of the leagues of the barons in Burgundy and Champagne?'

This quite clearly signified, 'Sire, these are the questions about which I am busy, and there are many others too, which I could reel off as I say my beads. Do you think you can get on without me?'

The Hutin, anxious and apparently taken aback, turned towards his uncle Valois as if asking for support.

'Messire de Marigny, the King has not called us together to deal with these matters,' said the Count of Valois. 'He will listen to them later.'

'If I am not advised of the agenda of the Council, Monseigneur, I cannot be expected to guess it,' replied Marigny.

'The King, Messire,' continued Valois as if he had not heard the interruption, 'the King wishes to hear our views upon the most important anxiety which, as a good sovereign, he can have: that of his posterity and the succession to the throne.'

'That is precisely it, Messire,' said The Hutin, trying to assume a tone of grandeur in order to express a desire from which it was lacking by its very nature. 'My first duty is to provide for the succession to the throne and for that I need a wife . . .'

He stopped short.

'The King, therefore, has come to the conclusion that he must marry again,' went on Valois. 'And his attention is fixed, after long consideration, upon Madame Clémence of Hungary, niece to the King of Naples. We wish to have the benefit of your advice before sending an embassy.'

The phrase 'we wish' sounded disagreeably in the ears of many of those present. Was it Monseigneur of Valois who reigned?

Philippe of Poitiers inclined his long head on one side. 'That is why,' he thought, 'they have begun by buttering me up with a peerage of the realm! As long as Louis did not marry again, I was second in the line of succession after the little Jeanne, who is suspected of being a bastard. If he takes another wife, and she gives him further children, I shall count for nothing. And they have decided this without consulting either Charles or myself, who are in the same position as Louis, with imprisoned wives.'[11]

'What is Monseigneur de Marigny's opinion of this proposal?' he asked in order to be disagreeable to Valois.

At the same time, he was knowingly committing a gross breach of etiquette towards his elder brother, because in principle it was the sovereign, and the sovereign alone, who asked the councillors to give their opinions. There would have been hell to pay if such a breach had occurred at a Council of King Philip's.

But today everyone seemed to be taking individual command, and since the new King's uncle was taking it upon himself to dominate the Council, the brother might well take the liberty of doing as much.

Marigny leant forward with his bull-like forehead, and it was clear that he was about to charge.

'Since the King's consideration has turned in the direction of Madame of Hungary, she must naturally have great queenly qualities,' he said. 'But, apart from the fact that she is Monseigneur of Valois's niece, which naturally suffices to make us love her, I do not clearly see how this alliance will profit the kingdom. Her father, Charles Martel, has been dead a long time, having been King of Hungary only in name; her brother Charobert [unlike Monseigneur of Valois, who affected the Italian pronunciation of these names, Marigny said them in French] has at last achieved a year or two ago, after fifteen years of fighting and intriguing, the Magyar crown which still sits rather loosely upon his head. All the fiefs and principalities of the House of Anjou have already been distributed among the family, which is so numerous that it spreads across the world like oil upon a cloth, and it might soon be thought that the royal family of France was but a branch of the line of Anjou. One can certainly not expect from such a marriage an enlargement of the kingdom, as King Philip always desired, nor any help in war if it were to become necessary, since all these remote princes have enough to do to retain their own possessions. In other words, Sire, I am certain that your father would have opposed a union in which the dowry was nebulous rather than assured.'

Monseigneur of Valois had gone crimson with anger; his knee began shaking under the table. Everything that had been said was directed against him, each phrase had a perfidious tendency.

'It is all very fine, Messire de Marigny,' he cried, 'to make the dead speak from the tomb. I shall reply that a queen's virtue is worth a province! The splendid alliances you wove so cleverly with Burgundy, and to which you so craftily persuaded my brother, have not turned out so well that you can set yourself up as a judge in these matters; or that you can expect to be consulted once again. Shame and sorrow resulted for everyone concerned.'

'That is the truth!' cried The Hutin sharply.

'Sire,' replied Marigny with almost imperceptible contempt, 'you were still very young when your marriage was decided upon by your father, and Monseigneur of Valois did not seem so opposed to it then. He made all haste, and without too close an investigation, to marry off his own son to Madame Marguerite's sister, in order to relate himself more nearly to her and to you.'

Valois was forced to admit the impeachment and found no answer. His face became more blotched than ever. He had, in fact, believed himself extremely clever to marry his elder son, Philippe, to the younger sister of Marguerite, who was known as Jeanne the Little, or Jeanne the Halt, because she had one leg shorter than the other. And now Marguerite was in prison, and the cripple a member of his family.[12]

'Women's virtue, like their beauty, is a passing thing, Sire,' went on Marigny. 'But provinces are permanent. And

Monseigneur of Poitiers cannot dispute the fact that we possess the Franche-Comté.'

'Is this Council,' asked Valois roughly, 'to be devoted to listening to Messire de Marigny praising himself, or to the advancement of the King's wishes?'

Tempers were rising; the discussion had become a paying off of old scores.

'In any case, Monseigneur,' replied Marigny, 'it would make more sense not to put the cart before the horse. We may consider all the princesses on earth for the King. I can well understand his impatience. But we have first to get him unmarried from his present wife. The Count of Artois appears not to have brought back the answers you expected from Château-Gaillard,' he continued in order to show that he was well informed. 'The first requirement for an annulment is a Pope . . .'

'The Pope you have been promising us for the last six months, Marigny, has not yet materialized out of this phantom conclave. Your envoys have so successfully bullied and defenestrated the cardinals at Carpentras that, raising their soutanes, they have fled across country and can no longer be found. You have little reason to think it a stroke of genius! Had you shown greater moderation, and that respect due to the ministers of God, which is so alien to you, we would not be in our present difficulty.'

'Up till now I have succeeded in preventing the election of a Pope who would be the creature of the King of Naples, because King Philip particularly wished that there should be one useful to France.'

Men who love power are not only dominated, as is

generally supposed, by an appetite for wealth and honours. Above all they are influenced by an objective taste for the creation of events, for controlling their occurrence, for acting upon the world with effectiveness and for being always in the right. Wealth and honours are no more than the signs and tools of their influence.

Marigny and Valois were both men of this particular stamp and, in Council, the successful man from the middle classes had nearly always won the day over the Prince of the Blood. Only Philip the Fair had succeeded in keeping these two adversaries at arm's length, using the political understanding of the one and the military ability of the other to the best advantage.

Louis X was completely submerged by the storm; the argument was going much too rapidly for him, and he was unable to forget certain painful memories of the previous night.

Monseigneur of Evreux intervened in an endeavour to quiet their tempers, and brought forward a formula which might conciliate the two positions.

'If, in exchange for a marriage with the Princess Clémence, we obtained from the King of Naples an agreement that the Pope should be French,' he proposed, 'and elected with all speed ...'

'Certainly, Monseigneur,' said Marigny more calmly, 'such an agreement would have certain benefits; but I very much doubt whether we can get it.'

'Nevertheless, let us send an embassy to Naples if that be the King's wish.'

'Most assuredly, Monseigneur.'

MAURICE DRUON

'Bouville, what do you advise?' said The Hutin suddenly, in order to give an appearance of continuing the discussion in hand.

Fat Bouville started. He had made an excellent Chamberlain, overseeing the expenditure and managing the household with precision, but his mind was not capable of any great flights. Philip the Fair hardly ever spoke to him in Council except to order him to open the windows.

'Sire,' he said, 'you are seeking a wife from a noble family; they maintain all the old traditions of chivalry. We should be honoured to serve such a Queen ...'

He stopped, interrupted by a glance from Marigny which seemed to say, 'You are betraying me, Bouville!'

Hugues de Bouville, a Norman like Marigny, was five years the elder. It was in his household, as an equerry, that Marigny had begun his career. The equerry had not been slow to surpass his lord, but had always faithfully dragged his old master after him in his extraordinary rise.

Fat Bouville lowered his head. He was so devoted a servant of the crown and so dazzled by royal majesty that, when the King spoke to him, he could not but approve. That The Hutin was an idiot was not apparent to him; he was *The King* and Bouville was prepared to lavish upon him all the zeal that he had shown towards Philip the Fair.

This servility received its immediate recompense, for The Hutin decided, to everyone's surprise, that Bouville should be sent to Naples.

Moreover, there was no opposition. The Count of Valois, believing that he could arrange everything by letter, thought that a mediocre but tractable man was exactly the ambassa-

92

dor he required. While Marigny thought, 'All right, send him then. He has as much cunning as a child of three. You'll see what the results will be.'

So, blushing, the good servant found himself charged with an important mission he had never expected.

'Don't forget, Bouville, that I must have a Pope,' said the young King.

'Sire, I shall have no other idea in my mind.'

Louis X was impatient for his departure. He wished his messenger already upon the road. He suddenly seemed to gain authority.

'On your way back you will pass through Avignon,' he went on. 'You will do your best to hasten the conclave. And since the cardinals, so it appears, are to be bought, you will get Messire de Marigny to furnish you with sufficient gold.'

'Where shall I find the gold, Sire?' asked the latter.

'Good God, in the Treasury of course!'

'The Treasury is empty, Sire, that is to say there is enough in it only to cover the necessary expenses between now and the Feast of Saint Nicholas, no more.'

'What do you mean, the Treasury is empty?' cried Valois. 'Why haven't you told us this before?'

'I wished to begin with it, Monseigneur, but you prevented me.'

'And why, in your opinion, is it empty?'

'Because, Monseigneur, the revenue from taxes does not easily accrue from a starving people. Because the barons, as you will be the first to realize,' said Marigny, his voice rising insolently, 'refuse to pay the dues which they had agreed. Because the loan from the Lombard companies has been exhausted by the war in Flanders, the war you so strongly recommended . . .'

'And which you wished to terminate upon your own authority,' cried Valois, 'before our knights could find an opportunity of glory and our finances of profit. If the kingdom has drawn no advantage from the peculiar treaties you went there to conclude, I imagine that that does not hold good for you, Marigny, because it is not your habit to overlook your own advantage in any business you undertake. I know this to my own detriment.'

He was alluding in this last phrase to an exchange of lands which had taken place between them in 1310, when Valois had asked Marigny to yield him his lordship of Champrond against that of Gaillefontaine, and had ever afterwards considered himself cheated.

'Nevertheless,' said Louis X, 'Bouville must set out as soon as possible.'

Marigny, without appearing to pay the slightest attention to the King's last words, cried, 'Sire, I would wish Monseigneur of Valois to elaborate what he has just said upon the subject of the treaties of Lille or, alternatively, to retract his words.'

A terrifying silence fell over the Council. Would the Count of Valois dare repeat straight out the appalling accusations he had just brought against his brother's Coadjutor.

Monseigneur of Valois did so dare.

'I tell you to your face, Messire, as everyone says behind your back, that the Flemish bought you to effect the retreat of our army, and that you embezzled money which should have been paid over to the Treasury.'

Marigny rose to his feet. Indignation had paled his

blotchy skin, and he now adopted the pose of his statue in the Mercer's Hall.

'Sire,' he said, 'I have listened today to more than a man of honour should hear in the whole course of his life. I possess what I do only from the benefits that the King, your father, lavished upon me for the services I rendered as his lieutenant for sixteen years. I have now been accused in your presence of embezzlement, of commerce with the enemies of the kingdom; nor has any voice been raised in my defence, not even yours, Sire. I demand that a commission be appointed to look into the accounts for which I am responsible to you and to you alone.'

Anger is contagious. Louis X suddenly grew irritated with the attitude Marigny had displayed since the opening of the Council, the manner with which he had thwarted his proposals, treated him like a small boy, and made him feel all too clearly how inferior he was to his father.

'Very well, Messire, the commission will be appointed,' he replied, 'since you demand it yourself.'

By these words he separated himself from the only minister capable of commanding in his stead and of directing the policy of his reign. Mediocrities can tolerate being surrounded only by flatterers who conceal their mediocrity. France was to pay through long years for this momentary resentment.

Marigny picked up his file, filled it with his documents, and went to the door. This action increased The Hutin's irritation.

'From now on,' he added, 'you will have no further concern with our Treasury.'

'I shall take the greatest care not to, Sire,' said Marigny, leaving the room.

And his feet could be heard fading down the length of the corridor.

Valois was triumphant, surprised almost at the speed with which his enemy's fall had been brought about.

'You are wrong, Brother,' said the Count of Evreux; 'you cannot browbeat a man of that sort.'

'I had good reason,' replied Valois; 'and you will soon be grateful to me for it. Marigny is a blot upon the face of the kingdom. He had to be squashed as soon as possible.'

'Well, Uncle,' asked The Hutin, reverting to his one anxiety, 'when will you send the embassy to Madame Clémence?'

As soon as Valois had promised that Bouville would set out within the week, he closed the meeting. He wanted to stretch his legs.

2

Marigny Remains Rector-General

AS HE WENT HOME, preceded as usual by three sergeant-mace-bearers, and followed by two secretaries and an equerry, Monseigneur de Marigny did not as yet comprehend what had occurred, how destiny had turned so abruptly against him. He was blinded by anger. 'That impudent rascal accuses me of having taken bribes over the treaties,' he said to himself. 'He's a fine one to talk! And as for this little King, who has got the brains of a flea and the surliness of a wasp, who says not one single word in my defence, but instead takes the Treasury out of my control!'

He rode on, unaware of the streets and the people he passed, unobservant of the hostile faces of those forced to make way for him. He was not loved. He had governed men from so high a position and for so long that he had lost the knack of looking at them.

Having reached his house in the Rue des Fossés-Saint-Germain, he leapt from his horse without awaiting the help of his equerry, walked quickly across the courtyard, threw his cloak over the arm of the first servant he met and, still holding his file of documents, mounted the stairs leading to the first floor.

His house was less like a private residence than a government office: heavy furniture, huge chandeliers, thick carpets, lavish hangings, nothing but solid furnishings designed to last. An army of servants were at his beck and call.

Enguerrand de Marigny opened the door of the room in which he knew he would find his wife. She was playing by the hearth with a miniature Italian dog, a dog with a grey clipped coat, resembling a tiny horse. Her sister, Dame de Chanteloup, a talkative widow, sat beside her.

From her husband's appearance, Madame de Marigny knew at once that something was wrong.

'Enguerrand, my dear, what has happened?' she asked.

Jeanne de Saint-Martin, goddaughter of the late Queen Jeanne, wife of Philip the Fair, lived in a state of perpetual admiration for the man she had married, and her devotion to him was the centre of her life.

'What has happened,' replied Marigny, 'is that, now the master is no longer there to hold them in check, the hounds have attacked me.'

'Is there anything I can do?'

He replied that he could well look after himself so harshly that Madame de Marigny's eyes filled with tears. Enguerrand was immediately remorseful. He took her by the shoulders, kissed her forehead at the edge of her ash-blonde hair and said, 'I know very well, Jeanne, that I have no one to love me but you!'

Then he went to his study, and threw his documents on a chest. His hands were trembling, and he very nearly dropped a candelabra he wanted to move. He swore, and then walked up and down between the window and the fire, giving his anger a chance to simmer down.

'You have taken the Treasury from me, but you have forgotten the rest. Just wait a little; you won't break me as easily as that.'

He rang a handbell.

'Send me four guards at once,' he said to the servant who answered.

The men came running from the guardroom, holding their belilied staves in their hands. Marigny gave them their orders.

'You go and find me Messire Alain de Pareilles, who should be at the Louvre. You, find my brother, the Archbishop, at the Episcopal Palace. You, Messires Guillaume Dubois and Raoul de Presles, and you, Messire le Loquetier. Find them wherever they may be. I shall await them here.'

The messengers departed and Enguerrand opened the door of the room in which his secretaries worked. 'I want to dictate,' he said.

A clerk came to him, carrying his tablet and his pens.

'Sire,' began Marigny, standing with his back to the fire, 'in the condition in which I am, now that God has called to Himself the greatest King France has ever known . . .'

He was writing to Edward II, King of England, and son-in-law of Philip the Fair by his marriage to Isabella. Since 1308, the date of the union he had taken a hand in bringing about, Marigny had had numerous opportunities of rendering Edward political and private services. The marriage was not going well, and Isabella complained of her husband's abnormalities. The situation in Guyenne was still serious ... Marigny, together with his enemy, Charles of Valois, had been selected to represent the King of France at the coronation at Westminster. In 1313 the English King, on a visit to France, had thanked the Coadjutor with a life-pension of a thousand pounds a year.

Now Marigny needed King Edward's help and was writing to ask him to intervene in his favour. He managed to convey in his letter the benefits that would accrue to him provided the policy of France should not change direction. Those who had worked together for the peace of empires should remain united.

The clerk hastened to dry the parchment and present it for signature.

'Am I to send it by the couriers, Monseigneur?' he asked.

'No. This will be taken to its destination by my son. Send one of your underlings for him, if he is not in the house.'

The secretary went out, and Marigny unclasped the collar of his robe; he felt his neck swelling at the thought of action.

'How sad for the kingdom,' he said to himself. 'What a state they will bring it to, if they are not opposed. Have I done so much only to see all my efforts brought to nothing?'

Like all men who have exercised power for a long time, he had come to identify himself with the country, and to consider every attack made upon him personally as a direct attack upon the interests of the State.

As things were, he was not far wrong; but he was nevertheless prepared to act against the interests of the kingdom as soon as its direction was taken out of his own hands.

It was in this state of mind that he received his brother Jean de Marigny. The Archbishop, his thin body clothed in a clinging violet gown, had a studied manner which the Coadjutor disliked. He wanted to say to his younger brother, 'You can give yourself airs with your canons if you like, but don't do it with me who has seen you slobbering your soup and blowing your nose in your fingers.'

In a very few words he summed up what had happened at the Council he had just left, and without hesitation gave him his orders in the same unanswerable tone of voice he used to his secretaries.

'I don't want a Pope just yet, because as long as there is no Pope I have the King in my power. There must be no managed conclave prepared to obey Bouville's orders. There must be no peace for the cardinals at Avignon. Let them fight and argue; you arrange it, Jean, till I give you further orders.'

Jean de Marigny, who had begun by sharing his brother's anger, looked gloomy when the conclave was mentioned. He thought for a moment, contemplating his handsome bishop's ring.

'Well, what are you thinking about?' Enguerrand asked.

'Brother,' said the Archbishop, 'I find your plans somewhat against the grain. In sowing further discord in the conclave than there is already, I run the risk of alienating the friendship of a certain candidate who, very well placed at this moment to win election to the Papacy, would give me, as soon as elected, a cardinal's hat.'

Enguerrand burst out, 'Your hat! This is a fine time to speak of it! If you ever do get a hat, my poor Jean, it is I who will give it you, as I gave you your mitre. But if you propose joining my enemies against me, you will soon be going, not only without a hat, but without shoes, a mere miserable monk, exiled to some monastery. You seem to have forgotten rather too quickly what you owe me, for instance, that unfortunate situation concerning the embezzlement of the Templars' possessions, from which I rescued you two months ago. And, by the way, have you succeeded in laying your hands upon that unfortunate receipt you gave the banker Tolomei, by means of which the Lombards made me climb down when I wanted to raise their taxes?'

'Of course, Brother,' replied the Archbishop untruthfully.

But he immediately hauled down his flag.

'What must I do?' he asked.

'You must send messengers whom you can trust beyond question, I mean people who are in your power for one reason or another and are so placed as to be afraid of my displeasure. They must spread two contradictory rumours; on the one hand, pretending to the French that the new King proposes to allow the Holy See to return to Rome; on the other, telling the Italians that he intends imprisoning the next Pope in the neighbourhood of Paris. Let them sow all the discord of which clerics are capable among themselves. Our good Bouville will lose himself in a vacuum. Bertrand de Got shook the cardinals a little too much; but we shall try a different tactic upon them: the fear of what does not exist. They don't care for each other now, I want them to hate each other, and blame each other for their mutual faults. Let me know how things go week by week, if I cannot be informed of a situation day by day. Does our young Louis X want a

Pope? He shall have one, when the time comes, but certainly not just any Pope through whom we might lose at a single blow all that King Philip and I have taken so long to extract from two previous Pontiffs. If you can, arrange matters so that your envoys do not know each other.'

Thereupon he dismissed his brother so as to see his son who was waiting outside the door. Louis de Marigny, as so often happens in families, resembled the Archbishop more than he did his father. He was slender, much too concerned with his personal appearance, and rather too elaborately dressed.

Son of a personage before whom the whole kingdom bowed down, godson moreover of Louis The Hutin, he did not know what it was to have to struggle to satisfy his wants. He was shallow and liked to affect that appearance of nobility which is more commonly assumed in the second generation than the tenth; and if he greatly admired his father, to whom he owed everything and who dominated him from such a height, he still blamed him for a certain coarseness of manner. The young man had but one quality, or rather but one vocation: he loved horses, and knew how to manage them as if chivalry had been in his blood for two centuries.

'Go and get ready, Louis,' said Enguerrand. 'You are leaving at once for London to deliver a letter.'

The young man's face expressed annoyance.

'Cannot my departure be put off till tomorrow, Father, or couldn't a courier go instead? I am due to hunt tomorrow in the Bois de Boulogne, only a small occasion of course because of Court mourning, but . . .'

'Hunting! It's about time you began thinking of something

else but hunting,' cried Marigny. 'Can I never ask my family, who owe me everything, to do the least thing without their looking sulky? You may as well know that I am being hunted at this moment! And if you don't help me, I shall be skinned alive and you too. If a courier would have done, I could have thought of it myself! I am sending you to the King of England, and I have things to say to him which I cannot put in writing. Does that sufficiently flatter your vanity to persuade you to give up a day's hunting?'

'Forgive me, Father,' said Louis de Marigny. 'I did not understand.'

Marigny took up the case which enclosed the letter.

'You know King Edward from having seen him a year or so ago in Paris. You will say the following to him in person: "Monseigneur of Valois wishes to have complete authority for himself. I fear, if he succeeds in acquiring it, that he will alter the agreements the two kingdoms have come to over Guyenne. Moreover, Valois wishes to remarry the new King to a princess of Anjou-Hungary, which will align his alliances towards the south rather than the north." That is all. Let the King of England ponder these two matters! I will keep in touch with him concerning any developments there may be.'

Marigny gazed at his son for a moment. 'Our royal Edward,' he thought, 'has a great appreciation of masculine beauty. Perhaps he will not be altogether insensible to our messenger's appearance.'

'Take with you only two equerries and such servants as are essential. Don't have too showy a train so long as you are in France. And you may draw two hundred, no, one hundred pounds from my treasurer; that will suffice.'

There was a double knock at the door.

'Messire Alain de Pareilles has arrived,' said a guard.

'Show him in. Goodbye, Louis; a good journey to you.'

Enguerrand de Marigny embraced his son, a thing he did but rarely. Then he turned towards Alain de Pareilles who was coming in, took him by the arm and, leading him to a seat by the hearth, said, 'Warm yourself, Pareilles, the cold is appalling.'

The Captain-General of the Archers had iron-grey hair, features heavily lined by time and war, and he had seen so much fighting, so many alarms and excursions, so much torture and execution that he could no longer be surprised by anything. The hanged of Montfaucon were to him an accustomed spectacle. In the last year alone he had led the Grand Master of the Templars to the pyre, the Aunay brothers to the wheel, and the royal Princesses to prison. But he was also in charge of the Corps of Archers and Sergeants-at-Arms in all the fortresses, and was thus responsible for preserving order throughout the kingdom. Marigny, who never addressed any member of his family in the familiar second person, used it to this old friend, the faultless, unyielding instrument of his power.

'Alain, I've got two missions for you and they must be carried out without delay,' said Marigny. 'You will go yourself to Château-Gaillard and give the fool in command of it a good shaking up. By the way, what is his name?'

'Bersumée, Robert Bersumée,' replied Pareilles.

'You will tell Bersumée that he must continue to conform to the instructions I gave him in the past with the consent of King Philip. I know that the Count of Artois has been there.

This is directly contrary to orders. If he were to be sent there, he or another, it should go through me. Only the King may go there; and there's not much risk of that. There must be no visits to Madame Marguerite, not a letter, nothing at all! You can tell the fool that I'll have his ears cut off if he doesn't obey me.'

'What are you proposing to do with Madame Marguerite?' asked Pareilles.

'For the moment she is a hostage. She must not be allowed to communicate with anyone, and let her safety be well looked to. I need her alive, and for a long time yet. If her way of life is having a bad effect upon her health, let it be made easier. The second order I have for you is this: as soon as you come back from Normandy, you will leave for the south. You will have sent ahead of you three hundred men from the Paris reserves to await you at Orange. Arrived there, you will take command of them and install them in the fort of Villeneuve, opposite Avignon. I want you to make a considerable stir about taking possession of the place. Make your archers march six times round the ramparts. Seen from beyond the river, they will look as if they numbered two thousand. I want the cardinals to shiver in their robes, and it's for their benefit I am organizing this masquerade. It will complement the trick I'm playing on them by other means. When you have done this, leave your men in position and return.'

'By God, that suits me well, Messire Enguerrand,' said Alain de Pareilles. 'To go and give that fool a piece of my mind and put the fear of God into those red-clothed asses will be a pleasant change from inspecting the Palace guard; and here . . .'

He stopped, hesitating to go on, and at last came out with what he had upon his mind.

'. . . and here, to tell you the truth, Enguerrand, there is an atmosphere which I don't care for.'

He sadly shook his iron-grey head.

'All the same, you must stay here,' replied Marigny. 'I fear that the servants of King Philip will have much to suffer in the days ahead. I need you in command of the Archers. You need not warn the Constable about the movement of troops I have ordered; I'll tell him myself. Goodbye, Alain.'

Then he went into his study where the justiciars he had sent for and some others as well, such as Briançon and Bourgenai, who had come of their own accord at the news, had gathered. Their familiar voices fell silent at his entry. The walls of the room were furnished with carved desks equipped with ink-horns and writing-tablets from which depended weights to hold the parchments flat. Upon swivelled reading-desks lay files and documents. These furnishings made the room look like a chapel or a monastic library.

'Messires,' said Enguerrand de Marigny, gazing with emotion upon his friends, 'you were not done the honour of being summoned to the Council which I attended this morning. We shall now hold a very private Council among ourselves.'

'We shall lack only King Philip,' said Raoul de Presles with a melancholy smile.

'Let us pray that his soul will come to our aid. He did not doubt us,' replied Marigny.

Then with renewed anger he cried, 'I have been asked to submit my accounts to examination, Messires, and I have had the Treasury removed from my control. I therefore wish to produce a very accurate account. Issue orders to every bailiwick and seneschalship that all accounts must be paid, beginning with the smallest debts. Let all supplies be paid for, all work in progress, everything that has been ordered in the name of the crown. Let everything be paid till there is no gold left, even where delay is possible.'

The others had already grasped the game he was playing. Enguerrand cracked his finger-joints as if he were in process of strangling someone. 'Monseigneur of Constantinople wishes to take over the Treasury, does he?' he cried. 'Much good may it do him! He'll have to look elsewhere for the money to pay for his intrigues!'

3

Charles of Valois

IF THE ATMOSPHERE WERE stormy on the left bank at Monseigneur de Marigny's, the contrary was true on the right bank at the Count of Valois's house.

A conscious sense of pride lay over the whole household. The most junior equerry felt that he had ministerial authority for rebuking the footmen, the women ordered people about more tyrannically than before, and the children screamed more loudly.

Everyone knew, or wished to show that he knew; everyone was sharing in advance in the events that were taking place, and in his own way; there were widespread boasting, backstairs whisperings, much importunate flattery and general running to and fro; the baronial party was triumphant.

Seeing the number of people who, on the very first morning after the dramatic Council, crowded into the rooms to show that they were faithful supporters of the winning party,

one might have thought that the real Court was not at the
Palace of the Cité, but at the Hôtel de Valois.

Moreover, it was a kingly residence! There was no beam in
the ceilings that was not carved, nor a hearth whose monumental chimney-piece was not decorated with the escutcheons
of France and Constantinople. The stone floors were covered
with oriental rugs, and the walls with Cyprian tapestries
embroidered with gold. On tables and sideboards silver and
carved silver-gilt stood side by side with enamels and precious
stones.

Chamberlains, newly important, gravely passed each other
instructions, and there was no one down to the last writing-
clerk who did not endeavour to assume a dignified air.

The ladies-in-waiting to the Countess of Valois gossiped
in a group about Canon Etienne de Mornay who, after
Monseigneur of Valois, was the man of the hour. A whole
following, effervescent, busy, flattering, came and went,
stood in the window embrasures and discussed public affairs.
Everyone was there, making pretence of having been
summoned, for Monseigneur of Valois was, in fact, holding
consultations in his study.

Even the fabulous Sire de Joinville had been seen to
arrive supported by a white-bearded equerry. A phantom
from another age, the years had turned him into a tottering
skeleton. The ancient Seneschal of Champagne, who had
accompanied Saint Louis upon the crusade of 1248, had been
the principal witness at the proceedings which had led to his
canonization, and had recently dictated his memoirs though
his memory was now beginning to fail, was ninety-one years
old. Half-blind, his eyes watery, his limbs trembling, and

his understanding not very clear, though still flattered that he should be remembered, he brought to the Count of Valois, by his presence alone, the moral support of the ancient chivalry and of the old feudal world.

The smell of power was abroad in Paris and it seemed that everyone wished to sniff it.

But behind this façade of prestige there was a canker hidden: money, its hideous lack, its pursuit, which for years now Charles of Valois had ceaselessly maintained. Remorselessly led on by his temperament to wish to take first place, he had lived above his resources, accumulating debts till he was scarcely able to pay the interest upon them.

The luxury in which he lived was fabulously expensive. And then there was his numerous and terrible family. Mahaut de Châtillon, his third wife, loved the most extravagant clothes and could not have borne that another woman should be better dressed than herself. Philippe, his favourite son, since he had been knighted was continuously buying suits of armour, fine light English surcoats, Cordovan boots, lances of wood from the north, and German swords.

A prolific progenitor, Monseigneur of Valois had thirteen daughters by his three marriages! Those who were already married had caused Charles to get into debt so that their weddings might match in splendour the crowns with which they were allying themselves. As for the others, marriage portions had to be thought of if they were to find suitable husbands.

As for the chamberlains, equerries, stewards and servants, they were both numerous and excessively rapacious. It was impossible to prevent their wasting everything, and stealing more. To feed the whole crowd of them, meat arrived on the scale of whole carcasses at a time, and vegetables and groceries by the cartload.

Not long before, playing the liberal by enfranchising the serfs of his estates – because his brother had obliged him to – against compensation, Valois had been able to meet part of his debts. But serfs can only be liberated once; and if, with the change of reign, the King's uncle longed to take the affairs of the kingdom into his own hands, it was as much to restore his credit as to satisfy his lust for power.

Some battles leave the conqueror as poor as the conquered. Monseigneur of Valois now had control of the royal treasury; but the treasury was empty.

And while on the ground floor the crowd was warming and refreshing itself at his expense, Valois, in his study, receiving visitor after visitor, was searching for some means of filling not only his own coffers, but also those of the State.

As he led the redoubtable Count of Dreux, with whom he had been discussing the situation in the bailiwicks west of Paris, to the top of the staircase, he heard a commotion below, mingled with cries of surprise.

It was Robert of Artois who, in the centre of an admiring circle, was twisting a horseshoe in his hands. Someone had just said in his presence that King Philip had been able to do it in his youth, and the giant wanted to demonstrate that this particular talent was common in his family. The veins swelled in his temples with the effort but the iron bent and men nodded their heads with respect while the women uttered little cries of wonder.

Monseigneur of Valois appeared upon a sort of interior balcony which overhung the Great Hall. At once all those present raised their heads towards him like a nestful of young birds waiting to be fed.

'Artois!' called Valois. 'I would like to have a word with you.'

'I am at your disposal, Cousin,' replied big Robert.

He threw the twisted horseshoe to an equerry who very nearly received it on his head, and hastened to join the King's uncle in his study.

The room had the proportions of a cathedral. A huge tapestry, embroidered in silver and gold, pictured upon the walls an embarkation for a crusade. Ivory statues, pictures, thin carved shutters standing open, goblets encrusted with gems, all gave the room an air of even greater luxury than the rest of the house. Upon a little table stood a chessboard of jasper and jade, mounted in silver and set with precious stones; one set of pieces was of jasper and the other of rock-crystal.

'Well,' cried Valois, 'do you think your man will come? He seems very dilatory.'

Heavy, massive in appearance, his colour high, superbly dressed to the point of bad taste, he walked to and fro, his expression anxious, among the treasures of which most had not yet been paid for.

'Well, Cousin, I sincerely hope he does come!' replied Artois. 'I am no less anxious to see him than you are, I can assure you, because if he gives us a favourable answer, I propose making you a request.'

'What may that be?'

'Now that you have control of the royal treasury, could it not pay me some of what it owes me?'

Valois raised his arms towards the ceiling.

'Don't you realize, Cousin,' Artois went on, 'that for the last seven years I have not been paid the five thousand pounds of revenues from my county of Beaumont, which was graciously given me supposedly in recompense for having Artois taken away, though it already belonged to me! Just think what that means! Thirty-five thousand pounds due to me. What am I expected to live on?'

Valois put his hand on Robert's arm with the protective gesture that was habitual to him.

'Cousin,' he said, 'for the moment the great urgency is to find the money to send Bouville on his way. The King is hourly demanding it. After that, I promise you, your affairs are the first I shall attend to.'

But his face grew dark with anxiety. To how many people had he made the same promise since the day before?

'The trick Marigny has played on us, emptying the coffers by making payments, will be his last, I promise you,' he cried. 'I'll have him hanged, do you understand, Robert! I'll have him hanged! Where do you think the revenues from your country have gone? Into his pocket, my good Cousin, into his pocket, I tell you!'

Since he had succeeded in giving the Rector-General of the kingdom a first blow, there were no limits to Valois's rage, and he continually found new causes for complaint against him.

In his eyes Marigny was responsible for everything. Had a burglary been committed in Paris? It was Marigny's fault because his police were not properly organized, perhaps even went shares with the burglar. Had Parliament issued a decree to the disadvantage of a great lord? Marigny had dictated it. Had a husband discovered his wife's misconduct? Again it was Marigny's fault, because of the incredible relaxation of morals that had taken place since he had been in power. It was even doubtful whether Marigny had not been the instigator of the royal Princesses' adultery, and if Philip the Fair were not dead through his fault.

'Anyway, do you think that your Siennese will accept?' asked Valois suddenly.

'Yes, yes. He will ask for security, but he'll accept, you'll see.'

Artois listened, never growing tired of watching his cousin, at once amused and fascinated. Valois was his own particular 'great man', the only being with whom he would have consented to exchange personalities. The giant, devoted to no one but himself, nevertheless felt almost capable of devotion to Valois.

For someone whose nature was not utterly dissimilar, Monseigneur of Valois's personality was indeed a fascinating one, and to watch the way he lived and behaved was something of a spectacle. This great lord was an extraordinary personage, impatient, tenacious, crafty, simple, physically courageous, but weak in the face of flattery, and above all animated by an ambition that nothing, neither honours nor privileges, could ever appease.

Others would have been perfectly satisfied with being Lord of Valois, Peer of France, Count of Alençon, of Chartres, of Perche, of Anjou, of Maine, premier peer of the kingdom besides. But not he; he was tortured by the longing to be king. At the age of thirteen he had received the crown of Aragon, to which he had pretensions as a descendant of Jaime the Conquistador, but had not been able to retain it. At twenty, placed at the head of the French armies by his brother, he had ravaged Guyenne. At thirty-one, summoned by his father-in-law, the King of Naples, to pacify Tuscany, where the Guelfs and Ghibellines were at each others' throats,[13] he had succeeded in acquiring from the Pope the indulgences of a Crusade, with the title of Vicar-General of the Christian World and Count of Romagna, while at the same time he extracted from the Florentines, whom he had utterly ruined, two hundred thousand golden florins as a reward for doing them the honour of going away and ceasing to pillage.

Widower of Marguerite of Anjou-Sicily, he had hastily remarried a Courtenay, with whom he had fallen madly in love as soon as he grasped the fact that she brought him by inheritance the fabulous title of Emperor of Constantinople. Alas, he had not reigned, since the two Paleologi, who shod in purple occupied the throne of Byzantium, if they had many difficulties within their empire, nevertheless took little heed of the busybody at the other end of the Christian world, who had begun to talk as if he were the ruler of the universe.

Again in 1308, after a series of extraordinary manoeuvres, Valois had become a candidate for the crown of the Germanic Holy Roman Empire without obtaining a single vote at the election. There was no available sceptre towards which he did not extend his hand across the world.

Now, at forty-four, he was not yet cured of his Byzantine dreams, nor of his German ones either. In his thoughts he counted up all the crowns he had nearly worn, without hesitating to include that of France. To acquire the last so little had been needed: merely that Philip the Fair should have had no children or that they should have died in infancy.

And when at times Valois exclaimed, 'My life is over! The fates have always betrayed me!' it was because he believed that he could have reconstituted under his own domination, from Spain to the Bosphorus, the Roman world as it had been a thousand years before under the Emperor Constantine.

The great megalomaniac lord had the temperament of an adventurer, the manners of a parvenu and the prescience of a founder of a dynasty. The thirteen Valois kings who were to be his descendants and reign over France for two hundred and fifty years would all have in their blood, Charles V excepted, certain characteristics of his crazed nature. But he was foredoomed to miss everything: he would die four years before the throne of France became vacant and his son succeeded to it.

'And that's what I'm reduced to, Cousin!' he cried at this juncture with theatrical despair. 'Imagine having to depend on the goodwill of a Siennese banker in order to be able to restore some kind of order to the affairs of the kingdom!'

4

Who Rules France?

AT LENGTH THE VISITOR Charles of Valois was awaiting was announced, and Artois assumed his most polite manner to receive Messire Spinello Tolomei.

'Friend banker,' he cried going towards him, his hands extended, 'I owe you a great deal of money and I have always promised you that I would pay you as soon as fortune favoured me.'

'Very good news indeed, Monseigneur,' replied the banker.

'Well, then! I can begin by showing the gratitude I owe you by procuring you a royal client.'

Tolomei saluted Valois with a profound inclination of his head, saying, 'Who does not know Monseigneur at least by sight and renown. He is well remembered at Sienna.'

He had left there the same kind of memories as he had left in Florence, at least to the extent that, the town being smaller, he had taken only seventeen thousand florins for 'pacifying' it.

Olive-skinned, pendulous of jowl, his left eye closed – it was supposed that he opened it only when he was speaking the truth, and it was therefore rarely seen – his grey, well-groomed hair falling low upon the collar of his dark green robe, Messire Tolomei waited to be asked to sit down. Having looked him up and down for a moment, Monseigneur of Valois complied.

Since the death of old Boccanegra, Tolomei had been elected by his colleagues, as had been expected, Captain-General of the Lombard Companies of Paris, a high-sounding title which had no military significance but gave its holder a more certain power than that of the Constable. His function was the secret control of a third of the banking operations in the kingdom, and it is well known that in these matters who can control a third controls the whole.

'There will be great changes in France now, friend banker,' said Robert of Artois. 'Messire de Marigny, who is no more a friend of yours, I believe, than he is of ours, finds himself very awkwardly placed.'

'I know,' murmured Tolomei.

'Moreover, I have told Monseigneur,' went on Artois, 'that, since he needs the assistance of a financier, he can do no better than come to you whose ability and loyalty I know so well.'

Tolomei smiled politely; but he thought mistrustfully, 'If they were going to offer me the management of the Treasury, they would not be paying me so many compliments.'

'What can I do to serve you, Monseigneur?' he asked, turning to Valois.

'What a banker usually does, Messire Tolomei,' replied

Valois with that fine arrogance he always assumed when he was going to ask for money.

'That can mean a number of things,' replied the Siennese. 'Have you funds you wish to lay out in good merchandise which will double its price in the next six months? Or do you wish to acquire an interest in merchant shipping? It is developing very rapidly at the present time when so much that we need must be brought in by sea?'

'No, it is nothing of that kind; I shall consider such matters later on,' Valois replied quickly. 'For the moment, what I require of you is to procure me some fresh money for the Treasury.'

Tolomei looked disconsolate.

'Alas, Monseigneur, in spite of my great desire to serve you, that is the one thing I cannot do. My friends and I have been bled white in recent times. None of the money the Treasury borrowed from us for the war in Flanders has yet been returned to us. Private accounts' – Tolomei glanced at Artois – 'bring us in nothing, nor do the advances we have made upon them; and to tell you the truth, Monseigneur, my coffers are a bit rusted at the locks. How much do you need?'

'Not much. Ten thousand pounds.'

The banker raised his hands in a gesture of horror.

'*Santo Dio!* Where shall I find them?' he cried.

These were only preliminaries, and Artois had foreseen that Tolomei, as usual, would plead poverty, say that he was stripped to the bone and groan more loudly than Job on his dunghill. But Valois, who was in a hurry, wanted to demonstrate his authority and assumed a tone which generally succeeded in imposing his will.

'Come, come, Messire Tolomei!' he cried. 'Don't talk like that. I have sent for you on business, and in order that you should practise your profession as you have always practised it, with profit I suspect.'

'My profession, Monseigneur,' replied Tolomei, his eye shut, his hands comfortably crossed upon his stomach, 'my profession is to lend; not to give. And for a long time now I have done nothing but give without return. I can't make money out of thin air and have not found the philosopher's stone.'

'Don't you want to help me get rid of Marigny for you? It would be to your own interest, I should have thought!'

'Monseigneur, to pay tribute to one's enemy when he is powerful and then to pay it again so that he should no longer be so, is a double operation which, you will agree, brings in very little return. Moreover, I should want to know what the consequences would be, and if I have a chance of getting my money back.'

Charles of Valois then launched into the great homily he had given all comers since the day before. He intended, if only he were given the means to do it, to suppress all the 'novelties' introduced by Marigny and his middle-class justiciars, restore the authority of the great lords, and re-establish order and prosperity in the kingdom by returning to the old feudal rights which had made the grandeur of the kingdom of France. Order! As happens with all political blunderers, the word was ceaselessly upon his lips, and nothing could have persuaded him to admit that the world had changed even a little in the last century.

'Before long,' he cried, 'I assure you we shall have

returned to the good old customs of my ancestor Saint Louis!'

As he spoke, he pointed to a sort of altar, upon which stood a reliquary in the form of a human foot containing a bone from the heel of his grandfather; the foot was of silver and the nails inset in gold.

The remains of the King-Saint had been cut up into pieces, since each member of the family and each royal chapel desired to possess a portion. The top of the skull was preserved in a fine bust of goldsmith's work in the Sainte-Chapelle; the Countess Mahaut of Artois, in her castle at Hesdin, possessed several hairs as well as a fragment of the jaw; and so many slivers and splinters of bone, so much debris, had been dissipated in this way that one might well wonder what could be left in the tomb at Saint-Denis. If all the pieces had been reassembled, the surprising discovery would undoubtedly have been made that the King-Saint had doubled in size since his death.[14]

Having asked permission, the Captain-General of the Lombards rose and devoutly kissed the big toe of the silver foot. Then, returning, he asked, 'Why do you require exactly ten thousand pounds, Monseigneur?'

Valois was compelled to explain that Marigny's orders had succeeded in emptying the Treasury and that the money was required for Bouville's mission.

'At Naples. Yes,' said Tolomei. 'Yes, we do much business with Naples through our cousins the Bardi. To marry the King. Yes, yes, I perfectly understand, Monseigneur. At length to reassemble the conclave. Alas, Monseigneur, a conclave is more expensive than a palace, and how much less solid! Yes, Monseigneur, yes, I understand.'

Then, when Valois had at last revealed all that was in his mind to the fat little man who always pretended ignorance in order to have things more clearly explained, Tolomei said, 'All that is very well thought out Monseigneur, and I wish you every success from the bottom of my heart; but I see no assurance that you will succeed in marrying the King, nor that you will have a Pope, nor even, if these things do happen, that I should see my gold again, supposing that I were in a position to provide it.'

Valois looked irritably at Artois. 'What an odd little man you have brought me,' he seemed to be implying, 'and having talked at this length, am I to get nothing in the end?'

'Listen, banker,' cried Artois, rising, 'you may not have this sum of money, but I know very well that you can get it for us if you want to. What interest do you require? What favours do you want?'

'But none, Monseigneur, no favours at all,' protested Tolomei; 'neither from you, you know it very well, nor from Monseigneur of Valois, whose protection is so dear to me. I am merely trying to think how I can help you.'

Then, turning, once again towards the silver foot, he added softly, 'Monseigneur of Valois has just said that he wants to return to the good old custom of Monseigneur Saint Louis. But what does he mean by that? Are all the old customs to be brought back into use?'

'Certainly,' replied Valois not well understanding what the other was leading up to.

'For instance, is the right of the great barons to mint money within their domains to be reintroduced?'

The two lords looked at each other as if a great light had

suddenly dawned upon them. How had they failed to think of that one before?

Indeed, the unification of the currency throughout the kingdom, as well as the royal monopoly in issuing it, were institutions of Philip the Fair. Before that, the great lords minted or had minted for them, concurrently with the royal coinage, their own gold and silver coins which had currency within their domains; and they drew huge profits from the privilege. And those who, like the Lombard bankers, furnished the raw metal and played the exchanges between one province and another found it equally profitable.

Charles of Valois at once saw himself re-establishing his fortune.

'Do you also mean, Monseigneur,' went on Tolomei, still gazing at the reliquary as if he were valuing it in his mind, 'that you will re-establish the right to private war between the barons?'

This was another feudal custom which Philip the Fair had abolished so as to prevent the great vassals from causing bloodshed, at the slightest excuse, within the kingdom in order to regulate their differences, establish their glory, or banish their boredom.

'Oh, if we could do that again,' cried Robert of Artois, 'I should soon recover my county from my bitch of an Aunt Mahaut.'

'If you need arms for your troops,' said Tolomei, 'I can obtain them for you at the lowest possible prices from the Tuscan armourers.'

'Messire Tolomei, you have exactly expressed the things

I want to accomplish,' cried Valois, 'and that is why I ask you to join with me in all confidence.'

He had already made the banker's suggestions his own, and within the hour would announce them as his own ideas.

Tolomei was also dreaming in his own way, for great financiers are no less imaginative than great conquerors, and it is a mistake to think that behind their calculations there exist no abstract thoughts of power.

The Captain-General of the Lombards already saw himself supplying the great barons of the kingdom with raw gold, and encouraging their differences in order to sell them arms.

'Well,' asked Charles of Valois, 'have you now decided to supply me with the money I want?'

'Perhaps, Monseigneur, perhaps; that is to say, I cannot give it to you myself, but I can find it for you in Italy, which is particularly lucky since it is precisely there that your embassy is going. I will guarantee it, which is a big risk, but I am prepared to take it, from the desire I have to serve you. Naturally, Monseigneur, it will be necessary for a man of mine, bearing letters of credit, to accompany your envoy so as to take charge of the money and account for it.'

Monseigneur of Valois frowned; these conditions did not please him at all; he would have preferred to receive the money direct and keep some of it to meet his own most urgent needs.

'You see, Monseigneur,' said Tolomei, 'I shall not be alone in this matter; the Italian companies are still more cautious than we are, and I must give them every assurance that they are not being duped.'

In fact, what he really wanted was to have an agent with

the expedition who could report to him everything that happened.

'And who will you send who will not cut a poor figure beside Messire de Bouville?' asked Valois.

'I shall see, Monseigneur, I shall see. I have but few people.'

'Why,' asked Artois, 'do you not send the boy who went to England for me?'

'My nephew Guccio?' asked Tolomei.

'That's the one, your nephew. He's intelligent, shrewd and good-looking. He'll be able to help our friend Bouville, who undoubtedly speaks but little Italian, upon the journey. I assure you, Cousin,' said Artois to Valois, 'that the boy is worthy of the job.'

'I shall miss him in my business,' said the banker, 'but that can't be helped. Monseigneur, I give him to you. It's fated that you should always get what you want of me.'

When Messire Spinello Tolomei had left the study, Robert of Artois stretched himself and said, 'You see, Cousin, you see I was not mistaken.'

'And do you know what made up his mind for him? It was that!' replied Valois, indicating with a graceful gesture his grandfather's foot. 'Thank God, all respect for what is noble has not been lost in France. The kingdom can be set to rights.'

That night a young man was overcome with mingled satisfaction and impatient hope; it was Louis The Hutin when his uncle told him that Bouville's embassy would leave before two days were out.

But another young man, when given the same news by his uncle, appeared less delighted; he was Guccio Baglioni.

'What, Nephew!' cried Tolomei. 'Here you are offered a

wonderful journey, the opportunity of seeing Naples, the Court of Naples, of living among princes, making friends among them – if you are not *un idioto completo*! – of seeing a conclave – and a conclave is a most remarkable thing – of learning much and enjoying yourself and you make *la faccia lunga* as if I were breaking bad news. You're spoilt, my boy, and you don't recognize your opportunities. Alas, the younger generation! Why, when I was your age, I should have leapt with joy and be already busy with my packing! To look as you do, there must be some girl you don't want to leave; am I right?'

Young Guccio's olive complexion grew a little darker, which was the sign that he was blushing.

'Well, well, she'll wait for you, if she loves you,' went on the banker. 'Women are made for waiting. One always finds them again. And if you are afraid that she does not love you enough, profit by those you will meet on the journey. There is but one thing one never finds again; that is youth, and time to travel about the world.'

As he looked at his nephew, Spinello Tolomei thought to himself, 'How strange life is! Here is this boy who, barely arrived from Sienna, went to London upon the intrigues of Monseigneur of Artois which brought the scandal of the Princesses of Burgundy to a head and forced The Hutin to separate from his wife; and now he is going off again to Naples to find him another wife. There must be some affinity in the stars between my nephew and the new King; their destinies seem to be linked. Who knows, perhaps Guccio will become a very great personage? I must ask Martin, the astrologer, to study these matters with care.'

5

A Castle by the Sea

THERE ARE CITIES THAT defy the centuries; time does not change them. Empires succeed each other, civilizations leave their remains in them like geological strata, but they preserve their character through the ages, their peculiar ambience, the sound and rhythm which distinguish them from all other cities upon earth. Naples is one of these cities, and appears to the traveller today, as it was in the Middle Ages, and doubtless a thousand years before, half-African, half-Latin, with its terraced alleys, its street-cries, its smells of olive oil, charcoal, saffron and frying fish, its sun-coloured dust, the sound of bells ringing on the necks of horses and of mules.

The Greeks founded it, the Romans conquered it, the barbarians despoiled it, the Byzantines and the Normans each in turn took possession of it as masters. But they did no more than modify a little the architecture of its houses and add certain superstitions, a few legends, to the traditions of its streets.

The population is neither Greek, Roman nor Byzantine; the people are Neopolitan in perpetuity, a population distinct from all others in the world. Their gaiety is but a façade concealing the tragedy of poverty, their magniloquence an accent relieving the monotony of the daily round, their leisure a virtue in refusing to pretend to be busy when there is in fact nothing to do; its population is life-loving, meeting the setbacks of fate with guile, with a gift of speech and a contempt for all things military because peace never becomes boring.

At this time the Princes of Anjou had reigned over Naples for fifty years. The two permanent signs of their rule were the woollen industry in the suburbs and the residential quarter they had built by the sea, dominated by the huge Castel Nuovo, the work of the French architect Pierre de Chaulnes, an immense pile rising above the skyline which the Neapolitans, subject for thousands of years to phallic superstitions, had immediately baptized, because of its shape, *il Maschio Angiovino*, the Male Angevin.

One morning at the beginning of January 1315, in a room high in this castle, floored with huge white paving-stones, Roberto Oderisi, a young Neopolitan painter of the Giotto school, was gazing at the portrait he had just finished. Standing motionless before his easel, a paint-brush held horizontally between his teeth, he could not tear himself away from the contemplation of his picture upon which the fresh paint still shone with a liquid light. He was wondering whether a touch of some paler yellow, or perhaps of a yellow slightly more orange, would not have rendered better the brilliance of the golden hair, whether the forehead was pale enough, whether the eye, the exquisite, blue, rather round eye, was lifelike. The drawing was correct, most certainly, the drawing was perfect! But the expression? Upon what does expression depend? A mere white dot upon the iris? A heavier shadow at the corner of an eyelid? How could one ever, merely by placing ground colours in juxtaposition, capture the reality of a face and the strange variations of light upon the contours of forms? Perhaps after all it was not the eye but a matter of the proportions between the eye and the nose, perhaps not even a question of proportion, a translucence lacking at the nostril, or perhaps some relation that he had failed to establish between the sedate contour of the lips and the droop of the eyelids.

'Well, Signor Oderisi, is it finished?' asked the beautiful Princess who was his model.

For a week she had spent three hours a day sitting still in this room, while her portrait was being painted for the Court of France.

Through the huge ogival window, now wide open, could be seen the spars of ships of the orient trade rocking gently at their moorings, and beyond them the prospect of the Bay of Naples, an immense vista of sea, astonishingly blue under the glare of the sun and the eternal shape of Vesuvius. There was a soft breeze and the day was gorgeously fine.

Oderisi took the paint-brush from between his teeth.

'Alas,' he replied, 'it is finished.'

'Why alas?'

'Because I shall now be deprived of the happiness of seeing Donna Clemenzia every morning, and it will be as if the sun has gone out.'

This was merely a minor compliment, for to tell a Neapolitan woman, whether she be princess or merely serving-maid in a hotel, that one will fall gravely ill at not seeing her again is but the minimum obligation of courtesy.

'Besides, Madam, besides,' he went on, 'I say alas because this portrait is not a success. It does not reproduce the beauty of the reality.'

One might have thought that he was in fact displeased with himself; and indeed, in criticizing himself, he was sincere. He was suffering the despair of the artist before his finished work, when he thinks, 'There, I must leave my picture as it is, because I can do no better, yet it is inferior to my conception, to what I had dreamed of accomplishing!' This young man, no more than seventeen years old, had already the characteristics of a great painter.

'May I see it?' asked Clémence of Hungary.

'Of course, Madam, but don't criticize me too severely. Alas, it is my master Giotto who should have painted you.'

Indeed, Giotto had been sent for by a courier despatched across the length of Italy. But the Tuscan master, who was that year busy painting the fresco of the life of St Francis of Assisi upon the walls of the choir of Santa Croce of Florence, had replied, from the summit of his scaffolding, that his young Neapolitan disciple should be offered the commission.[15]

Clémence of Hungary rose to her feet and, with a susurration of the stiff folds of her silken dress, went to the easel. Tall, thin, lissom, she had more grandeur than grace, and perhaps more nobility in her demeanour than femininity. But the somewhat severe impression created by her demeanour was compensated by the purity of her features, by the tender wondering look in her eyes, and by a peculiar radiation which suffused and emanated from her.

'But Signor Oderisi,' she cried, 'you have painted me as more beautiful than I am!'

'I have done no more than draw your features, Donna Clemenzia, though I have also tried to paint your soul.'

'Well, I should wish to see myself as you see me, and that my looking-glass had as much talent as you.'

They smiled at each other, mutually thanking each other for the compliments.

'Let us hope that this portrait of me will please the King of France. I mean my uncle, the Count of Valois,' she added, somewhat confused.

She had blushed. At twenty-two she still blushed often and, knowing it, looked upon it as a weakness. How often had her grandmother, Queen Marie of Hungary, not said to her: 'Clémence, when one is a princess and may become a queen, one really does not blush!'

Good God, was it really conceivable that she might become a queen? With her eyes upon the sea, she dreamed of her distant cousin, of this unknown king who had asked her to be his wife, and of whom she had heard so much during the last fortnight, ever since an official ambassador had arrived from Paris at a time when he was least expected.

The fat Bouville had managed to present the young Louis X as an unhappy prince, who had been betrayed and who had suffered, but who was endowed with a handsome face and every good quality of mind and heart. As for the Court of France, it was quite as pleasant as the Court of

Naples, mingling as it did family happiness and the pomps of majesty. Nothing could have seemed more seductive to a young woman of Clémence of Hungary's nature than the thought of healing the mental wounds of a man who had suffered through the betrayal of an unworthy woman, and who was also hard hit by the premature death of a father whom he had adored. As far as Clémence was concerned, love was inseparable from fidelity. And, above all, she had the additional pride of having been chosen. For a fortnight she had lived in a state of beatitude and was overflowing with gratitude towards the Creator of the universe.

A wall-hanging, embroidered with emperors, lions and eagles, was pulled aside, and a slim young man with a thin nose, ardent, gay eyes, and very dark hair, entered bowing.

'Oh, there you are, Signor Baglioni,' cried Clémence of Hungary in a happy voice.

She very much liked the young Siennese who appeared to serve Bouville as secretary, and seemed also to be one of the heralds of her happiness.

'Madam,' said Guccio Baglioni, 'Messire de Bouville has sent me to ask if he may have his daily audience with you?'

'Most certainly,' replied Clémence; 'you know that it is always a great pleasure to me to see Messire de Bouville. But come over here and tell me what you think of the picture which is now finished.'

'I say this, Madam,' replied Guccio, having remained silent for a moment before the picture; 'that this portrait is wonderfully faithful and that it parades before the eye the most beautiful woman that I have ever admired.'

Oderisi, his forearms stained with ochre and vermilion, drank in the praise.

'But are you not in love with some French woman, as I understood?' asked Clémence smiling.

'Certainly, I am in love,' said Guccio rather surprised.

'Well, in that case, Messire Guccio, you are either insincere towards her or towards me, for I have always heard that for someone in love there is no more beautiful face in the world than the loved one's.'

'The lady who has my love and who returns it,' replied Guccio quickly, 'is certainly the most beautiful woman in the world . . . after you, Donna Clemenzia, and to state the truth is not to fail in love.'

Clémence amused herself by teasing him a little. For since he had been in Naples, lived at Court, and found himself concerned in the preparations for a king's marriage, the nephew of banker Tolomei was inclined to adopt the airs of a hero of chivalry overcome with love for a distant beauty, and was prone, at times, to sigh in the most touching way. In fact, his passion was kept happily subordinate to the journey; his melancholy had disappeared after two days of travel and he had not lost thereby a single pleasure the mission could afford him.

Princess Clémence, already half-affianced, had suddenly become aware of curiosity and sympathy for the love affairs of other people; she wanted every young man and every young girl on earth to be happy.

'If God wills that I should go to France' – like everyone about her, she spoke of the proposal in elaborate circumlocutions – 'I shall have the greatest pleasure in meeting her of whom you think so much and whom you will, I think, marry.'

'Oh, Madam, pray heaven that you come to France! You will have no better servant than I and, I am sure, no more devoted servant than she.'

And he bent his knee with the grandest air in the world, as if he were kneeling before the ladies' box at a tournament. She thanked him with a gesture of her hands; she had beautiful, tapering hands, a little too long perhaps, like those of saints in frescoes.

'Oh, what splendid subjects I shall have there, what charming people they are,' she thought, fascinated by this little Italian who, in her eyes, had become the representative of the whole of France. She felt almost guilty in his presence; because of her, he had had to leave his love; because of her, a young girl in France must suffer separation.

'Will you tell me her name,' she went on, 'or is it a secret?'

'It can be no secret from you, if it please you to know it, Donna Clemenzia. Her name is Marie, Marie de Cressay. She is of noble lineage; her father was a knight; she awaits me in her castle thirty miles from Paris. She is sixteen years old.'

'Well, I wish you all happiness, Signor Guccio; be happy with your beautiful Marie de Cressay.'

When he had left her, Guccio positively danced down the corridors. He already saw the Queen of France attending his wedding. It was, however, still necessary that Donna Clemenzia should become queen, and also that the Cressay family should agree to give him, a young Lombard – that is to say in the eye of public opinion rather more than a Jew but rather less than a true Christian – Marie's hand in marriage!

He was suddenly aware, too, that for the first time he was seriously thinking of marriage with the beautiful lady of the manor of Neauphle whom he had seen in fact but twice in his life. It is thus that imagination can in the end determine destiny, and it but needs our future actions to be given shape in speech so that we are obliged to give them the reality of accomplishment.

Guccio found Hugues de Bouville in the apartment he had been given as a lodging, surrounded by heavy furniture decorated with painted leather. The official Ambassador of the King of France was in process of turning himself about in search of a good light, looking-glass in hand, to tidy himself and smooth his greying locks. He was wondering whether he should have his hair dyed. Travel enriches the young; but is not always without disquiet for those in their sixth decade. The Italian air had completely intoxicated Bouville. The austere man had betrayed his wife in Florence and had wept. But when he had betrayed her again in Sienna, where Guccio had found two childhood friends who had become prostitutes, fat Bouville had ceased to be afflicted with remorse. In Rome he had felt twenty years younger. Naples, prodigal of facile pleasures, provided one had a little gold in one's belt, had been an enchantment. What elsewhere would have been considered vice, here took on a disarmingly natural, an almost naïve aspect. Young pimps of twelve years old, bronzed and ragged, boasted of the charms of their elder sisters with an antique eloquence, then sat like good little boys in the antechamber scratching their feet. Besides, one had the feeling of doing good when one paid for a whole family's food for a week. And then the pleasure of walking about without an overcoat in the month of January! Bouville had dressed himself in the latest fashion and now wore surcoats with the sleeves striped horizontally in two colours. Of course he had been robbed at every street corner! But how inexpensive were the pleasures of life!

'My dear fellow,' he said when Guccio entered, 'do you know that I have lost so much weight that it is even possible I shall recover my figure?'

This remark was audacious, to say the least of it, since, to every eye but his own, Bouville's figure was as round as a butter dish.

'Messire,' said the young man, 'Donna Clemenzia is ready to receive you.'

'I hope the portrait isn't finished?' said Bouville.

'It is, Messire.'

Bouville sighed heavily.

'Well, that is the sign that we must return to France. I regret it, because I have developed a feeling of friendliness towards this country, I admit, and I would willingly have given the painter a few florins to prolong his labours. Well, well, even the best of things comes to an end.'

There was something conspiratorial in the way they smiled at each other. And, as they went to the Princess's lodgings, fat Bouville even took Guccio affectionately by the arm.

Between these two men, so different in age and origins, a true friendship had been born and had burgeoned upon their journey. For Bouville, the young Tuscan was indeed the symbol of their journey, with its freedoms, its discoveries and its renewed youth. And, through Bouville, Guccio travelled in the train of a great lord, and lived familiarly with princes.

They revealed unknown worlds to each other and were each other's perfect complement, forming a curious relationship in which the adolescent more often than not was the greybeard's cicerone.

Thus they entered the presence of Donna Clemenzia; but their expressions of careless happiness disappeared as soon as they saw the old Queen-Mother Marie of Hungary. With her granddaughter and Oderisi on either side of her, she was looking with displeasure at the portrait.

The two visitors went forward hesitantly, for everyone walked carefully in the presence of Marie of Hungary.

She was seventy years old. Widow of the King of Naples, Charles II, the Lame, she had had thirteen children and had already seen about half of them to their graves. These maternal activities had given her person a certain breadth, and her bereavements had marked the shape of her toothless mouth. She was tall, grey of complexion, white of hair, with a general expression of strength, decisiveness and authority which had not diminished with the years. She had worn a crown since her birth. It was this aged Queen, related to the whole of Europe, who had claimed the vacant throne of Hungary for her descendants, and had fought for twenty years that they might obtain it.

Now that the son of her eldest son was King of Buda, her second son, the deceased bishop, was on the point of being canonized, her third, Robert, reigned over Naples and Apulia, her fourth was Prince of Torrento, her fifth Duke of Durazzo, and her surviving daughters were married one to the King of Majorca, the other to the King of Aragon, Queen Marie, nevertheless, did not as yet appear to have finished her

task; she was concerned with her granddaughter, the orphan
Clémence, whom she had brought up.

Turning abruptly to Bouville, whom she had perceived as
a mountain-hawk marks down a chicken, she signed to him
to approach.

'Well, Messire,' she asked, 'what do you think of the
portrait?'

Bouville stood before the easel in meditation. He was
looking less at the Princess's face than at the two shutters
which had been constructed to protect the portrait during its
journey, and upon which Oderisi had painted on one side the
Castel Nuovo and on the other side the great window of
the chamber with its view of the bay of Naples. Gazing at this
landscape, which he must leave with so much regret, Bouville
was already subject to nostalgia.

'Its artistry appears to me beyond reproach,' he said at last.
'Though perhaps the frame is somewhat too plain to enclose
so beautiful a face. Do you think perhaps that a golden
festoon . . .'

He was trying to delay his departure for a day or two.

'That is of no importance, Messire,' interrupted the aged
Queen. 'Do you think that it is a good likeness? You do. That
is the important thing. Art is a perfectly frivolous affair and
I should be astonished if King Louis cares tuppence about
garlands. It is the face that will interest him, am I not right?'

As opposed to the whole Court, who spoke of the marriage
only by circumlocution, and pretended that the portrait
was for Monseigneur of Valois because of the love he bore
his niece, Marie of Hungary did not mince her words. She
dismissed Oderisi saying, 'You have done your work well,

giovonotto; you will be paid what is due to you by the treasurer. And now go back to painting your church and make sure that the devil is particularly black and the angels peculiarly bright.'

And in order to get rid of Guccio, she ordered him to help the painter carry his brushes.

Then, when they had gone, with low bows which she scarcely acknowledged, she went on, 'And so, Messire de Bouville, you are leaving for France.'

'With infinite regret, Madam, and with all the kindnesses that have been shown me here . . .'

'But,' she interrupted him, 'your mission here is finished. Almost, anyway.'

She fixed Bouville with her dark eyes.

'Almost, Madam?'

'I mean to say that the business has been arranged in principle and that the King, my son, has given you his consent. But this consent, Messire' – and owing to a sort of nervous tic which frequently attacked her, the tendons of her neck jutted into relief – 'this consent, and don't forget it, is always dependent upon a certain condition. For though we are highly honoured by our cousin the King of France's request, though we are always ready to love him with Christian loyalty and to give him numerous progeny, because the women of our family are fruitful, it is nevertheless a fact that our definite answer depends upon your master being free of Madame of Burgundy, and that quickly.'

'But we shall have the annulment soon, Madam, as I have had the honour to assure you.'

'Messire,' she said, 'we are now talking between ourselves.

Do not assure me of something that is not yet accomplished. When will you receive the annulment? Upon what grounds will you obtain it?'

Bouville coughed to hide his embarrassment. The blood began mounting to his cheeks.

'That is Monseigneur of Valois's business,' he replied, endeavouring to assume an air of ease. 'He will manage things in the best possible way and is certain of obtaining it immediately.'

'Yes, yes,' grumbled the old Queen, 'I know my son-in-law! When it is a question of words he is invincible and all his geese are swans.'

Even though her daughter Marguerite had died in 1299, and Charles of Valois since then had twice remarried, she continued to call him 'my son-in-law' as if his other unions were of no account.

Standing apart by the window, looking out across the sea, Clémence felt embarrassed at being present at this conversation. Must love be burdened by these preliminaries which resembled discussions about a treaty? After all, it was a question of her happiness, of her life. To become Queen of France seemed to her an unhoped for destiny, one which she was prepared to await with patience. Already she had waited till the age of twenty-two, wondering whether she should not enter a nunnery! So many matches, judged insufficiently good, had been refused on her behalf, without her opinion being asked. She thought that her grandmother was taking too intransigent a tone. Afar off in the bay a ship of the line was setting sail for the coast of Barbary.

'Upon my return journey, Madam, I am to go by Avignon,

with instructions from the King,' Bouville was saying. 'And I assure you that we shall shortly have the Pope we now lack.'

'I would like to believe you,' replied Marie of Hungary. 'But we want everything arranged by the summer. We have other offers for Clémence; other princes desire her for wife. We cannot imperil her future, nor consent to a longer delay.'

The tendons of her neck jutted out once more.

'You must know,' she went on, 'that Cardinal Duèze is our candidate at Avignon. I very much hope that he is also the candidate of the King of France. You will obtain the annulment all the more quickly should he become Pope, because he is entirely in our confidence and owes us a great deal. Moreover, Avignon is Angevin territory of which we are suzerain, under the King of France of course. Don't forget it. Go and take leave of my son the King, and may all turn out as you wish. But before summer, I repeat, before summer!'

Bowing, Bouville withdrew.

'Madam, my grandmother,' said Clémence in an anxious voice, 'do you think . . .'

The old Queen tapped her on the arm.

'It is all in the hands of God, my child,' she replied, 'and nothing happens unless it is His wish.'

And she too went out.

Left alone, Clémence thought, 'Perhaps King Louis has other princesses in mind. Is it really sensible to put so much pressure upon him, and may he not make his choice elsewhere?'

She was standing in front of the easel, her hands clasped

at her waist, having automatically adopted the pose of the portrait.

'Could a king really take pleasure,' she asked herself, 'in placing his lips upon those hands?'

6

Chasing Cardinals

HUGUES DE BOUVILLE, GUCCIO and their escort took ship
next day at dawn. Busy with their preparations, they had
slept little, and it was with the melancholy disquiet which
follows upon too short a night that, leaning side by side upon
the rail of the sterncastle, they watched Naples, Vesuvius
and the islands receding. Fleets of white sails were leaving
the shore for the day's fishing. Then they were upon the
high seas. The Mediterranean was superbly calm; there was
only gentle breeze enough to give the ship way. Guccio,
who had not embarked without a certain alarm, since he
remembered his detestable crossing of the Channel the year
before, was delighted not to feel seasick; and it needed no
more than twenty-four hours for him to become proud of
his own valour, and to compare himself in some sort with
Messire Marco Polo, the Venetian sailor, whose voyages to
the country of the Great Khan were beginning to be known
and read pretty well throughout the world. Guccio came and

went from forecastle to sterncastle, learning nautical terms and imagining himself an adventurer, while the head of the mission was still regretting the wonderful city from which he had had to drag himself away.

Messire de Bouville recovered some of his vitality only five days later when they disembarked at Aigues-Mortes.

This port, from which Saint Louis had once set sail upon a crusade, and whose building had been finished only under Philip the Fair, was France once more.

'Come on,' said the fat man, doing his best to throw off his nostalgia, 'we must now set about our urgent tasks.'

The weather was sharp and cloudy, and Naples already seemed no more than the memory of a dream.

Forty-eight hours later they came to Avignon. The journey on horseback, with twelve equerries and the servants of the escort, had been no sinecure, particularly for Guccio, who dared not for an instant risk letting the iron-bound chests containing the gold delivered by the Bardi of Naples out of his sight.

Messire de Bouville had caught a chill. He spent his time cursing a country which no longer seemed to him his own, and in which the slightest shower seemed to be personally directed against himself.

Their arrival, upon the second evening, amid great gusts of *mistral,* was a sad disappointment, since there was not a single cardinal in Avignon. And this was most odd in a city where a conclave was, in principle, supposed to be in session! No one could give the envoys of the King of France any information, no one knew anything, no one wished to know anything. It was only by going to the garrison of Villeneuve, which was at the end of the bridge upon the other bank of the Rhône, that at ten o'clock at night Bouville learnt from an officer, sulky at having been awakened, that the conclave had returned to Carpentras.

'This captain of archers,' said Bouville to Guccio, 'is not very forthcoming towards those who come in the King's name. I shall report him when we return to Paris.'

Carpentras is thirty-five miles from Avignon and it was impossible to think of going on there during the night. The Papal palace[16] was closed and no one replied to their knocking. The two men returned to the inn where they had supped and where they had to share a communal room with their escort. The whole company slept pell-mell before a fire amid a strong smell of boots. Alas, how far away were the beautiful girls of Italy!

'You lacked firmness in dealing with that captain,' said Guccio, showing for the first time some irritation with Bouville. 'You should have ordered him to give us lodging.'

'It's quite true, but I didn't think of it,' replied fat Bouville. 'I am not firm enough.'

The following morning everyone was in a bad temper, which grew worse when they reached Carpentras; there was not the shadow of a cardinal there either. Moreover, it was freezing. Also, added to everything else, they had a curious feeling of insecurity, of being the victims of a plot, for, when Bouville and his men had scarcely left Avignon at dawn, two horsemen had passed them, without saluting, galloping hard towards Carpentras.

'How very odd,' Guccio had remarked; 'one might think

those fellows are determined to reach our destination before we do.'

The little city of Carpentras was deserted; the inhabitants appeared to have gone to ground or to have fled. 'It is here that Pope Clement died,' said Bouville. 'Indeed, the atmosphere of the place seems far from gay. Or is this apparent emptiness due to our arrival?'

At the name of Clement V, Guccio had made the sign against the evil eye, and touched the relics he wore about his neck through the thickness of his cloak. He remembered the Templars' curse.

At last, in the cathedral, they found an old canon who at first pretended to take them for travellers, who wished to make their confessions, and led them towards the sacristy. He was deaf, or pretended to be so. Guccio's manner was absent; he was concerned for his money-chests, and also afraid for his own skin. He put his hand to his dagger, ready to stab the old canon at the first alarm. The old fellow, after having had every question repeated half a dozen times, having reflected, put his head on one side and wiped the dust from his threadbare habit, at last consented to inform them that the cardinals were at Orange. He had been left behind all alone.

'At Orange!' cried Messire de Bouville. 'But, good God! These are not prelates but carrier pigeons! Are you quite certain that they are there?'

'Certain?' replied the old canon, shocked by the oath uttered in the sacristy. 'Certain? Of what can one be certain in this world except of the existence of God? However, I think you will find the Italians at Orange.'

Then he fell silent, as if he feared having already said too much. He certainly had some angry thoughts in mind, but did not dare vent them.

Guccio wished only to leave Carpentras; the town oppressed him and he did all he could to hurry their departure.

But hardly had Bouville and Guccio gone a couple of miles than two horsemen passed them once again; this time there was no room for doubt that this riding to and fro was occasioned by their presence.

Bouville, suddenly becoming warlike, wished to fall upon the two horsemen, but Guccio would not have it.

'Our cavalcade is too slow, Messire Hugues, for us ever to catch them up, and I cannot leave my chests behind.'

At Orange they learnt, without much astonishment, that the members of the conclave were not there, that they were probably to be found at Avignon.

'But we have passed by Avignon,' cried Bouville, losing his temper with the clerk who was giving them the information, 'and it was as bare as the palm of my hand. What about Monseigneur Duèze? Where is Monseigneur Duèze?'

The clerk replied that Monseigneur Duèze, since he was Bishop of Avignon, must certainly be there. The Provost of Orange, by an unfortunate coincidence, happened to be away that day and the underling who was taking his place had no instructions to attend to the comfort of the new arrivals. They had to pass another whole evening in an extremely dirty inn, which looked out upon a field of ruined and overgrown houses which seemed to them excessively ugly. Sitting opposite a Bouville foundering from fatigue, it began to seem to Guccio that he must take the expedition

in hand if they were ever to reach Paris with or without
results.

In every mishap they saw a sign that they were being
dogged by ill-luck. One of the men of the escort had got a
broken leg from the kick of a horse and would have to be left
behind; the pack-horses, which had had no proper rest, were
beginning to get sore backs; it was becoming urgent that
all the horses should be reshod; Messire de Bouville had a
terrible cold in the head, and talked rather too much about
a certain lady in Naples, wondering whether she had really
loved him sincerely. During the whole of the following
day he showed so little energy that he made no difficulty
about letting Guccio take over his responsibilities.

'I shall never dare appear before the King,' he groaned, 'but
how on earth, I ask you, can one make a Pope when every
soutane flies at our approach! I shall never be able to sit in the
Council again, my poor Guccio, never again. The failure of
this one mission destroys my life's work.'

He fussed continually. Was Madame Clémence's portrait
properly packed, had it been damaged by the rain?

'I'll look after things, Messire Hugues,' replied Guccio
authoritatively. 'And the first thing to do is to find a lodging;
you appear to me to be in considerable need of one.'

Guccio went off to find the Captain of the Town and took
the high tone with him that Bouville should have done in the
first place. He sounded so high and mighty in his strong
Italian accent, as he detailed the titles of his chief and those
he thought proper to attribute to himself, was so convincing
in explaining their requirements, that in less than an hour
a palace was emptied and placed at their disposal. Guccio

installed his people in it and put Bouville into a well-warmed bed. When the fat man, who made the doubtful excuse of a chill to avoid taking decisions, was snugly under the blankets, Guccio said, 'I don't like this atmosphere of trickery with which we are surrounded. I want now to put the gold in a safe place. There is an agent of the Bardis here; and I propose depositing it with him. Then I shall feel in a much better position to find your cardinals for you.'

'My cardinals, my cardinals!' grumbled Bouville. 'They're no cardinals of mine, and I'm as fed up with their tricks as you are. We'll talk about it when I have had some sleep, if you like, because at the moment I feel utterly chilled. Are you quite certain of your Lombard? Can we trust him? After all, the money belongs to the King of France.'

Guccio took a high tone with him.

'Will you please believe, Messire Hugues, that I am as much concerned about the money as if it belonged to a member of my own family; can you understand that?'

He went straight off to the bank which was in the Sainte-Agricole quarter of the town. The Bardi agent – who was, moreover, a cousin of the head of this powerful company – received Guccio with the cordiality due to a nephew of an important colleague, and went himself to put the gold into the strong-room. They exchanged signatures; then the Lombard led his visitor into his parlour so that Guccio might tell him of his difficulties. Standing before the hearth was a thin rather stooping man who turned round at their entry.

'Guccio! *Che Piacere!*' he cried, *'come stai?'*

'Ma . . . *caro* Boccaccio! *Per Bacho! che fortuna!*'

They fell into each other's arms.

You always meet the same people travelling because, of course, it's always the same people who travel.

There was nothing very singular about Signor Boccaccio's presence here, since he was a traveller for the Bardi company. The good luck lay simply in the fact of meeting him on that particular day. Guccio and Boccaccio had made part of the journey to London together the year before; they had become intimate friends; Guccio knew that Boccaccio had a child by a French mistress.

While the Lombard of Avignon was ordering spiced wine for them, Guccio and Boccaccio talked delightedly like old friends.

'What are you doing here?' asked Boccaccio.

'I'm chasing cardinals,' replied Guccio, 'and I don't mind telling you that they're far from easy game.'

Upon which he recounted the whole story of their mission, the misadventures they had had these last days, and raised a good laugh at the fat Bouville's expense. He himself felt singularly cheered; he felt at home here, as if he were in the circle of his own family.

If you are always prone to meet the same people, it is true too that the same people always do you a good turn and get you out of difficulties.

'You need not be astonished,' said Signor Boccaccio, 'at not finding your Monsignori. They have been instructed to take care, and everyone who comes from the Court of France, or says he does, puts them to flight. Last summer Bertrand de Got and Guillaume de Budos, the nephews of the late Pope, arrived here, sent by your friends Nogaret and Marigny, supposedly to take their uncle's body back to Cahors. They

brought with them a mere five hundred soldiers, a somewhat excessive number of bearers for a single corpse! The
gallant soldiers had been sent to force the election of a Pope
who was not to be Cardinal Duèze, and their arguments
were not altogether of a gentle kind. One fine morning their
eminences' houses were all sacked while they were sitting in
conclave in the convent of Carpentras. The cardinals had to
escape through a breach in the wall into the open country and
run for their lives. They haven't forgotten it yet.

'You can add,' said the Bardi cousin, 'that the garrison of
Villeneuve has been reinforced, and that the cardinals fear
from moment to moment to see the archers cross the bridge.
They thought that your arrival was the signal. And do you
know who the horsemen were who so continuously passed
you? Undoubtedly Archbishop Marigny's people. They are
clearly infesting the whole of these parts at the moment. I
don't know exactly what they are after, but it is not the same
thing as you are.'

'You and Bouville,' went on Boccaccio, 'will achieve
nothing here on behalf of the King of France; moreover you
run the risk of swallowing a dose of poison one night and
never awakening again. At this moment, coming from the
King of Naples is no recommendation to the cardinals, or
to some of them at least! You have just come from there,
haven't you?'

'Straight from there,' replied Guccio, 'and we even have
old Queen Marie's blessing to see Cardinal Duèze as soon as
possible.'

'Good God, why didn't you say so at once! I can arrange
an interview with Duèze, who is an odder fish than you

might expect. I can arrange it for tomorrow, if you like.'

'You know where to find him, do you?'

'He has never left here,' said Boccaccio, laughing. 'Go back to your lodging, and I will bring you news before nightfall. Have you, by chance, any money for him? Good. He often needs it and owes us quite a bit.'

Three hours later Signor Boccaccio knocked on the door of the palace where Bouville lodged. He brought fairly good news. The following morning at about nine o'clock Cardinal Duèze would be taking a constitutional at a place called Pontet, so named because of a little bridge there, two and a half miles north of Avignon. The Cardinal agreed to meet, as if by chance, the Seigneur de Bouville, should the latter happen to be passing through the place and provided he was not accompanied by more than six men. The men of the escort were to remain upon the boundaries of a large field, while Duèze and Bouville conversed in the centre of it, out of sight and hearing. The Cardinal of the Curia delighted in making mysteries.

'Guccio, my boy, you are saving me and I shall always remember to be grateful to you,' said Bouville, whose chill seemed to recover with hope renewed.

The following morning, therefore, Bouville, accompanied by Guccio, Signor Boccaccio and four horsemen, went to Pontet. The day was foggy, hiding the contours of the land and deadening sound; the locality was as deserted as one could wish. Messire de Bouville had put on three coats, which made him appear even fatter than usual. They had to wait for some time.

At last, out of the fog, came a small group of horsemen

surrounding a young man riding a white mule. He leapt athletically from his mount. He was wearing a black cape beneath which showed red robes, his head was covered by a cap with ear-flaps and lined with white fur. He came towards them with a quick, almost dancing step through the wet grass, and it was only then that the young man was recognizable as Cardinal Duèze. His adolescence was seventy years old. Only his face, hollow of cheek and of temple, and the white eyebrows upon his dry skin, betrayed his age; and his eyes had a sort of watchful intensity which was no longer that of youth.

Bouville also walked forward and met the Cardinal by a little wall. The two men looked at each other a moment, mutually surprised at each other's appearance, which in no way accorded with their expectations. Bouville, with his innate respect for the Church, had expected to meet a prelate of majestic appearance, somewhat unctuous perhaps, but not this elf bouncing out of the fog. The Cardinal of the Curia, who had imagined that an old warrior like Nogaret or Bertrand de Got had been sent to him, gazed with stupefaction at this fat man covered with as many layers of clothes as an onion has skins, who was noisily blowing his nose.

It was the Cardinal who spoke first. His voice always surprised those who had never heard it before. Muffled like a funeral drum, breaking when it rose to a higher register, rapid and smothered, it seemed to come not from him but from someone close by for whom one instinctively looked.

'So you come, Messire de Bouville, on behalf of King Robert of Naples, who does me the honour of his Christian confidence. The King of Naples, the King of Naples,' he repeated. 'You were Great Chamberlain to King Philip, who was not very favourably disposed towards me; though I really do not know why, since I acted as he wished at the Council of Vienna in order to have the Templars suppressed.'

'I believe, Monseigneur,' replied Bouville, who was taken aback by this opening, 'that you were opposed to stigmatizing Pope Boniface, or at least his memory, with heresy; and King Philip did not forget it.'

'Really, Messire, it was asking too much. Kings are never aware of how much they require of one. When one runs the risk of becoming one day a Pope oneself, one naturally cannot be expected to create precedents of that nature. When a King himself succeeds to the throne, he does not proclaim that his father was a traitor, an adulterer and a plunderer. Boniface died mad, of course, refusing the sacraments and uttering the most horrible blasphemies. But what would the Church have gained by establishing his shame. And as for Pope Clement V, my venerated benefactor – you know that I owe the little I am to him, and that we were both born at Cahors – Pope Clement was certainly of this opinion. Monseigneur de Marigny does not like me either; he has done everything to oppose me, particularly these last weeks. I don't understand what it's all about! Why do you wish to see me. Is Marigny still as powerful in France as he was, or does he merely pretend to be so? It is said that he is no longer in power, and yet everyone continues to obey him.'

The Cardinal was a strange man making use of a criminal's technique to bring about a meeting with an ambassador, and then from the first moment discussing brass tacks as if he had known him all his life. Moreover, speaking rapidly in a smothered voice, his delivery was irregular, and his argument disconnected. Like many autocratic old men, he followed the line of his own thought without taking into consideration whether it was being followed.

'The truth is, Monseigneur,' replied Bouville, who did not want to engage in an argument about Marigny, 'that I have come to express to you the wish of King Louis and of Monseigneur of Valois that a Pope may be elected as early as possible.'

The Cardinal raised his white eyebrows.

'A fine wish,' said Duèze, 'when my election has been prevented for the last nine months by corruption, trickery and force. But you may as well know that I am in no particular hurry! For the last twenty years I have been working on my *Theasaurum Pauperum,* and I shall require a good six years more to finish it, without taking into account my *Art Transmutatoire,* which treats of alchemy, and my *Elixir des Philosophes,* more occult still, which I should much like to see finished before I die. I am busy enough with these things, and I am not so anxious for a tiara which would overweigh me with duties. No, really, I am in no hurry. But has there been a change of policy in Paris? Nine months ago I had collected nearly every vote, and it was the King of France who lost them for me. Do they now want to see me become Pope after all?'

Bouville was in some difficulty, since he did not know Whether it was Jacques Duèze or another whom Monseigneur of Valois wished for. He had been told 'a Pope.'

'But certainly, Monseigneur,' he replied mildly. 'Why not you?'

'In that case something important is to be demanded of

me, or at any rate from whoever is elected,' said the Cardinal. 'What is it?'

'The fact is, Monseigneur, the King requires an annulment,' said Bouville.

'In order that he may remarry with Clémence of Hungary?'

'How do you know that, Monseigneur?'

'The Inner Council at which this was decided took place five weeks ago, did it not?'

'You are very well informed, Monseigneur. I cannot imagine how you acquire your information.'

The Cardinal did not reply and merely looked heavenwards as if he saw angels passing.

'An annulment,' he whispered to himself. 'Certainly, one can always annul. Were the doors of the church properly open on the marriage day? You were present and you don't remember, isn't that so? Yes, it may well be that others remember that they were inadvertently closed. Your King is a very close cousin of his wife's. It is possible that they omitted to ask for a dispensation. On those grounds one could unmarry nearly every prince in Europe; they are related to each other on every side, and one has but to look at the results of their unions to realize the fact, this one is lame, that one deaf, and another impotent. If from time to time there were no sin or misalliance among them, they would very soon become extinct from scrofula or debility. Moreover, I shall refer to all this in my *Thesaurum*, in order to encourage the poor not to follow the example of the great.'

'The French royal family,' replied Bouville somewhat vexed, 'are all in very good health, and our princes of the blood are as robust as blacksmiths.'

'Of course, of course, but when illness does not attack their bodies, it attacks their minds. And many of their children die in infancy. No, really, I am in no hurry to become Pope.'

'But if you should become it, Monseigneur,' said Bouville, trying to recapture the thread, 'would the annulment seem possible before summer?'

'To annul is less difficult,' said Jacques Duèze dryly, 'than to recover the votes that have been lost to me.'

The conversation was going round in a circle. Bouville looked towards his men at the end of the field and much regretted that he could not call Guccio or perhaps Signor Boccaccio, who seemed so clever. The fog was beginning to thin a little. Bouville was tired of standing and his three coats were beginning to weigh him down. He automatically sat down on the little wall which consisted of flat stones placed one upon another, and wearily asked, "Well, Monseigneur, what is the situation at the moment?'

'The situation?' said the Cardinal.

'Yes, I mean the state of the conclave?'

'The conclave? But there isn't one. Cardinal Albano . . .'

'You mean Messire Arnaud d'Auch, late Bishop of Poitiers?'

'That is he.'

'I know him; he came a year or so ago to Paris as Papal Legate to pass sentence on the Grand Master of the Templars.'

'That's the man. Being Cardinal Camerlengo, it is up to him to summon us; he has managed not to do so since Messire de Marigny forbade him to.'

'But if, in the end . . .'

At that moment Bouville suddenly realized he was sitting

down while the prelate was still standing, and he quickly rose and apologized.

'No, no, I beg you, Messire,' said Duèze, making him sit down again.

And with an agile movement he came and sat down next to him upon the wall.

'If the conclave was reconstituted,' went on Bouville, 'what decision would it come to?'

'None. And why this is so is perfectly clear.'

Perfectly clear to Duèze, of course, who, like every candidate for election, ran over the number of votes in his favour ten times a day, but less simple for Bouville who had some difficulty in understanding what followed, quavered out as it was in that voice from the confessional.

'The Pope has to be elected by two-thirds of the votes. We are twenty-three at the conclave; fifteen Frenchmen and eight Italians. Of those eight, five are for Cardinal Caetani, Boniface's nephew, irremediably. We shall never win them over. They want to avenge Boniface, hating the Crown of France and everyone who, either directly or through Pope Clement, my venerated benefactor, has served it.'

'And the other three?'

'Hate Caetani; these are the two Colonna and Orsini. A family affair. Since none of the three is powerful enough to have any hope for himself, they are favourable to me to the extent that I am an obstacle in Caetani's way, unless of course they were promised that the Holy See would be returned to Rome, which might make them agree among themselves and leave them free to assassinate each other afterwards.'

'And the fifteen Frenchmen?'

'Oh, if the Frenchmen voted the same way, you would have had a Pope a long time ago! But only six are for me, the King of Naples having, through my offices, been generous to them.'

'Six Frenchmen,' Bouville said, 'and three Italians, that makes nine.'

'Yes, Messire. That makes nine, and we need sixteen to have the required number. You will realize that the other nine Frenchmen are not numerous enough to elect the Pope Marigny wants.'

'We need to find another seven votes. Do you think that any of them could be acquired for money? I have the means to provide you with funds. How much do you suppose it would cost per cardinal?'

Bouville thought that he had managed the affair extremely cleverly but, to his surprise, Duèze did not appear to receive his proposal with any particular alacrity.

'I do not believe,' he replied, 'that the French cardinals we require will respond to that particular argument. It is not that honesty is a major virtue in all of them, nor that they live lives of austerity; but the fear they have of Messire de Marigny places them for the moment above the things of this world. The Italians are greedier, but hate rules them in place of avarice.'

'I see,' said Bouville. 'Everything rests with Marigny and the power he has over the nine French cardinals.'

'Yes, Messire, everything today depends upon that. Tomorrow it may depend upon something else. How much gold can you provide me with?'

Bouville stared.

'But you have just told me, Monseigneur, that gold would be of no use to you!'

'You misunderstood me, Messire. The gold cannot help me to acquire new supporters, but I need it to keep those I have and for whom, so long as I am not elected, I can do nothing. It would be a pretty business if, when you have obtained for me the votes I lack, I should have lost in the meantime those who support me now!'

'How much money do you require?'

'If the King of France is rich enough to furnish me with five thousand pounds, I guarantee to use them well.'

At that moment, Bouville needed once more to blow his nose. The other took this for diplomatic craftiness and feared that he had mentioned too high a sum. It was the single point that Bouville made during the whole conversation.

'Even with four thousand,' whispered Duèze, 'I could manage for a time.'

He already knew that the gold would leave his purse only to meet his creditors.

'The Bardi,' said Bouville, 'will remit you the gold you require.'

'Let them keep it on deposit,' replied the Cardinal; 'I have an account with them. I will draw on it as necessity arises.'

Upon which he suddenly seemed in a hurry to remount his mule, assuring Bouville that he would not fail to pray for him and that he would be delighted to meet him again.

He extended his ring for the fat man to kiss, and then went off, dancing over the grass, as he had come.

'An odd Pope we shall have in him, occupying himself as he does with alchemy as much as with church matters,' thought Bouville as he watched him disappear. 'Is he suited to the vocation he has chosen?'

As far as he was concerned, Bouville was not too displeased with himself. He had been commissioned to see the cardinals, had he not? He had succeeded in meeting one of them. To find a Pope? This Duèze appeared to wish for nothing better. To distribute gold? He had done so.

When he rejoined Guccio and told him with a satisfied air the results of the interview, Tolomei's nephew cried, 'It seems to me, Messire Hugues, that you have succeeded in buying at a very high price the only cardinal who is already on our side.'

And part of the gold that the Bardi of Naples had lent, through Tolomei, to the King of France returned to the Bardi of Avignon to reimburse them for the money they had lent to the King of Anjou's candidate.

7

A Pope is Worth an Exoneration

THIN-LEGGED, AND RATHER lanky of body, his chin
sunk upon his breast, Philippe of Poitiers stood before The
Hutin.

'Sire, my Brother,' he said in a calm, cold voice which
somewhat recalled that of Philip the Fair, 'you must admit
the truth that has come to light in the inquiry; you cannot
deny truth when it stares you in the face.'

The Commission of Accountancy, set up to look into the
financial transactions of Enguerrand de Marigny, had finished
its labours the day before.

For many days, under the painstaking chairmanship of
Philippe of Poitiers, the Counts of Valois and Evreux, the
Count of Saint-Pol, Louis de Bourbon, the Canon Etienne
de Mornay, who was already beginning to take up his new
duties, though the title had not yet been given him, of
Chancellor to the Crown, the First Chamberlain, Mathieu de
Trye, and finally Archbishop Jean de Marigny, had read the

documents, searched the archives, studied line by line the Treasury Journal over a period of sixteen years, and had demanded subsidiary explanations and documentary proof. They had not spared themselves, and no avenue of investigation had been neglected. In an inquiry where so much hatred was involved, every possible line had been followed up.

And yet they had been able to find nothing to Marigny's disadvantage. His administration of the royal treasure and the public funds was discovered to be scrupulous and exact. If he were rich, it was merely due to the liberality of the late King and the fact that he had known how to invest his money profitably. But there was no evidence that he had ever confused, at least in matters of finance, his private interests with those of the State; still less that he had robbed the Treasury as his adversaries accused him of having done. Was this result really a surprise to Monseigneur of Valois? At most, his was the angry disappointment of a gambler who has lost. He had been obstinate to the end, the only one of the Commissioners, with of course Mornay who had echoed his words and denied the evidence.

Louis X had now the Commission's conclusions before him, supported by six votes to two, and yet hesitated to approve them; his hesitation deeply wounded his brother.

'Why did you make me Chairman of the Commission, Brother,' said Philippe, 'if you refuse to approve the report?'

'Marigny has many defenders who feel themselves bound up with his destiny,' The Hutin replied.

'I can assure you that he had none on the Commission, except perhaps his brother . . .'

'. . . and our uncle Evreux and yourself, perhaps?'

Philippe of Poitiers shrugged his shoulders but did not lose his calm.

'I do not see how my future,' he replied, 'could be bound up with Marigny's, and to suggest it is to insult me.'

'That is not what I meant to say at all, Philippe, certainly not.'

'I am not here to defend anyone, Louis, unless it be justice itself, and you should feel obliged to do the same since you are King.'

History repeats itself; there are situations strangely analogous. The same temperamental hostility that had existed between Philip the Fair and his youngest brother, Charles of Valois, was repeated in Louis X and Philippe of Poitiers. But the characteristics were curiously inverted. Face to face with a brother who really ruled, the envious Valois had largely played the part of a mischief-maker; now it was the elder who seemed unable to exercise power properly, and the younger who had a sovereign's mind. And as Valois, in his vanity, had during twenty-nine years said to himself, 'Ah, if I were King . . .' so today Philippe of Poitiers began to say to himself, and with greater justice, 'I should certainly do better in his place.'

'Furthermore,' said Louis, 'there are a number of factors that displease me. This letter I have received from the King of England, recommending me to repose the same confidence in Marigny that our father did, and elaborating the services he has rendered to both our kingdoms . . . I do not care to have my actions dictated to me.'

'Do you refuse to take good advice merely because it is given you by our brother-in-law?'

Louis X's large lustreless eyes refused to meet his brother's.

'Let us await Bouville's return. One of the equerries sent on ahead has reported that he will arrive today.'

'What has Bouville to do with your decision?'

'I want news from Naples, and about the conclave,' said The Hutin with growing impatience. 'I do not wish to oppose our uncle Charles at the very moment he is arranging for his niece to be my wife and is creating a Pope for me.'

'So, at the caprice of our uncle, you are prepared to sacrifice an honest minister, and remove from power the only man who understands today how to run the affairs of the kingdom? Take care, Brother; you will find it difficult to make a compromise. You have noticed how, while we were investigating Marigny's accounts, as if he were a dishonest servant, everyone in France has continued to obey him as they did in the past. You will either have to restore him to complete power or destroy him utterly, pronouncing him guilty of invented crimes, punishing him for his loyalty; that would be to act contrary to your own interests. Marigny may take another year to make a Pope for you; but he will give you one who is in conformity with the interests of the kingdom, as for instance the late Bishop of Poitiers, whom I know well since he comes from my own county! Our uncle Charles will promise you a Holy Father from day to day; but without doubt he will be able to move no more rapidly, and in the end will get some Caetani who wants to go back to Rome, appoint your Bishops from there, and direct affairs in France.'

Louis gazed at Marigny's exoneration, which Philippe of Poitiers had prepared, as it lay before him.

'*And thus approve, commend and receive the accounts of Sire Enguerrand de Marigny* (Valois had demanded and obtained that the titles of the Rector-General should not be included) *and hold him exonerated, he and his heirs, of all receipts made by the administration of the Treasury of the Temple, the Louvre and the King's Exchequer.*'

The parchment only lacked the Royal signature and the affixing of the seal.

'Brother,' went on the Count of Poitiers, 'you have made me a peer of your realm in order to help you and give you counsel. As a peer I counsel you to approve it. It is an act demanded by justice.'

'Justice is the prerogative of the King,' cried The Hutin with that sudden violence he was apt to show whenever he felt he was supporting a bad case.

'No, Sire,' calmly replied he who was to become Philip the Long. 'The King belongs to justice, is its expression, and is there to see that it triumphs.'

Bouville and Guccio reached Paris in the late afternoon. The capital was already in the grip of frost and the early darkness of a winter evening.

They found the First Chamberlain, Mathieu de Tryc, waiting for them at the Porte Saint-Jacques. He saluted his predecessor on behalf of the King and informed him that he was awaited at the Palace.

'What! Without time for a rest?' said Bouville ill-temperedly. 'I'm as tired as I'm dirty, my good friend, and it's a miracle I can still stand upon my feet. I'm too old for these journeys.'

He was not pleased at being so hurried. He had thought to dine a last time with Guccio in some private room in a good inn, so that they would have the opportunity to assemble clearly their ideas upon the results of their mission, and be able to say to each other the many things for which there is never time during forty days of travelling, and which one always feels the need to express on the last night, as if there will never be another opportunity.

They had to part in the street without affectionate good-byes, since Mathieu de Trye's presence embarrassed them. Bouville was a prey to overwhelming nostalgia; he was subject to the melancholy of things past; looking at Guccio, as he went on his way, he realized that the wonderful Neapolitan days were disappearing with him, that the miraculous time of recovered youth he had been privileged to know in the autumn of his days was over. His new shoot of life was lopped off and would burgeon no more.

'I have not thanked him enough for all he has done for me, and for the pleasure his company has afforded me,' thought Bouville.

He had not even noticed that Guccio had taken with him the money-chests which, less the expenses of the expedition and the cardinal's bonus, contained the remainder of the Bardi gold; thus, whatever happened, the Tolomei bank would make sure of its commission.

Not that this prevented Guccio also from having a certain feeling of emotion upon leaving fat Bouville, since in people who are well endowed to conduct business the sense of personal interest never obliterates sentiment.

Upon entering the Palace, Bouville became aware of a

number of things that displeased him. The servants upon
his path appeared to have lost the precision of discipline he
had imposed upon them in King Philip's time, that air of
deference and ceremony, present in their least gesture, which
manifested the honour they felt in belonging to the royal
household. There had been a lowering of standards.

But when the late Great Chamberlain found himself in the
presence of Louis X, he lost his critical faculty; he was in
the presence of the King and thought of nothing but bowing
sufficiently low.

'Well, Bouville,' said The Hutin, giving him the curtest
of welcomes, somewhat to the fat man's distress, 'how is
Madame of Hungary?'

'Most formidable, Sire; she frightened me. But she has
astonishing intelligence for her age.'

'What's her appearance like, her looks?'

'Most majestic, Sire, though her teeth have all gone.'

The Hutin's face expressed horror. Charles of Valois, who
was standing beside his nephew, burst out laughing.

'My dear Bouville,' he cried, 'the King is not asking you
about Queen Marie, but about Madame Clémence.'

'Oh, I beg your pardon, Sire!' said Bouville, blushing.
'Madame Clémence? But I will show her to you.'

'What? You don't mean to tell me you've brought her back
with you?'

'No, Sire, merely her portrait.'

And he had Oderisi's portrait brought in and placed upon a
table. The two shutters which protected the portrait were
opened; candles were brought near.

Louis went slowly, cautiously, towards it as if towards

something dangerous which might explode in his face. Then he smiled and looked at his uncle, his expression happy.

'It's a beautiful country, Sire, if you only knew it,' said Bouville, seeing Naples depicted once more upon the two shutters.

'Well, Nephew, have I deceived you?' cried Valois. 'Look at that complexion, that honey-coloured hair, that noble pose! Look at her throat, Nephew, what an exquisitely feminine throat!'

He praised his niece as a horse-coper his wares at a fair.

'And I must tell the King,' added Bouville, 'that Madame Clémence is still more beautiful in the flesh than she is upon canvas.'

Louis fell silent; he seemed to have forgotten the presence of the other two. Head thrust forward, shoulders stooping, he was absorbed in a curious tête-à-tête with the portrait. In Clémence's eyes he recognized a certain affinity with Eudeline's expression, a sort of patient dreaming, a serene kindliness; even their colouring was not without a certain resemblance. There was an Eudeline, but born of kings, about to become a queen. For a moment Louis tried, in his imagination, to superimpose upon the portrait the face of Marguerite, her wide full forehead, her dark hair curling about it, her olive skin, her eyes that so easily turned hostile. And then that other face disappeared and Clémence's remained triumphant in its calm beauty, and Louis felt certain that beside this fair princess he need fear no bodily impotence.

'Oh, she is beautiful, really beautiful!' he said at last. 'I am very grateful to you, Uncle. Bouville, I give you two hundred pounds per annum from the Treasury as a token of gratitude for your embassy.'

'Oh, Sire,' murmered Bouville gratefully, 'I have been sufficiently rewarded by the mere honour of serving you well.'

'And so now we are affianced,' went on The Hutin. 'It only remains for me to get unmarried; we are affianced . . .'

He walked up and down in agitation.

'Yes, Sire,' said Bouville, 'provided you are free of your present wife before summer.'

'I have every intention of being so! But who has made that condition?'

'Queen Marie, Sire. She has other offers for Madame Clémence, and though yours is undoubtedly the most important and the most desirable, she does not wish to commit herself further than that.'

The Hutin's expression grew sombre and Bouville thought that his pension of two hundred pounds was on the point of disappearing. But the King had turned questioningly to Valois, who looked astonished.

Valois, during Bouville's absence and unknown to him, had been in postal contact with Naples by courier, and he had assured his nephew that his engagement was in process of being definitely concluded without any time-limit.

'Is this a condition that Madame of Hungary made at the last moment?' he asked Bouville.

'Yes, Monseigneur.'

'She only said it to make us hurry and give herself importance. If by any chance, though I think it unlikely, the annulment took longer, Madame of Hungary would most certainly prove patient.'

'I cannot tell, Monseigneur; she made the condition in a firm, decided manner.'

Valois felt a certain uneasiness, and tapped the arm of his chair with his fingers.

'Before summer,' murmured Louis, 'before summer ... and what point has the conclave reached?'

Bouville then gave an account of his peregrinations about the district of Avignon, trying not to cut too ridiculous a figure. He did not mention how he had succeeded in meeting Cardinal Duèze. He equally forbore to mention Marigny's activities; he felt a certain repugnance about accusing his oldest friend, and accusing him wrongly moreover. For Bouville admired Marigny, feared him too, and knew that he possessed political perceptions that he himself was utterly incapable of grasping. 'If he is acting thus, it is because he has good reason to do so,' he thought. 'I must not risk judging him wrongly.' He contented himself with underlining the fact that the Pope's election depended above all upon the wishes of the Rector of the kingdom.

Louis X listened with the greatest attention, his eyes fixed upon Clémence's portrait.

'Duèze, yes,' he said. 'Why not Duèze? He is prepared to give me my annulment at once. He lacks four French votes. So you assure me, Bouville, that only Marigny can arrange matters and provide me with a Pope?'

'It is my firm belief, Sire.'

The Hutin went slowly towards the table where lay the parchment his brother had given him containing the Commission's findings. He took up a goose-quill and dipped it in the ink.

Charles of Valois's face turned pale.

'Nephew,' he cried, leaping forward, 'you are not going to exonerate the rogue?'

'In spite of you, Uncle, there are those who affirm his accounts to be honest. Six of the lords appointed to make the examination are of that opinion; only your chancellor shares yours.'

'Nephew, I implore you to wait. The man is deceiving us as he deceived your father,' cried Valois.

Bouville wished that he were not present.

Louis gazed at his uncle with stubborn, malicious eyes.

'I have told you that I need a Pope,' he said, 'and since my lords assure me that Marigny is honest . . .'

As the other was about to make further objections, Louis rose to his feet and with great authority in his voice, but a certain failure of memory, said, 'The King belongs to justice, in order to . . . in order to . . . in order to see that it triumphs.'

And he signed the exoneration. Thus it was due to his disloyalty towards the King, if not to France, over the matter of the conclave, that Marigny owed the fact that his fidelity in financial administration was recognized.

Valois left the room, wild with anger he could no longer have kept under control. 'I would have done better,' he thought, 'to find him some girl twisted of body and hideous of face. He would be in no such hurry then. I've been tricked.'

Louis X turned to Bouville.

'Messire Hugues,' he said, 'let Messire de Marigny be summoned at once.'

8

A Letter's Fate

A GUST OF WIND SMOTE the narrow window, and Marguerite of Burgundy drew hastily back, as if the far heavens wished to strike her.

Day was breaking uncertainly over the forest of Andelys. It was the hour when the first guard was mounted upon the battlements of Château-Gaillard. Nothing in the world can be more melancholy than some mornings of high wind in Normandy, when huge black clouds drive in from the west, bearing with them the promise of heavy rain. The tops of the trees are bowed like the curved spines of frightened, fleeing horses.

Sergeant Lalaine came to unlock the door half-way up the staircase, which isolated the cells of the two Princesses; and Private Gros-Guillaume deposited two wooden bowls of steaming gruel upon the stool. He went out again, dragging his feet and without a word.

'Blanche!' called Marguerite, going to the spiral staircase.

There was no answer.

'Blanche!' she cried again more loudly.

The silence that followed filled her with despair. At last there was a rustling of a skirt in the staircase, and the sound of wooden clogs upon the steps. Blanche came in, staggering, worn out; in the room's grey light her clear eyes seemed fixed in that expression of absent concentration which is common to the eyes of the mad.

'Have you been able to sleep a little?' Marguerite asked.

Blanche did not reply but, going to the jug of water that stood near the bowls, she knelt and tipping the jug to her mouth, drank a long draught. For some time now she had performed the ordinary acts of living eccentrically.

None of Bersumée's furniture remained in the room. The Captain of the Fortress had taken it all back as soon as, two months before, he had received, by means of a somewhat bullying visit from Alain de Pareilles, Marigny's order to keep to his original instructions. Gone was the worn tapestry that had been hung upon the walls for the pleasure and in honour of Monseigneur of Artois; gone was the table from which the imprisoned Queen had eaten in her cousin's presence. A pallet, its mattress stuffed with husks of dried peas, had replaced the bed.

But, since Marigny had let it be known that he was concerned for the survival of Madame Marguerite, Bersumée took care that the fire was kept alight, the blankets sufficiently warm and the food adequate at least in quantity.

The two women sat down side by side upon the pallet, their bowls upon their knees.

Blanche, making no use of her spoon, lapped up the

buckwheat gruel straight from the bowl like a dog. Marguerite did not eat at all. She was warming her hands round the wooden bowl; this was the only good moment of her day, the last sensual pleasure that remained to her in her prison. She closed her eyes, utterly concentrated upon the miserable satisfaction of getting a little warmth into the palms of her hands.

Suddenly Blanche rose to her feet and threw her bowl of gruel across the room. The gruel spilt upon the floor where it remained, turning sour, for a week.

'What is the matter with you?' asked Marguerite.

'I shall throw myself downstairs, kill myself, and you will be here alone, alone!' screamed Blanche. 'Why did you refuse? I can't go on, do you understand, I can't go on. We shall never get out of here, never, because you didn't consent. It's your fault, it's your fault, from the very start. But you'll stay here alone, all alone.'

She was going mad, or making herself mad, which is in itself a form of lunacy.

To prisoners hope disappointed is worse than waiting. Blanche had thought that she was to go free through Robert of Artois's visit. But nothing had happened, except that the amenities their cousin's visit had obtained for them had been discontinued. From then on the change in Blanche had been terrifying. She had ceased to wash herself; she had grown thin; she alternated between moods of sudden fury and crises of weeping which left long furrows down her dirty cheeks. Unceasingly, she hurled reproaches at Marguerite, even accused her of having pushed her into the arms of Gautier d'Aunay out of sheer viciousness, and then angrily demanded that she should write to Paris accepting the proposal that had been made her. They had grown to hate each other.

'All right, die then, since you have not the courage to fight!' exclaimed Marguerite.

'Fight for whom, for what? Fight against walls . . . Fight that you may be Queen? Because you still think you will be Queen, don't you?'

'But if I do accept, you fool, it is I who will go free, not you!'

'Alone, alone, you'll be alone!' repeated Blanche, hearing nothing that was said to her.

'Good! I want nothing better than to be alone!' cried Marguerite.

The last two months had also affected her more than the preceding half-year. As the days went by and nothing happened, she often thought that her refusal had been a mistake, that the weapon she thought was hers would turn out to be of no use to her.

Blanche ran towards the staircase. 'All right, let her break every bone in her body! I shall no longer have to hear her screams and groans! She won't kill herself, but at least she'll be taken away,' Marguerite said to herself.

Then, at the last moment, as Blanche reached the door, she cried, 'Blanche!'

She went to her and took her by the arm. For a moment they looked at each other, Marguerite's brilliant, questioning dark eyes gazing into the blue, bewildered eyes of Blanche. Then Marguerite said wearily, 'All right, I'll write the letter. I've come to the end of my tether too.'

Leaning out into the staircase, she shouted, 'Guards, summon Captain Bersumée.'

Nothing answered her but the winter wind shaking the tiles upon the roofs.

'You see,' said Marguerite, shrugging her shoulders, 'even when I want to do it ... I shall ask to see Bersumée or the Chaplain when they bring us our dinner.'

But Blanche ran down the stairs and started hammering on the lower door, screaming that she wanted to see the Captain. The archers of the guard interrupted their game of dice and one of them replied that he would be sent for.

Bersumée arrived soon afterwards, his wolfskin cap pulled down to the solid line formed by his eyebrows. He listened to Marguerite's request.

Pens, parchment? What were they needed for? The prisoners had no right to communicate with anyone whatsoever, neither verbally nor in writing, those were the orders of Monseigneur de Marigny.

'I must write to the King,' said Marguerite.

To the King? Well, that certainly set Bersumée a problem. Did 'anyone whatsoever' include the King?

Marguerite spoke with such haughtiness and persuasion that, in the end, he weakened.

'Very well, but be quick about it,' she cried.

It suddenly seemed to her that sending this letter, which she had refused to write for so long, was of desperate urgency.

Since the Chaplain was absent that particular morning, Bersumée himself returned with writing materials which he had found in the sacristy.

As she was about to begin the letter, Marguerite felt a last hesitation. It filled her with a sensation of panic. Never again, if by good fortune her case were to be reopened, could she plead not guilty or pretend that the brothers Aunay had made false confessions under torture. She would have deprived her daughter of every right to the crown.

'Go on, go on!' Blanche whispered in her ear.

'Whatever happens, things could be no worse,' murmured Marguerite.

And she began to compose her renunciation.

'I recognize and declare that my daughter Jeanne is not the child of the King, my husband. I recognize and declare that I have always refused my body to the said King, my husband, with the result that there never has been any physical relationship between us . . . As has been promised me, I await translation to a convent in Burgundy . . .'

Bersumée, suspicious, stood beside her while she wrote; then, when she had finished, he took the letter and studied it for a moment, but it was only a pretence since he was unable to read.

'This must reach Monseigneur of Artois as soon as possible,' said Marguerite.

'Oh, Madam, that alters matters. You said that it was for the King.'

'To Monseigneur of Artois that he may remit it to the King!' cried Marguerite. 'My God, you're a fool! Can't you see what is written in the address?'

'Oh, very well. But who is to deliver the letter?'

'Good God, you of course!'

'But I have no orders.'

Their relations had seriously worsened of late. Marguerite

no longer hesitated to tell Bersumée what she thought of him, while Bersumée treated her with contempt because she had not succeeded in regaining her freedom.

He took all day to decide what to do. He asked the advice of the Chaplain, who was in any case aware that his pens had been taken from the sacristy. There was a variety of reasons for his doing so; it was generally said that Marigny had fallen into disgrace and even that the King intended to bring him to trial. One thing was sure: if Marigny continued to send instructions, he certainly no longer sent money, and Bersumée had received neither his own nor his men's pay. It was a good opportunity to go and find out what was happening.

The following morning, therefore, having put on his steel helmet and given Sergeant Lalaine, under pain of death, orders to permit no one whatever to enter or leave Château-Gaillard during his absence, Bersumée, having mounted his dappled half-bred percheron, took the road to Paris.

He arrived in the middle of the afternoon of the following day. It was raining in torrents. Muddy to the eyes, Bersumée stopped at a tavern near the Louvre to fortify himself and reflect a little. All along the road his head had ached from anxiety. How was he to know whether he was doing the right thing or not, acting for or against his own promotion? And the dilemma was represented by two names: Artois and Marigny; Artois and Marigny. By infringing the orders of the latter, what did he stand to gain from the former?

Providence looks after fools as it does drunkards. While Bersumée was warming his stomach before the fire, a great clap on his jerkin-clothed back put a stop to his meditations.

It was Sergeant Quatre-Barbes, an old companion in arms,

who had just come in and recognized him. They had not seen each other for six years. They embraced, stood back to look each other up and down, embraced again and loudly demanded wine to celebrate their meeting.

Quatre-Barbes, a thin fellow with black teeth and a squint, was a Sergeant of the Company of Archers of the Louvre nearby. He was a regular at this tavern. Bersumée envied his living in Paris. Quatre-Barbes envied Bersumée his having been promoted more quickly than himself and his being now Captain of a Fortress. Everything therefore went well between them, since they envied each other's lot!

'Good God! Do you mean to say you guard Dame Marguerite? You old bastard, I bet you have a good time!' cried Quatre-Barbes.

From questioning each other they became confidential, then passed to the problems that so much concerned Bersumée. What truth was there in the rumour of Marigny's disgrace? Quatre-Barbes must know, living as he did in the capital and more particularly in the Louvre, which was under the Rector-General's control! It was thus that Bersumée learnt, much to his terror, that Monseigneur de Marigny had triumphed over the difficulties in his path, that three days earlier the King had recalled him and embraced him in the presence of several barons, while handing him his exoneration, and that he was now as powerful as ever.

'If I were Marigny, I know very well what I should do,' said Quatre-Barbes.

'This damned letter's put me in the hell of a mess,' thought Bersumée.

Wine liberates the tongue. Bersumée, taking care that no

one near them should hear, admitted to his newly recovered friend why he was there and asked his advice.

The Sergeant sat for a long moment with his nose in his mug, then replied. 'In your place, I should go to the Palace and see Alain de Pareilles, who is your chief, and ask his advice. At least you'll be covered.'

The afternoon had gone in talking and drinking. Bersumée was a little drunk, and felt relieved that a decision had been made for him. But it was too late to go and present himself to the Captain-General of the Archers. Quatre-Barbes was not on guard that night. The two companions supped where they were; then the Sergeant, as was inevitable upon the arrival of an old friend from the country, led Bersumée to visit the prostitutes who, since the ordinance of Saint Louis, were congregated in the streets behind Notre-Dame, their hair dyed that they might be clearly distinguished from honest women.

Thus Marguerite of Burgundy's letter which, in principle, was to change the succession to the throne of France, remained the whole night sewn into Bersumée's jerkin, upon a chest in a brothel.

In the early morning Quatre-Barbes invited Bersumée to come and wash in his quarters in the Louvre; towards nine o'clock, brushed, clean and close-shaven, Bersumée presented himself at the guard-house of the Palace and had himself announced to Alain de Pareilles.

The Captain of the Archers showed no hesitation whatever when Bersumée told him of the situation. He passed his fingers through his iron-grey hair, and asked, 'From whom do you receive your instructions?'

'From Monseigneur de Marigny, Messire.'

'Who, over me, commands all the royal fortresses?'

'Monseigneur de Marigny, Messire.'

'To whom must you refer upon every question?'

'To you, Messire.'

'And above me?'

'To Monseigneur de Marigny.'

Bersumée felt that delightful sensation of protection, that resumption of childhood, that the good soldier knows in the presence of someone of higher rank than his own.

'So,' concluded Alain de Pareilles, 'it is to Monseigneur de Marigny that you must deliver your letter. But take care to put it into his own hands.'

Half an hour later, in the Rue des Fossés-Saint-Germain, it was announced to Enguerrand de Marigny, who was working in his study with his secretaries, that a certain Captain Bersumée, coming from Messire de Pareilles, wished to see him.

'Bersumée ... Bersumée ...' said Enguerrand. 'Ah yes, of course! That's the fool in command at Château-Gaillard. I'll see him.'

And he indicated that he wished to be left alone.

Extremely nervous at being shown in to the Rector of the kingdom, Bersumée took from his jerkin the letter addressed to Monseigneur of Artois. Since it was not sealed, Marigny read it at once with earnest attention, his face showing no expression whatever.

'When was this written?' he asked.

'The day before yesterday, Monseigneur.'

'You have done very well to bring it to me. I compliment

you. Assure Madame Marguerite that her letter will be sent on to the right quarter. And if she should have a mind to write others, see that they take the same route. How is Madame Marguerite?'

'As well as can be expected in prison, Monseigneur. But she certainly stands up to it better than Madame Blanche, whose mind appears to be somewhat deranged.'

Marigny made a vague gesture which indicated that no one's state of mind was of any significance in the affair.

'Look after their bodily health; see that they are fed and warm.'

'By the way, Monseigneur . . .'

'Yes, what is it?'

'I am rather hard up for money at Château-Gaillard. I have received none to pay my men with, nor myself.'

Marigny shrugged his shoulders; he was not at all surprised. For the last two months everything had been going to wrack and ruin.

'I will give orders to your bailiwick,' he said. 'The cashier will bring your account up to date before the week's out. How much are you personally due?'

'Fifteen pounds and sixpence, Monseigneur.'

'You shall receive thirty at once.'

And Marigny rang for his secretary to show Bersumée out and pay him the wages of obedience.

Left alone. Marigny read Marguerite's letter over again with great care, thought for a moment, and then threw it into the fire.

With a satisfied smile he watched the parchment curling up in the flames; at that moment he felt himself to be in reality the most powerful personage in the kingdom. Nothing escaped him; he held everyone's fate in the palm of his hand, even the King's.

PART THREE

THE ROAD TO MONTFAUCON

I

Famine

THE WRETCHEDNESS OF THE people of France was greater that year than it had been for a hundred past, and a scourge that had ravaged previous centuries reappeared: famine. In Paris the price of a bushel of salt was ten silver pennies, and twelve bushels of wheat sold for sixty pence, a price never before reached within living memory. This increase in prices was primarily caused by the disastrous harvest of the preceding summer, but was also largely contributed to by the disorganized state of the administration, by the disturbances created in a number of provinces by the barons' leagues, by people panicking and therefore hoarding, and by the cupidity of speculators.

February is undoubtedly the most difficult month in a year of scarcity. The last supplies from the previous autumn are exhausted, and so is the physical and mental resistance of human beings. Cold is joined to hunger. It is the month which has the highest death rate. People despair of ever seeing the spring again; in some despair becomes despondency and in others turns to hatred. As the road to the cemetery becomes familiar, everyone begins to wonder when his own turn will come.

In the country dogs that could no longer be fed were eaten, and cats had become wild again and were hunted like game. For lack of fodder cattle were dying and people fought over the carrion. Women plucked frozen grass for food. It was common knowledge that the bark of the beech made a better flour than that of the oak. Day by day young people were being drowned beneath the ice on the lakes attempting to catch fish. There were practically no old people left. Carpenters, weak and emaciated as they were, were in constant employment making coffins. The mills had ceased to grind. Mothers who had gone insane still held in their arms the corpses of their children who clutched a handful of rotten straw in their dead fingers. From time to time a monastery could be importuned; but charity itself was powerless, for there was nothing to buy except shrouds for the dead. Tottering crowds evacuated the countryside for the towns in the vain hope of finding bread; but they only met another procession of skeletons who, coming from the towns, seemed to be walking towards the Last Judgement.

Things were in this state in those regions normally considered rich as well as in the poorer ones, in Valois as well as in Champagne, in Marche as in Poitou, in Angoumois, in Brittany, and even in Beauce, even in Brie, even in the Île-de-France. It was the same at Neauphle and at Cressay.

Guccio, on his way from Avignon to Paris with Bouville, had noted the evidences of the state of the country but, since he had lodged only with Provosts or in royal castles, had provisions for the journey, good gold in his pocket to meet the exorbitant prices of the inns, and had been in a hurry to get back, he had not seen want near at hand.

He was no more aware of it when, three days after his return, he was trotting along the road that leads from Paris to Neauphle. His travelling cloak, lined with fur, was warm, his horse going well, and he was going towards the woman he loved. He spent the time polishing phrases for the beautiful Marie in his head, perhaps to tell her how he had spoken of her to Madame of Hungary, future Queen of France, and that the thought of her had never left him, which was in fact the truth. Because chance infidelities do not prevent one thinking, indeed rather the contrary, of the person to whom one is being unfaithful; indeed it is the most frequent manner of being faithful that men have. Then he was going to describe to Marie the splendours of Naples. He felt himself, as a result of his journey, clothed in an aura of importance and high diplomacy; he intended to make himself loved.

It was only when he reached the neighbourhood of Cressay, because he knew the district well and had a tenderness for it as the scene of his springtime love-making, that Guccio began to become aware of things other than himself.

The deserted fields, the silent villages, the rare column of smoke from a hovel, the absence of livestock, the few thin and filthy people he met, and above all the looks they gave him, began to give the young Tuscan a feeling of disquiet and insecurity which grew stronger with every step he took. And when he entered the courtyard of the old manor upon the banks of the Mauldre, he had an intuition of disaster. There was no cock upon the midden, no lowing from the cowhouse, not the bark of a dog. The young man went forward but no one, servant or master, appeared to greet him. The house seemed dead. 'Have they left?' Guccio wondered. 'Have their goods been seized and have they been sold up during my absence? What can have happened? Or has the plague been raging in these parts?'

He tied the reins of his horse to a ring in the wall – he had brought no servant with him for so short a journey so as to be the freer – and went into the living-house. He found himself face to face with Madame de Cressay.

'Oh, Messire Guccio!' she cried. 'I thought . . . I thought . . . and so you have come back . . .'

There were tears in Dame Eliabel's eyes, and she sought support from a piece of furniture as if faint with the surprise of seeing him. She had lost a stone and a half and aged by ten years. Her dress now hung about her where before it had stretched tautly across her breast and hips; her complexion had turned grey, her cheeks were sunken and quivered beneath the widow's veil framing her face.

In order to dissimulate his astonishment at seeing the change in her, Guccio looked round the Great Hall. Heretofore it had had all the appearance of a dignified way of living in spite of straitened means; today it revealed utter poverty, a dusty and chaotic penury.

'We are in no condition to receive a guest,' said Dame Eliabel sadly.

'Where are your sons, Pierre and Jean?'

'Hunting, as they are every day.'

'And Marie?' asked Guccio.

'Alas!' said Dame Eliabel, lowering her eyes.

Guccio felt icy claws at his head, his throat and about his heart.

'*Ch'e successo?* What has happened?'

Dame Eliabel shrugged her shoulders in a gesture of despair.

'She is so low,' she said, 'so weak that I can no longer hope for her recovery, nor even that she will see Easter.'

'What is the matter with her?' said Guccio, feeling the claws relax because he had at first imagined the worst.

'The same thing that is the matter with all of us and of which we are all dying in these parts! Hunger, Signor Guccio. And you can well imagine, if stout bodies such as mine are so exhausted that they are afraid of falling, what ravages hunger inflicts upon a constitution like my daughter's, which is still immature.'

'But good God, Dame Eliabel,' cried Guccio, 'I thought that famine only affected the poor!'

'And what else do you think we are but poor?' replied the widow. 'We are in no better case merely because we are noble and own a tumbledown manor house. For squires like us, all our wealth consists in our serfs and the work they do. How can we expect them to feed us, when they haven't anything to eat themselves and come to die before our door with outstretched hands. We have had to kill off our livestock in order to share it with them. Add to that that the Provost has been requisitioning, here as elsewhere, upon orders from Paris, so he said, doubtless to feed his Sergeants-at-Arms, for they are still fat. When all our peasants have died, what will remain to us but to follow their example? Land in itself is worth nothing; it is only valuable if it is worked, and putting corpses into it won't make it productive. We no longer have any servants either male or female. Our poor lame old man . . .'

'The one you called your carver?'

'Yes, our carver . . .' she said with a sad smile. 'Well, he left us for the cemetery a few weeks ago. It was in keeping.'

'Where is she?' asked Guccio.

'Marie? Upstairs in her room.'

'May I see her?'

The widow hesitated a moment; even in disaster she preserved a sense of convention.

'Yes, certainly,' she said, 'I will go and prepare her for your visit.'

She went upstairs with heavy steps and a moment later called Guccio. He reached the top of the stairs in a few strides.

Marie de Cressay was lying in a narrow bed in the old-fashioned way, the bedclothes not tucked in and the mattress and cushions piled so high behind her back that her body seemed to be at an angle to the ground.

'Signor Guccio . . . Signor Guccio . . .' Marie murmured.

Her eyes looked bigger for the blue shadows that surrounded them; her long chestnut and gold hair was spread out over the velvet pillow. Upon her thin cheeks and fragile neck her skin had a disquieting transparency. And the impression that she had formerly given of having drunk the sunlight had disappeared, as if a great white cloud had come to rest over her.

Dame Eliabel left them, to avoid showing them her tears;

and Guccio wondered whether the lady of the manor knew, if Marie in her illness had admitted the love she bore in her heart.

'*Maria mia*, my beautiful Marie,' said Guccio going close to the bed.

'There you are at last, come back at last. I was so afraid, oh so very afraid, of dying without seeing you again.'

She looked at Guccio with searching intensity, and her eyes were anxiously questioning.

'What is the matter with you, Marie?' he asked, because he didn't know what else to say.

'Weakness, my beloved, mere weakness. And the great fear I had that you had abandoned me.'

'I had to go to Italy on the King's service, and leave so suddenly that I had no chance of letting you know.'

'On the King's service . . .' she murmured.

The anxious, silent questioning still lay behind her eyes. And Guccio suddenly felt ashamed of his good health, his furred clothes, the heedless weeks he had spent in travelling. Ashamed even of the Neapolitan sun and of the vanity which had filled him till an hour before, of having lived among the great of the world.

She stretched out her beautiful emaciated hand towards him; and Guccio took it in his; and their fingers met once again, wonderingly, and at last were intermingled in a clasp, a surer promise of love than any kiss, as the two stranger hands were joined in the same prayer.

The dumb questioning faded from Marie's eyes and her eyelids drooped.

They stayed thus a moment without speech; the girl felt

that she was drawing renewed strength from Guccio's fingers.

'Marie,' he said suddenly, 'look what I have brought you!'

He took from his purse two stars of wrought gold encrusted with pearls and cabuchon precious stones, which it was at that time fashionable for rich people to sew into the collars of their coats. Marie took these jewels and carried them to her lips. And Guccio felt a tightening of the heart, for gold, however exquisitely wrought by the most cunning of Venetian goldsmiths, cannot relieve hunger. 'A pot of honey or preserved fruits would have been a better present today,' he thought. He was seized with a great longing to act.

'I am going to find something to cure you,' he cried.

'That you should be here, that you should have been thinking of me, I ask for nothing more . . . Are you going already?'

'I shall be back in a few hours.'

He was at the door.

'Your mother, does she know?' he asked in a low voice.

Marie shook her head.

'I was not certain enough of you to reveal our secret,' she murmured; 'I shall do it only when you wish me to.'

Going down into the Great Hall, he found Dame Eliabel with her two sons who had just come in from hunting. Their faces unshaven, their eyes bright with fatigue, their clothes torn and ill-repaired, Pierre and Jean de Cressay also bore about them the marks of distress. They showed Guccio all the joy they felt in seeing a friend once more. But they could not escape a certain jealousy and envy in seeing the young Lombard's prosperous appearance, particularly, moreover, as he was younger than they were. 'Clearly a bank gets on better than the nobility,' thought Jean de Cressay.

'Our mother will have told you everything, and you have seen Marie . . .' said Pierre.

'A crow and a fieldmouse are the only results of our hunting this morning. And a fine soup for a whole family we shall make out of them! But what can you expect? There are snares everywhere. One can promise a peasant a beating for hunting as much as one likes, but they would rather be beaten and have a little game to eat. One can well understand it; in their place we should do the same.'

'I hope at least that the Milanese falcons I brought you last autumn render you good service?' asked Guccio.

The two brothers looked away in embarrassment. Then Jean, the eldest and more surly of the two, at last brought himself to say, 'We had to surrender them to Provost Portefruit so that he would leave us our last pig. Besides, we no longer had anything to set them on.'

He was ashamed and very unhappy to have to admit the use to which they had put Guccio's present.

'You were perfectly right,' the latter said; 'when I have a chance, I will try and get you others.'

'That dog of a Provost,' cried Pierre de Cressay in fury, 'I can promise you he has not improved since the time you snatched us out of his clutches. By himself he is worse than the famine and doubles its disastrous effects.'

'I am very ashamed, Messire Guccio, of the stringent fare I am asking you to share with us,' said the widow.

Guccio refused with the utmost delicacy of politeness, alleging that he was awaited for dinner at the bank of Neauphle.

'The important thing is to find proper food for your

daughter, Dame Eliabel,' he added, 'and not to let her die.
I am going to get some.'

'We are extremely beholden to you for your thought, but
you will find nothing, except grass along the roads,' replied
Jean de Cressay.

'Oh well!' cried Guccio, tapping the purse that hung from
his belt, 'I am not a Lombard if I don't succeed in doing
something.'

'Even gold is useless now,' said Jean.

'That's what we shall see.'

It was fated that Guccio, whenever he met this family,
should play the role of knight-errant, rather than that of the
creditor he still was for a debt of three hundred pounds,
which remained undischarged since the death of the late
squire of Cressay.

Guccio rode towards Neauphle, persuaded that the clerks
of the Tolomei branch would arrange things for him. 'If I
know them, they will have hoarded prudently or at least
know where to go if one has the means of paying.'

But he found the three clerks huddled round a peat fire;
their faces were waxen and their heads hung low.

'For the last two weeks there has been no business, Messire
Guccio,' they said. 'We don't even have one client a day.
Loans are not being repaid and there would be no advantage
in ordering distraint: you can't seize nothing. Food?' They
shrugged their shoulders.

'We are shortly going to feast off a pound of chestnuts,'
said the manager, 'and lick our lips for the next three days.
Is there still salt in Paris? It's the lack of salt above all from
which people are dying. If you could only send us a bushel!

The Provost of Montfort has some, but he won't distribute it. He lacks for nothing, I promise you; he has plundered all the neighbourhood as if the country were at war.'

'What, that man again! He's a disaster, that Portefruit!' cried Guccio. 'I shall go and find him. I've already checkmated him once, the thief.'

'Messire Guccio . . .' said the manager, wishing to persuade the young man to prudence.

But Guccio was already outside and mounting his horse. He felt a surge of hatred in his breast such as he had never known before.

Because Marie was dying of hunger, he suddenly found himself on the side of the poor and suffering; and he might have guessed from that alone that his love was real.

He, a Lombard, born with a silver spoon in his mouth, had taken up his position beside the poor. Now he noticed that the walls of the houses seemed redolent of death. He felt himself at one with these families staggering behind their coffins, with these men whose skin was drawn tight across their cheekbones and whose eyes had become like those of beasts.

He was going to strike his dagger into Provost Portefruit's stomach; he had made up his mind. He was going to avenge Marie, avenge the whole province and accomplish an act of simple justice. Of course he would be arrested, he wanted to be, and the affair would make a great stir. Uncle Tolomei would move heaven and earth; he would go and see Monseigneur de Bouville and Monseigneur of Valois. The case would come before the Parliament of Paris, even before the King. And then Guccio would shout aloud, 'Sire, that is why I killed your Provost . . .'

After galloping for some three miles his imagination grew somewhat calmer. 'Remember, my boy, that a corpse pays no interest,' Messire Tolomei was in the habit of saying. And in the last resort people fight well only with weapons that are proper to them, and if Guccio, like every Tuscan, know how to manage a short blade reasonably well, it was not his speciality.

He slowed his pace, therefore, at the entrance to Montfort-l'Amaury, calmed both his horse and his temper and went to the Provost's office. As the sergeant of the guard did not show him all the courtesy he should have done Guccio took from his pocket a safe-conduct, sealed with the private seal of Louis X, which Tolomei had obtained through Valois for his nephew's mission to Italy.

It was drawn up in pretty wide terms: 'I require all my bailies, seneschals and provosts to give aid and assistance . . .' Guccio counted on being able to use it for a long time to come.

'On the King's service!' said Guccio.

At the sight of the royal seal the Provost's sergeant immediately became courteous and zealous, running to open the doors.

'You will feed my horse,' Guccio ordered.

People over whom you have once had the advantage nearly always consider themselves defeated in advance when they find themselves in your presence again. However difficult they may wish to be, it is no use; water always flows in the same direction. This was the situation between Master Portefruit and Guccio.

His flesh quivering like brawn, his mind in a state of some

anxiety, the Provost came to greet his visitor. Reading the safe-conduct, 'I require all my bailies . . .' did nothing to decrease his anxiety. What could this young Lombard's secret business be? Was he come to make inquiries, to inspect? Philip the Fair had in the past had these mysterious agents who, under cover of some other business, traversed the kingdom, making their reports, then suddenly a head would fall, a prison door open.

'Ah, Messire Portefruit, before going any further I wish to inform you,' said Guccio, 'that I have made no mention in high places of the matter of the Cressay succession duty, which brought about our meeting a year ago. I looked upon it as a mistake. This to ally your anxiety.'

It was indeed an admirable method of reassuring the Provost! It was to tell him clearly and at once: 'I am reminding you that I caught you out in flagrant dishonesty, and that I can make it known whenever I wish.'

The Provost's fat moonlike face paled a little, except for the birthmark, violet and prominent, which grew disgustingly at the corner of his forehead. His eyes were small and yellow. The man must have had some liver disease.

'I am grateful to you, Messire Baglioni, for the view you take,' he replied. 'It was indeed all a mistake. Besides, I have had the accounts erased.'

'Did they need erasing?' remarked Guccio.

The other realized that he had uttered a dangerous folly. Decidedly this young Lombard had the gift of confusing him.

'I was just about to sit down to dinner,' he said, in order to change the subject as quickly as possible; 'will you do me the honour of joining me?'

He was beginning to show himself obsequious. Dignity impelled Guccio to refuse; but cunning suggested his acceptance; people never give themselves away so easily as at dinner. Besides, Guccio had eaten nothing and come far since morning. So, having left Neauphle in order to kill the Provost, he found himself sitting comfortably next to him and using his dagger only to carve a beautifully roasted sucking-pig submerged in exquisitely thick, golden gravy.

The Provost's doing himself so well in the middle of a starving countryside was utterly scandalous. 'When I think,' Guccio said to himself, 'when I think that I came here to find food for Marie and that it is I who am doing the eating!' Every mouthful increased his hatred of Portefruit; and as the other, thinking to conciliate his visitor, had his finest provisions and rarest wines brought out, Guccio, at each bumper he was forced to accept, repeated to himself, 'I'll pay him out for all this, the pig! I'll see that he swings for it.'

Never was a meal eaten so hungrily and with such little advantage to him who offered it. Guccio missed no opportunity of putting his host ill at ease.

'I am told that you have acquired certain falcons, Master Portefruit?' he asked suddenly. 'Have you the right to hunt then, like nobles?'

The other choked in his goblet.

'I hunt with the nobles of the neighbourhood, when they are kind enough to ask me,' he replied quickly.

He tried once more to change the subject, and added, in order to say something, 'You appear to travel a lot, Messire Baglioni?'

'Indeed, a good deal,' replied Guccio off-handedly. 'I have

just come back from Italy where I was upon the King's business to the Queen of Naples.'

Portefruit remembered that at their first meeting Guccio had just returned from a mission to the Queen of England. Certainly this young man seemed to be much employed on expeditions to queens; he must be very powerful. Moreover, he somehow always managed to know the things one would have preferred to keep quiet.

'Master Portefruit, the clerks of the branch of my uncle's bank at Neauphle are reduced to great misery. I have found them ill from hunger, and they assure me that they can buy nothing,' declared Guccio suddenly. (And the Provost realized that they were coming to the object of the visit.) 'How do you explain that in a country ravaged by famine you impose tithes in kind, taking and seizing everything there is left to eat?'

'Oh, Messire Baglioni, this is a very serious matter for me and an extremely painful one, I promise you. But I must obey orders from Paris. I have to send three wagon-loads of food every week, as do all the other provosts hereabouts, because Monseigneur de Marigny is afraid of a rising and wishes to keep the capital quiet. As usual it is the countryside that suffers.'

'And when your sergeants-at-Arms collect sufficient to fill three wagons, they manage at the same time to fill a fourth and you keep that one for yourself.'

The Provost felt considerable distress. How very painful the dinner was turning out to be. He wondered whether he would manage to digest it properly!

'Never, Messire Baglioni, never! What will you think next?'

'Out with it, Provost! Where does all this come from?' cried Guccio indicating the spread before them. 'I know very well that these hams do not grow in your herbaceous borders. Nor do your Sergeants-at-Arms wax as fat as they are merely by licking the lilies on their staves!'

'Had I realized,' thought Portefruit, 'I would not have entertained him so well.'

'The fact is, don't you see,' he replied, 'that if order is to be maintained in the kingdom it is essential that those employed to watch over it should be properly fed.'

'Certainly,' said Guccio, 'certainly. You are speaking with great good sense. A man such as you, upon whom such important duties devolve, must obviously not reason like the common people, nor indeed act as they do.'

Suddenly he had become approving, friendly and appeared to accept his host's point of view entirely. Unconsciously he was imitating Monseigneur Robert of Artois, whom he had seen several times and whose manners had made a considerable impression on him. He almost went so far as to slap the Provost on the back. The other, who had drunk a good deal to give himself courage, fell into the trap.

'It's exactly the same with the taxes, isn't it?' went on Guccio.

'The taxes?' repeated the Provost.

'Yes, of course! You farm them, don't you? Naturally you have to live and pay your agents. So obviously you have to raise more than you hand over to the Treasury. What do you do about it? You double the tax, isn't that so? As far as I know, that is what every provost does.'

'More or less,' said Portefruit candidly, since he believed

that he was dealing, if not with an accomplice, at least with someone in the know. 'We are obliged to, of course. You must know that in order to obtain my position I had to grease the palm of one of Marigny's secretaries.'

'Really, a secretary of Marigny's?'

'Yes, indeed, and I continue to give him something on every Saint Nicholas's Day. I have to share, too, with my receiver, without mentioning what the bailie, my superior, takes off me. So, when all is said and done . . .'

'There does not remain all that much for you, I see . . . So, Provost, you are going to help me, as it is your duty to do, and I will propose a deal by which you will lose nothing. I must feed my clerks. Every week you will deliver to them salt, flour, beans, honey, and either fresh or dried meat which they need merely to exist, and for which they will pay at the highest Paris prices with a bonus of threepence in the pound. I am even prepared to give you fifty pounds in advance,' he said, shaking his purse till it rang.

The sound of the gold overcame the Provost's caution. He bargained a little, merely for bargaining's sake, and arranged the weights and quantities with Guccio, who calculated everything double in order to supply the Cressay family.

Since Guccio wanted to take some provisions away with him at once, the Provost led him into his larder which resembled a merchant's warehouse.

Now that he had made a deal, what point was there in further concealment? In fact he was not altogether displeased to have someone at last to whom he could show with impunity his wealth of foodstuffs, of which he was most certainly more vain than of his administrative titles. If he had become a provost through ambition, his real aptitudes were more suited to the business of a grocer. With his round face, his snub nose, and his short arms, he went to and fro among his casks of lentils and peas, sniffed his cheeses, and let his eyes rest caressingly upon his strings of sausages. Having just spent two hours dining, he looked as if he were already hungry again.

'The fellow deserves to be raided with clubs and pitch-forks,' thought Guccio. A servant prepared a large parcel of victuals which, enveloped in a cloth to cover them, Guccio attached to his saddle.

'And if by any chance,' said the Provost, showing him out, 'you should happen to go short yourself in Paris, I might as occasion offers be able to send you a wagon-load.'

'I'll think about it, Provost. Besides, you will not have to wait long to see me again. And in the meantime you may rest assured that I shall speak of you as you deserve.'

Thereupon Guccio left for Neauphle, and went to the bank where the clerks, when they heard his news, overwhelmed him with gratitude.

'And so,' said Guccio, 'every week someone will come from Cressay or you will arrange to take there, when night has fallen, half of what the Provost sends you. My uncle takes a great interest in that family, who stand better at Court than one might expect from appearances; take care that they lack for nothing.'

'Are they to pay cash or is it to be debited to them?' asked the manager.

'You will keep a separate account which I shall deal with myself.'

Ten minutes later Guccio arrived at the manor, triumphantly brandishing his parcel of provisions. When he went to her room and unpacked his acquisitions, Marie had tears in her eyes.

'Guccio, one might think you were a magician,' she cried.

'I would do much more to see you regain your strength, and for the joy of earning your love. You will receive as much again every week. Believe me,' he added smiling, 'it's less difficult than finding a cardinal in Avignon.'

This reminded him that he had not come to Cressay only to flirt. As they were alone, he took the opportunity of asking Marie if the casket he had left in her care the autumn before was still in the same place in the chapel.

'You will find it where we left it,' she replied. 'My greatest anxiety was that I would die without knowing what to do with it.'

'Don't worry about it any more; I am going to take it back with me. And for God's sake, if you love me, think no more of dying!'

'Not any more now,' she said, smiling.

Having assured her that he would return more often, he left her biting delightedly into dried plums.

Having gone down into the Great Hall, he told Dame Eliabel that he had brought back wonderful relics from Italy, that they were most efficacious, and that he wished to pray over them alone in the chapel so as to obtain Marie's recovery. The widow was astonished that so devoted, clever and busy a young man should at the same time be so pious. Clearly, he had every good quality.

Having obtained the key, Guccio went and shut himself up

in the chapel; there he went behind the little altar, found without difficulty the hinged stone and, searching among the sainted bones, whoever's they were, recovered the leaden casket which contained the receipt signed by Archbishop Marigny. 'Here's a good relic to cure the kingdom with,' he said to himself.

He replaced the stone and went out, wearing a somewhat sanctimonious expression.

Having received the thanks and embraces of the lady of the manor and her two sons, he at once set out upon the road to Paris.

Overcome with fatigue, he was compelled to sleep a few hours in the small village of Versailles. The next day he arrived back at his uncle's, to whom he told everything or, at least, nearly everything; that is, he did not much elaborate upon the steps he had taken on behalf of the Cressays, but he described the family and the actions of the Provost with such violence and indignation that the banker was surprised.

'I hope you have brought back the Archbishop's receipt?' asked Tolomei.

'Certainly, Uncle,' replied Guccio, handing him the leaden casket.

'Are you really telling me,' went on Tolomei, 'that this provost told you himself that he raises double taxes, of which he gives part to a secretary of Marigny's? Do you know which one?'

'I could find out. Portefruit believes now that I am a great friend of his.'

'And he says that the other provosts do the same?'

'Without hesitation. Isn't it a disgrace? They make of

hunger an infamous trade and they guzzle like pigs while the population starves round them. Oughtn't the King to be told?'

Tolomei's left eye, the one that was never seen, had suddenly opened, and his whole face took on a different expression, at once ironical and somewhat alarming. At the same time the banker rubbed his plump and pointed hands together.

'Excellent! This is very good news you bring me, my little Guccio; very good news indeed,' he said smiling.

2

Vincennes

THE MODERN MAN, WHEN he tries to imagine the Middle Ages, generally believes that he must make a terrific imaginative effort. The Middle Ages seem to him a dark period, lost in the mists of time, an era of the world upon which the sun never shone and in which lived a race of alien human beings, a society radically different from the one we know. But, indeed, we only have to look about us at our own world and read our newspapers every morning; the Middle Ages lie at our very door; they persist beside us today, and not only in a few monumental remains; they lie beyond the sea which borders our coasts, within a few hours' flying; they form part of what is still called the French Empire, and present our twentieth-century statesmen with problems they are unable to resolve.

Several Mohammedan countries in North Africa and the Middle East are precisely in a period of fourteenth-century development and can show us, in a number of respects, a reflection of what the European medieval world was like. Similar towns, their houses piled one upon another, narrow swarming streets, enclosing a few sumptuous palaces; the same extremes of appalling misery among the poor and of opulence among great lords; the same story-tellers at the corners of the streets, propagating both myths and news; the same population, nine-tenths illiterate, submitting through long years to oppression and then suddenly rebelling violently in murderous panic; the same influence of religious conscience upon public affairs; the same fanaticism; the same intrigues among the powerful; the same hate among rival factions; the same plots so curiously ravelled that their solution lies only in the spilling of blood! The conclaves of the Middle Ages must have closely resembled the present discussions among Moslem doctors of law. The dynastic dramas which marked the end of the direct line of the Capets correspond to the dynastic dramas which today disturb the Arab countries; and the thread of this story will be better understood if we say that it could be defined as a merciless battle between the Pasha of Valois and the Grand Vizier Marigny. The only difference is that the European countries of the Middle Ages were not fields of expansion for the interests of nations better equipped with technical methods and arms. After the fall of the Roman Empire colonialism was dead, at least in our part of the world.

'We haven't been able to meet him face to face but, good heavens, we'll take him in the flank,' the banker Tolomei had said in speaking of Marigny after the latter had returned to favour.

When Guccio had told him of the actions of the Provost of Montfort-l'Amaury, Tolomei reflected for two whole days; then, on the third, having put on his fur coat, his hat and cape, since it was raining cats and dogs that afternoon, he went to Valois's house. He found the King's uncle and his cousin Artois somewhat disconsolate, bitter in their talk, taking their defeat badly and dreaming of revenge.

'Messeigneurs,' said Tolomei, 'during these last weeks your actions have been such that, if you owned a bank or a business, you would have had to go into liquidation.'

He could permit himself this tone: he was owed ten thousand pounds, and the other two accepted his reprimand without replying.

'You didn't ask my advice,' went on Tolomei, 'so I didn't offer it to you. But I could have warned you that a man as powerful as Enguerrand would not dip his fingers into the King's coffers. If he has embezzled, it will be in some other way.'

Then, addressing himself directly to the Count of Valois, he said, 'I have given you a great deal of money, Monseigneur Charles, so that you might raise yourself in the King's confidence; you should return me that money at once.'

'You shall have it, Messire Tolomei,' cried Valois.

'When? I should not have the audacity, Monseigneur, to doubt your word. I am certain of my debt; but still, I must know by what means it will be repaid me; and moreover, it is no longer you who have charge of the Treasury, but Marigny once more.'

'And how do you suggest that we can make an end of the foul pig?' said Robert of Artois. 'We are as interested in doing so as you can be, believe me, and if you have any better ideas than ours, we'll be grateful for them.'

Tolomei smoothed the folds of his robe and crossed his hands on his stomach.

'Messeigneurs,' he replied, 'stop accusing Marigny. Cease clamouring that he is a thief, now that the King has announced that he is no such thing. For a time you must appear to accept the fact that he is in power, and then behind his back, make inquiries in the provinces. Don't put the royal officers in charge of this, because it is precisely against them that these inquiries must be directed; tell the nobles, both great and small, with whom you have power, to gather information everywhere upon the actions of the men Marigny has placed in the provostships. In many places taxes are raised of which only half go to the Treasury. What is not taken in money is taken in food and then marketed. Have this looked into, I tell you; and then get the King's authority, and Marigny's too, to convoke all the provosts, receivers of taxes and financial agents, that they may have their accounts examined before the barons of the kingdom. I tell you that if you do this, such monstrous embezzlement will be revealed that you will have no difficulty in putting the blame upon Marigny, without having to consider whether he is in fact guilty or innocent. And in doing so, Monseigneur of Valois, you will have all the nobles on your side, since they loathe seeing Marigny's Sergeants-at-Arms poking their noses into everything upon their fiefs; and you will also have on your side all the common people who are dying of hunger and want a scapegoat for their misery. There, Messeigneurs, is the advice I permit myself to give you and which, were I in

your place, I should take to the King. I can also assure you
that the Lombard companies, who have branches more
or less everywhere, can help you in your inquiries if you so
wish it.'

'The difficulty will be to persuade the King,' said Valois,
'because at the moment he is infatuated with Marigny and
also with his brother, the Archbishop, through whom he
expects to get a Pope.'

'As far as the Archbishop is concerned, you need have no
fears,' replied the banker. 'I have him in the. hollow of my
hand and I will tell you how when the moment arrives.'

When Tolomei had left, Artois said to Valois, 'That fellow
is decidedly cleverer than we are.'

'Cleverer ... cleverer ...' murmured Valois. 'What you
mean is that he puts in his precise merchant's language what
we had already thought.'

And for the second time they obeyed the instructions
which were given them by the powers of finance. Messire
Spinello Tolomei, with the ten thousand pounds for which he
had made himself guarantor with his Italian colleagues, was
allowing himself the luxury of ruling France.

But it took nearly two months to convince The Hutin. In
vain did Valois repeat to his nephew, 'Remember, Louis, your
father's last words. Remember that he said to you, "Get to
know the state of your kingdom as soon as possible." Well, by
convoking all the provosts and receivers, you will learn the
state. And our sainted ancestor, whose name you bear, also
gives you an example, for he held a great inquiry of this kind
in the year '47.'

Marigny approved such an assembly in principle, but he

did not think that the time was ripe for it. He always had a good reason for deferring it, justly objecting that a moment when the country was in a state of upheaval was not the time to withdraw all the King's agents from their posts at once and cast suspicion upon their administration.

However, the central authority was no longer solid, and it had to be recognized that there were two factions in France which were opposed, at variance and mutually destructive. Torn between these two parties, ill-informed, no longer knowing what was calumny and what reliable information, by nature incapable of clearly making up his mind, sometimes according his confidence to the left, sometimes to the right, Louis X never made a decision unless he was forced to, and thought that he governed when in fact he did no more than obey.

There was still no tiara looming in the sky above Avignon, where Marigny had put up candidates who made no progress against Cardinal Duèze.

At last, on March 19th, 1315, yielding to the violence of the baronial leagues, Louis X, upon the advice of the majority of his Council, signed the charter for the Norman lords, which was shortly to be followed by the charters for those of Languedoc, Burgundy, Picardy and Chartres in Champagne. These charters restored tournaments, private wars and gauges of battle. It was once more permitted for gentlemen 'to fight each other, to ride, to come and go, and to carry arms.' The nobility regained their freedom to divide up lands and create new vassals without having to refer to the King. Nobles could no longer be arraigned except before their peers. The Sergeants-at-Arms and the King's Provosts could no longer arrest criminals or directly indict them without first referring to the lord of the region. The middle classes and freed peasants could no longer, except in a few cases, leave the lands of their lords in order to claim the King's justice.

Finally, in the matter of military subsidies and the recruitment of troops, the barons reacquired a certain independence which allowed them to decide if they wished or not to take part in a national war, and how much they wished to contribute towards it.

Marigny and Valois, for once agreed, had succeeded in placing at the end of these charters a vague formula concerning the supreme royal authority and all that 'by ancient custom belonged to the sovereign prince and to no other.' This formula, in law, would have permitted a strong central power to annul everything that had been ceded clause by clause. But both in spirit and in fact all the institutions of the Iron King were destroyed. And The Hutin, inspired by Valois, countered with 'Saint Louis' whenever anyone mentioned 'Philip the Fair'.

Marigny, who had fought to the end to defend the work of sixteen years of his life, said upon that particular day, as he left the Council, that they had laid the foundations for great trouble in the land.

At the same time the Assembly of all the provosts, treasurers and receivers was called for the middle of April; special investigating officers, called 'reformers', were sent out; and when it became a question of where to hold the Assembly, Charles of Valois proposed Vincennes in memory of the King-Saint.

* * *

On the appointed day Louis X, his peers, his barons, his Council, the great officers of the Crown and the members of the Exchequer, came in state to the manor of Vincennes. They made an imposing procession which brought the people to their doors, while urchins, following, cried, 'Long live the King!' in the hope of a handful of sugar-plums. It had been bruited abroad that the King was to judge the tax-collectors, and nothing could have given the populace a keener pleasure. It was a warm April day and light clouds floated high above the forest trees. A true springtime in which hope might burgeon; if famine were still abroad, cold at least was over, and people told each other that the next harvest would be a good one if Jack Frost did not scorch the young corn.

The Assembly was held in the open air near the royal manor. There had been some difficulty in deciding which was Saint Louis's oak, since there were so many of them about. Some two hundred receivers, treasurers and provosts were regimented there, for the most part sitting on wooden benches, some cross-legged on the ground.

Under a canopy embroidered with the arms of France the young King, a crown upon his head, sceptre in hand, was seated upon a *faudesteuil*, a sort of fold-stool deriving from the chair of State which, from the origins of the French monarchy, served as the sovereign's throne when he was travelling. The arms of Louis X's *faudesteuil* were carved with the heads of greyhounds and the seat consisted of a red silk cushion. On each side of the King, the peers and barons were assembled and the members of the Exchequer sat behind trestle-tables. One after another the Royal functionaries were called up, carrying their account-books, together with the 'reformers' who had been placed in charge of their particular districts. The work of checking threatened to become extremely boring and Louis X, taking the proceedings patiently, was distracting himself by counting the wood-pigeons flying about the trees.

It was not long before it became clear that the accounts in nearly every case showed lavish squandering and traces of dishonesty and embezzlement, particularly during the immediately preceding months, since the death of Philip the Fair, and during the period when Marigny's authority had been undermined.

A certain excitement began to ripple among the ranks of the barons, and among the functionaries a certain fear. When it came to the turn of the Provosts and Receivers of Taxes for the region of Montfort-l'Amaury, Neauphle, Dourdan and Dreux, upon whom Tolomei had furnished the most precise evidences of guilt to the 'reformers', there were marked signs of anger from those in the King's neighbourhood. But the most indignant of the lords was Marigny, who showed his fury the most clearly. Suddenly his voice drowned all others, and he harangued his subordinates with a violence which made them bend their heads. He demanded restitution and promised punishment. Suddenly Monseigneur of Valois, rising to his feet, interrupted him.

'You are playing a fine part for our benefit, Messire Enguerrand,' he cried, 'but shouting so loudly at these scoundrels will do you no good, because they are the very men whom you have placed in these positions, they are devoted to you, and it is clear that you have shared their loot.'

Such absolute silence followed upon this declaration that a

dog could be heard barking in the neighbouring countryside. The Hutin did not know where to look; he had not been expecting an accusation of this kind.

Everyone held his breath as Marigny advanced upon Charles of Valois.

'Me, Monseigneur,' he said hoarsely. 'Me, have you dared to accuse me? If a single one of this riff-raff' (he indicated with his open hand the assembled receivers of taxes) 'if a single one of these bad servants of the kingdom can come out and affirm upon his conscience, swear upon his oath, that he has paid me any bribe, or given me the least part of his receipts, let him come forward.'

Then, pushed forward by Robert of Artois's great hand, a man advanced, trembling, short-armed, round of face, and with a hideous birthmark at the corner of his eyebrow.

'Who are you? What have you go to say? Do you want to be hanged?' asked Marigny.

Master Portefruit stayed silent, though he had been well briefed, first by Guccio, then by the Count of Dreux, Lord of Montfort, and finally by Robert of Artois into whose presence he had been brought the day before. His life was to be spared, and even the profits he had amassed, upon condition that he brought false witness against Marigny. 'Well, what have you got to say?' Valois asked in his turn. 'Do not be afraid of confessing the truth, because our well-loved King is here to listen and render justice.'

Portefruit went down on one knee before Louis X and, spreading wide his arms, said in so feeble a voice that there was difficulty in hearing him, 'Sire, I am most culpable, but I was compelled to act as I have by the secretary of Monseigneur de Marigny, who each year demanded a quarter of the taxes for the benefit of his master.'

Marigny kicked the Provost of Montfort aside with his foot, and the latter, having accomplished his filthy business, hastened to lose himself in the crowd.

'Sire,' said Enguerrand, 'there is no single word of truth in what that man has said; he is acting under instruction, but whose instruction? I see it all too clearly. I can be accused of ill-placed confidence in these rascals whose dishonesty has now been made apparent; I can be accused of not having sufficiently overseen them, of not having sent a round dozen of them to be broken on the wheel, and I will accept the blame, even though for the last four months I have had all disciplinary powers over them taken from me. But let no one accuse me of theft. This is the second time, Messire de Valois, and this time I will tolerate it no longer.'

Turning towards the King with a wide, dramatic gesture, the Count of Valois cried, 'Nephew, we have been deceived by a wicked man who has been too long in our counsels, and whose misdeeds have brought curses upon our house. He is the cause of the extortions of which the country complains and has, for the sake of his own private gain, made treaties with the Flemings to the country's shame. This was the cause of your father's falling into a depression from which he died before his time. It is Enguerrand who is responsible for his death. As for me, I am prepared to prove that he is a thief and that he has betrayed the kingdom, and if you do not have him immediately arrested, I swear to God that I will no longer appear at your Court nor at your Council.'

'It's a damned lie!' cried Marigny.

'Before God, it is you who are lying, Enguerrand,' replied Valois.

Thereupon, he threw himself at Marigny's throat, seized him by the collar, and these two men, these two wild beasts of whom one was Emperor of Constantinople and the other had his statue among those of the Kings, hurling insults at each other, raising the dust about them, began fighting like a couple of labourers in the presence of the whole Court and the whole administration of the Council.

The barons had risen to their feet, the provosts and receivers of taxes had moved backwards, tumbling their benches over in their terror. Suddenly there was a loud laugh. It was The Hutin who had been unable to play the role of Saint Louis to the end.

More infuriated by the laugh than by the shameful spectacle of the two combatants, Philippe of Poitiers came forward and, with unexpected strength, separated the two opponents and held them apart at the full extent of his long arms. Marigny and Valois were gasping, their faces crimson, their clothes torn.

'How dare you, Uncle?' said Philippe of Poitiers. 'Marigny, control yourself, I order you to do so. Go home and calm down.'

The strength and authority of this boy of twenty-one had its effect upon these men of double his age.

'Go, Marigny, I tell you,' insisted Philippe of Poitiers. 'Bouville! Lead him away.'

Marigny permitted himself to be led away by Bouville and went towards the gate of the manor of Vincennes. People scattered before him as if he were a fighting bull escaped from the *toril*.

Valois remained where he was; he was trembling with fury and kept repeating, 'I'll have him hanged; as true as I'm standing here, I'll have him hanged.'

Louis X had stopped laughing. His brother's intervention had given him an object lesson in authority. Moreover, he was suddenly aware that he had been tricked. He rose from his chair, drew his cloak about his shoulders and said sharply to Valois, 'Uncle, I must speak to you at once; please follow me.'

3

A Slaughter of Doves

'You gave me your assurance, Uncle,' cried Louis The Hutin, pacing nervously up and down one of the rooms of the Manor of Vincennes, 'you gave me your assurance that this time there was no question of accusing Marigny, and you have done it! It is taking too much advantage of my goodwill.'

When he came to the end of the room, he turned quickly about, and his cloak described a circle about his calves.

'How can one keep one's temper, Nephew, in face of such villainy?' replied Charles of Valois, still panting from his fight, and holding the pieces of his torn collar.

He was speaking almost in good faith and could now persuade himself that he had yielded to a spontaneous impulse, when in reality the comedy had been decided upon two months ago.

'You know very well that I need a Pope, and you know too that only Marigny can make one for me; Bouville has made that perfectly clear!' went on The Hutin.

'Bouville! Bouville! You believe only the information that Bouville brought back with him, and he saw nothing and understands nothing. The young Lombard who was sent with him to look after the gold has told me more than your Bouville about matters at Avignon. I assure you that Marigny will never succeed in making the Pope you need. In fact, he knows what you want and is putting every obstacle he can in the way of it, so that you will keep him in power. Where will you be tonight, Nephew?'

'I have decided to stay here,' replied Louis.

'Very well, before evening I shall bring you evidence which will destroy Marigny, and I think then that you will certainly finish by handing him over to me.'

Thereupon Valois left for Paris, taking with him Robert of Artois and the equerries who normally served him as escort. Upon their way they crossed the train of wagons which were bringing to Vincennes the beds, chests, tables, and crockery for the King's residence during the night; for at that date the royal castles were not permanently furnished, or were but barely so, and it was necessary to bring all that was wanted with an army of furnishers who arranged everything in a couple of hours.

Valois went back to his house to change his clothes while sending Robert of Artois to Tolomei's.

'Friend banker,' said the giant, 'the moment has come for you to give me that document you spoke of, which establishes the thefts committed by Archbishop Marigny from the possessions of the Templars. Monseigneur of Valois needs it within the hour.'

'That's all very fine, Monseigneur Robert. You are asking

me to give up a weapon which has already saved us once, me and all my friends. If it gives you the means of destroying Marigny, I shall be delighted. But, should Marigny unfortunately survive it, I am a dead man. And then, Monseigneur, and then, I have been thinking . . .'

Robert was boiling over during this conversation, because Valois had told him to make haste, and he knew the value of every wasted moment; but he knew too that by hurrying Tolomei he would obtain nothing.

'Yes, I have been thinking things over,' continued the latter. 'The good laws of the time of Monseigneur Saint Louis which are in process of being restored are an excellent thing for the kingdom; but I would like an exception made of the decrees under which the Lombards were chased out of Paris. My friends have spoken to me about it, and I would like an assurance that we shall not be disturbed.'

'But listen, Monseigneur of Valois has told you so; he supports you; he protects you!'

'Yes, yes, fine words, but we should prefer that this was all in writing. The Lombard companies of which I am, as you know, Captain-General, have respectfully prepared a request to the King asking him to confirm our customary privileges; and at this time, when the King is signing every charter placed before him, we much desire that he should sign ours. That done, Monseigneur, I shall most willingly place in your hands the document which can hang, burn or send to the wheel Marigny the younger or Marigny the elder, whichever you like, or indeed both of them at once.'

Artois hit the table with his fist, and the whole room shook.

'Enough of this bargaining, Tolomei,' he cried. 'I have told you that we cannot wait. Give me your petition, and I promise to get it signed; but give me the other parchment at the same time. We are on the same side and for once you must trust me.'

Tolomei, his hands crossed upon his stomach, sighed.

'Well,' he said, 'sometimes one has to take a risk; but really, Monseigneur, I personally don't like it.'

And he gave the Count of Artois, with the Lombard's petition, the leaden casket that Guccio had brought back from Cressay. Then he grew afraid and for many days was sick of his fear.

An hour later, at the Episcopal Palace, which was next door to Notre-Dame, the Counts of Valois and Artois entered noisily into the presence of Archbishop Jean de Marigny.

In an audience chamber with a vaulted roof, perfumed with incense, the young prelate extended his ring for them to kiss. Valois pretended not to have noticed the gesture, while Artois raised the Archbishop's fingers to his lips with such an air of impudence that one might have thought he was about to throw the whole hand over his shoulder.

'Monseigneur Jean,' said Charles of Valois, 'the time has come when you must tell us by what means you and your brother have managed to oppose so strongly the election of Cardinal Duèze at Avignon, so that the conclave resembles nothing more than a collection of phantoms.'

'But I count for nothing in the matter, Monseigneur, for nothing at all,' replied Jean de Marigny, growing pale but maintaining the unction in his voice. 'I am sure that my brother is acting for the best to help the King, and as for me,

I give what help I can, though the conclave depends upon the cardinals' wishes and not upon ours.'

'Very well!' cried Artois, 'if that is how things are, if Christianity can manage without a Pope, the Episcopal See of Sens and of Paris can doubtless manage without an Archbishop!'

'I don't understand you, Monseigneur Robert,' said Jean de Marigny, 'except that your words are threatening a Minister of God.'

'Was it God by any chance, Messire Archbishop, who commanded you to embezzle certain of the Templars' possessions which should have reverted to the Treasury, and do you think that the King, who is also God's representative upon earth, can tolerate a dishonest prelate upon the Cathedral throne of his capital city? Do you recognize this?' concluded Artois, pushing the document given him by Tolomei under the Archbishop's nose.

'It's a forgery!' cried the Archbishop.

'If it's a forgery,' replied Robert of Artois, 'let justice be done quickly. Bring a case before the King so that the forger may be discovered!'

'The majesty of the Church would have nothing to gain by it.'

'And you everything to lose, I think, Monseigneur.'

The Archbishop had sat down in a great chair and was gazing at the walls as if seeking a means of escape. He was caught in a trap, and felt his courage wavering. 'They will stop at nothing,' he said to himself; 'it really is a pity that all should be ruined merely for the two thousand pounds of which I was in need.' He felt the sweat starting beneath his violet vestments, and saw his whole life destroyed because of a deed already more than a year old, whose profits had already been dissipated.

'Monseigneur Jean,' said Charles of Valois, 'you are still young, and you have a great future before you in the affairs not only of the Church but of the kingdom. What you have done' (he took the parchment from Robert of Artois's hand) 'is an excusable folly at a time when all morality is in decline, and you acted, I imagine, under the influence of evil example. It would be a great pity that this fault, which merely concerns money, should blight the dignity of your fame or shorten your days. For, if by mischance this document were to be seen by the King, in spite of the pain we should all feel, it would lead you to the cloister . . . or to the stake. My opinion, Monseigneur, is that you are doing the kingdom a great deal more harm by lending your help to your brother's policies against the wishes of the King. If you are prepared to denounce this second error of yours, we shall hold you acquitted of the first.'

'What do you ask of me?' said the Archbishop.

'Abandon your brother's party, which is no longer worth anything,' said Valois, 'and come and confess to King Louis what you know of the wicked instructions you have received about the conclave.'

The prelate had feet of clay. He owed his elevation merely to his brother; he had been given a mitre and the most important episcopal throne in France that he might condemn the Templars, when most of the bishops refused the invitation and declined to sit in judgement. But he had panicked in front of Notre-Dame upon the day of Jacques de Molay's execution. At ordinary times he appeared strong; but he was a coward in the hour of crisis. His fear was such that it did not even give him time to think of his brother to whom he owed everything; he thought of no one but himself and entered easily upon the role of Cain to which he must have been destined since his birth. His treachery was to assure him a long life of honours under four successive kings.

'You have shown me the way of conscience,' he said, 'and I am ready, Monseigneur of Valois, to redeem my error in the way you suggest. I would merely be grateful if you would give me back that parchment.'

'Certainly,' said the Count of Valois, giving him the document. 'It is sufficient that the Count of Artois and myself have seen it; our evidence will be believed by the whole kingdom. You will accompany us to Vincennes at once; there is a horse ready for you below.'

The Archbishop sent for his cloak, his embroidered gloves and his hat, and went slowly, majestically, downstairs in front of the two lords.

'I have never seen,' murmured Robert of Artois to Valois, 'anyone grovel with such haughtiness.'

Every king, every man, has his pleasures, which more than any other action he performs reveal the profound tendencies of his nature. King Louis X had no liking for hunting or fencing or tournaments. From childhood he had enjoyed the game of tennis which was played with leather balls; but above all he enjoyed, when he was in the country, finding some barn or grain-store where, bow in hand, he could shoot doves on the wing as an equerry released them one by one from a basket.

He was engaged in this cruel sport when his uncle and his

cousin brought the Archbishop to him. The floor of the barn was littered with feathers and splashes of blood. A dove, nailed by a wing to a beam, was fluttering and screeching; others, better shot, lay on the ground, their thin claws folded and contracted upon their breasts. The Hutin exclaimed with joy each time one of his arrows pierced a victim.

'Another!' he called to the equerry, who opened the lid of the basket.

The bird flying in circles gained height; Louis drew his bow and if the arrow, missing its target, blunted itself upon the wall, he swore at the equerry for having carelessly released the dove at the wrong moment.

'Nephew,' said Charles of Valois, 'you seem to be more skilful today than ever, but if you wouldn't mind interrupting your exploits for a moment, I wish to talk to you about those grave matters we discussed.'

'Well, what is it now?' said The Hutin impatiently.

His brow was damp with sweat and he was excited by his sport. He saw the Archbishop, and signed to the equerry to leave the barn.

'Well, Monseigneur, is it true that you are preventing me from having a Pope?'

'Alas, Sire,' said Jean de Marigny, 'I have come to reveal certain things which I thought were done at your orders and which I am much pained to learn are in fact contrary to your wishes.'

Thereupon, with the greatest appearance of good faith in the world, and a certain unctuous emphasis in his tone of voice, he told the King of all the manoeuvres Enguerrand de Marigny had employed to prevent a meeting of the conclave and to raise obstacles to the election of Jacques Duèze.

'However hard it may be, Sire,' he concluded, 'to have to denounce the wicked actions of my brother, it is still harder for me to see him acting against the interests of the kingdom. I do not hold him in any particular consideration merely because he is a member of my family, since, when you have a vocation such as mine, you have no real family but in God and the King.'

'Really, the scoundrel almost brings tears to one's eyes,' thought Robert of Artois. 'The rascal knows how to use his tongue!'

A forgotten dove had perched on the edge of a window. The Hutin loosed an arrow, piercing the bird and breaking the window.

'Well, and where do I stand now?' he cried, turning sharply about.

Robert of Artois quickly led the Archbishop away and Valois remained alone with the King.

'Yes, where do I stand?' he repeated. 'I am betrayed on every side; people promise things and don't perform them. We are in the middle of April, the summer is but six weeks away, and you remember, Uncle, that Madame of Hungary said, "before summer". Will you succeed in making me a Pope within the next six weeks?'

'Speaking in all honesty, I no longer believe it can be done, Nephew.'

'Well then, you see how things are! What's going to happen to me?'

'I have advised you often enough since the winter to get rid of Marigny.'

'But since that wasn't done, wouldn't it be better to summon Enguerrand, reprimand him, threaten him and order him to act on the other tack? Isn't he the only man we can use?'

Panic-stricken and stubborn, The Hutin always came back to Marigny as the only possible solution. He was walking uncertainly to and fro in the barn; white feathers stuck to his shoes.

'Nephew,' said Charles of Valois suddenly, 'I have twice in my life been the widower of admirable women. It's a great injustice that you should not be the widower of a shameless one.'

'Yes, yes!' cried The Hutin. 'Oh yes! If only Marguerite were to die!'

Suddenly he stopped walking to and fro, looked at his uncle, and the two men stood quite still for a moment, their eyes fixed upon each other's.

'The winter was a cold one, prisons are not healthy places for women,' went on Charles of Valois, 'and it is a long time now since Marigny informed us of Marguerite's state of health. I am astonished that she has been able to stand the treatment she has received. Perhaps Marigny is concealing from you how ill she is, how near to death?'

There was once more silence between them. Valois's words matched The Hutin's most secret desires; but he would never have dared to be the first to express them. An accomplice was proposing himself who would relieve him of everything, even of speech, even of thought.

'You have promised me, Nephew, that you would surrender Marigny to me the day you have a Pope,' said Valois.

'I can give you him just as well, Uncle, the day I become a widower,' replied The Hutin.

Valois passed his ringed hands across his large cheeks and went on in a low voice, 'You must give me Marigny first, because he commands all the fortresses and forbids entry into Château-Gaillard.'

'Very well,' replied Louis X. 'He forfeits my protection. You can tell Chancellor de Mornay to give me any orders you think proper for signature.'

That very night, after the supper hour, when Enguerrand de Marigny was alone and preparing the memorandum he intended handing the King, demanding the right to challenge, that is to say the right to demand single combat with any person who dared maintain that he was a traitor or a perjuror, Hugues de Bouville came to see him. The old Grand Chamberlain of Philip the Fair seemed a prey to conflicting emotions, and his message seemed to be weighing upon him.

'Enguerrand,' he said, 'do not sleep in your own house tonight, they intend to arrest you; I know it from a sure source.'

He again addressed Marigny familiarly in the second person as he had done when his old friend had begun life in his household as an equerry.

'They won't dare,' replied Marigny. 'And who will come to arrest me, I ask you? Alain de Pareilles? Alain would never accept such an order. He would be more likely to withstand a siege in my house with his archers than allow a hair of my head to be touched.'

'You are wrong not to believe me, Enguerrand, and
you have made a mistake also, I assure you, in acting as you
have these last months. When you are placed as we are, to
act against the King, whatever the King may be like, is to act
against oneself. And I, too, am in process of acting against the
King at this moment out of the friendship I bear you and
because I wish to save you.'

The fat man was sincerely unhappy. His goodwill was
touching. A loyal servant of the sovereign, a faithful friend, an
official of integrity, respecting both the laws of God and those
of the kingdom, how was it, animated as he was by such
honest sentiments, that his voice lacked authority?

'What I have come to tell you, Enguerrand,' he went on,
'I have from Monseigneur Philippe of Poitiers who is your
only supporter at this hour. Monseigneur of Poitiers wishes
to place some distance between you and the barons whose
anger you have aroused. He has counselled his brother to
send you to govern some distant land, Cyprus for example.'

'Cyprus?' cried Marigny. 'What, allow myself to be shut
up in an island in the far seas, when I have governed the
whole kingdom of France? Am I to be exiled there? I shall
continue to walk the streets of Paris as a master, or I shall
die in them.'

Bouville sadly shook his black-and-white locks.

'Believe me,' he repeated, 'do not sleep at home tonight.
Whatever may happen, I at least will not have to reproach
myself with having failed to warn you.'

As soon as Bouville had gone, Enguerrand went and
discussed the visit with his wife and his sister-in-law, Dame
de Chanteloup. The two women were also of the opinion

that it would be wise to leave at once for one of the Norman provinces and then, from there, if the danger became obvious, go to a port and take refuge with the King of England, who was devoted to Marigny.

But Enguerrand flew into a rage.

'Good God,' he cried, 'have I no one but women and eunuchs about me!'

And then he went to bed as usual. He stroked his favourite dog, was undressed by his valet, watched him wind up the weight of the clock, still a rare possession in those days, for which he had paid a great sum. He turned over in his mind the last phrases of his memorandum, which he intended finishing the following morning, then went to the window, drew aside the curtain and gazed out at the roofs of the dark city. The night watch were passing down the Rue des Fossés-Saint-Germain, repeating every twenty paces, in their mechanical voices, 'This is the watch! . . . It is midnight . . . Sleep in peace! . . .'

As usual they were a quarter of an hour late by the clock.

Enguerrand was woken up at dawn by a loud noise of trampling in his courtyard, and by a knocking on his door. A panic-stricken equerry came to warn him that the archers were below. He sent for his clothes, dressed hurriedly and, at the top of the stairs, ran into his wife and son who were hurrying to him.

'You were right, Jeanne,' he said to his wife, kissing her forehead; 'I have never listened to you sufficiently in the whole of my life. You must leave this very day with Louis.'

'I would have gone with you, Enguerrand, but now I cannot leave the place where you will be made to suffer.'

'King Louis is my godfather,' said Louis de Marigny; 'I shall go at once to Vincennes.'

'Your godfather is weak-minded and the crown sits rather loose upon his head,' replied Marigny angrily.

Then, as it was dark upon the staircase, he cried, 'Hi there, footmen. Bring lights! Light up!'

And when his servants had come running, he descended the staircase surrounded by their torches like a king.

The courtyard was swarming with men-at-arms. In the doorway a tall figure in a coat of mail was etched sharply against the grey of early morning.

'How could you have consented to this, Pareilles? How could you have dared?' said Marigny, spreading wide his hands.

'I am not Alain de Pareilles,' replied the officer. 'Messire de Pareilles is no longer in command of the archers.'

He moved aside to let a thin man in a dark cloak come forward. It was Chancellor Etienne de Mornay. As eight years earlier Nogaret had come in person to arrest the Grand Master of the Templars, Mornay came in person today to arrest the Rector of the kingdom.

'Messire Enguerrand,' he said, 'I pray you to follow me to the Louvre where I have orders to imprison you.'

At the same hour the majority of the great middle-class justiciars of the preceding reign, Raoul de Presles, Michel de Bourdenai, Guillaume Dubois, Geoffrey de Briançon, Nicole Le Loquetier, Pierre d'Orgemont, were arrested at their houses and taken to various prisons, some to be put to torture, while a detachment was sent to Châlons to arrest Bishop Pierre de Latille, the friend of Philip the Fair's youth, the man whom he had so much wished to see during his last hours.

With them the Iron King's whole reign was put in thrall.

4

The Night Without a Dawn

WHEN, IN THE MIDDLE of the night, Marguerite of Burgundy heard the drawbridge lowered at Château-Gaillard, and a sound of horses' hooves in the courtyards, she did not at first believe that these noises were real. She had waited so long, dreamed of this moment ever since, through the letter she had sent to the Count of Artois, she had accepted her disgrace and consented to the abrogation of all her rights, both for herself and for her daughter, in exchange for the promised freedom which never came!

Ten weeks had gone by, ten weeks of silence, more destructive than hunger, more exhausting than cold, more degrading than vermin, more testing than loneliness. Despair had entered into Marguerite's soul, had affected her nerves and weakened her body. These last days she no longer moved from her bed, a prey to a fever which caused her acute depression. Her only movement was to take the beaker of water placed on the floor beside her and raise it to her lips. Her eyes wide open to the shadows of the tower, she passed the hours listening to the too-rapid beating of her own heart; and then, if her fever abated, if her forehead became momentarily cool, if her heartbeats relaxed their rhythm, she suddenly sat up, screaming, with the appalling feeling that she was on the point of death. The silence was filled with nonexistent sounds; the shadows were peopled with tragic memories which were spiritual rather than physical. Her reason was giving way under the delirium of insomnia. Philippe d'Aunay, the handsome Philippe, was not altogether dead; he stood beside her, his legs broken, his body bleeding; she held out her arms to him, unable to seize him. Nevertheless, lying there as she did, he seemed to be leading her along the path which leads from this world to God, though she was no longer aware of the world, nor able to see God. And this intolerable progress seemed to stretch out before her to infinity, to the Day of Judgement; perhaps indeed this was purgatory.

'Blanche!' she cried. 'Blanche! Here they are!'

Locks, bolts, and the hinges of doors were creaking in reality at the bottom of the tower; numerous footsteps sounded on the stone treads of the stairs.

'Blanche! Do you hear them?'

But Marguerite's weakened voice could not reach her cousin through the heavy door which, at night, separated the two storeys of their prison.

The light of a single candle dazzled the imprisoned Queen. Men were crowding through the doorway in numbers Marguerite could not compute; she saw only the giant in the red cloak, his clear eyes and his silver dagger, as he came towards her.

'Robert!' she murmured. 'Robert, you have come at last!'

Behind the Count of Artois a soldier was carrying a chair on his head which he placed by Marguerite's bed.

'Well, well, Cousin,' said Robert, sitting down. 'You do not appear to be in a very good state of health, and from what I can see and hear you are suffering from . . .'

'From everything,' said Marguerite. 'I no longer know whether I am dead or alive.'

'It was time I came. Everything will soon be over; you'll see. I have good news for you: your enemies are destroyed. Are you strong enough to write?'

'I don't know,' said Marguerite.

Artois, telling them to bring the light nearer, gazed attentively at the ravaged, haggard face, with its thin lips, its sunken, too-bright dark eyes, the hair plastered by fever across the prominent brow.

'Perhaps you can at least manage to dictate the letter the King wants. Chaplain!' he called, snapping his fingers.

A white robe with above it a blue, shaven crown came out of the shadows.

'Has my marriage been annulled?' asked Marguerite.

'How can it have been, Cousin, since you refused to do what you were asked?'

'I have not refused,' she said. 'I accepted . . . I accepted everything. I don't understand you any more. I don't know what you are talking about.'

'Fetch a jug of wine to give her strength,' said Artois, turning his head.

Someone left the room and his steps could be heard upon the stairs.

'You must make an effort, Cousin,' went on Artois. 'This is the moment when you must accept what I am going to say.'

'But I wrote to you, Robert; I wrote to you so that you might tell Louis everything you asked, that my daughter was not his . . .'

The world seemed to spin round her.

'When?' asked Robert.

'Ten weeks ago, ten weeks in which I have waited for you to free me.'

'To whom did you give the letter?'

'To Bersumée, of course.'

And suddenly Marguerite thought, panic-stricken, 'Did I really write? It's appalling, I can no longer remember. I can no longer remember anything.'

'Ask Blanche,' she murmured.

But at that moment there was a great noise at her side; Robert of Artois had risen to his feet, he had seized someone and was shaking him by the collar, shouting at the top of his voice. How his shouts reverberated in Marguerite's ears and echoed in her head!

'But I took it, Monseigneur. I took it myself,' replied Bersumée in a terrified voice.

'Where did you take it? To whom did you give it?'

'Let me go, Monseigneur, let me go, you're throttling me. I gave the letter to Monseigneur de Marigny. That was the order I received.'

There was the dull sound of a body hitting the wall.

'Is my name Marigny? When you are given a letter for me, must you give it to someone else?'

'He promised me, Monseigneur, that he would send it to you.'

'Fellow, I'll settle your account later,' said Artois. Then, turning back to Marguerite, he said, 'I never received your letter, Cousin. Marigny must have kept it.'

'Oh, well!' she said.

She was almost reassured. At least she knew now that she had written the letter.

At that moment Sergeant Lalaine came in, carrying the jug of wine. Robert of Artois watched Marguerite drink it.

'It might, really, have been easier if I had brought poison,' he thought; 'it was stupid not to have thought of it . . . she could have taken it in this . . . it's a pity, a pity I didn't know. Now it's too late; moreover, in her present state she cannot in any case have many days to live.'

He felt detached, almost sad. There was no battle to fight any more. There he sat, massive, his hands on his thighs, surrounded by soldiers armed to the teeth, before the pallet upon which a young woman lay in a state of exhaustion. Had he been able to hate her enough when she was Queen of Navarre and heiress to the throne of France? Had he not done everything he could to destroy her, travelling here and there, intriguing, spending money, combining against her in the English Court as well as the Court of France? He had hated her when she was powerful; he had desired her when she was beautiful. Even last winter, powerful baron that he was, she had still dominated him though she was no more than a miserable prisoner. Now the Count of Artois found that his triumph had led him further than he wished to go. The mission with which he had been charged by Valois, because he could trust no one else, was somewhat against the grain. He felt no pity, only the indifference of disgust, and a bitter weariness. So much force brought against a sick, defenceless, wasted body! Hate died in Robert because it no longer had an object which could measure up to his strength.

And indeed he sincerely regretted that the letter abstracted by Marigny had never reached him. Marguerite would have been shut up in a convent. It couldn't be helped; it was too late; the dice were thrown and things must be as they must.

'You see, Cousin,' he said, 'to what extent Marigny is your enemy and how he has plotted everything from the start. If it were not for him, you would never have been accused, nor would your husband, Louis, have treated you in this fashion. Marigny has done everything he could, since Louis became King, to keep you here, as he has done everything to bring about the destruction of the kingdom. But today, as you have heard, the wicked man has been arrested and I have come to hear your grievances against him so that both the King's justice and your pardon may be hastened on.'

'What must I say?' asked Marguerite.

She had raised her hand to her neck, because the wine she had drunk made her heart beat still faster and she felt as if her breast were about to burst open.

'I shall dictate on your behalf to the Chaplain,' said Robert; 'I know what you must say.'

The Chaplain sat on the floor, the writing-tablet upon his knees, the candle beside him illuminating the three faces from below.

'Sire, my Husband,' began Robert slowly so that he would not forget any of the text composed by Charles of Valois,

'I am dying of sorrow and sickness. I pray you to accord me your pardon, for if you do not do so quickly, I feel that I have but a little time to live and that my soul is taking wings from my body. Everything that has happened is the fault of Messire de Marigny, who wished to destroy me in your estimation and in that of the late King by a denunciation whose falsity I swear, and who by appalling treatment has . . .'

'A moment, Monseigneur,' said the Chaplain.

He had taken his scraper in his hand to smooth a roughness on the parchment.

'. . . reduced me,' continued Robert, 'to the miserable condition in which I now am. Everything is due to that wicked man. I pray you once again to save me from the condition in which I am, and I assure you that I have never ceased to be your obedient wife under the will of God.'

Marguerite raised herself a little on her pallet. She could not understand by what extraordinary contradiction it was now intended, after a year in prison, to make her appear innocent.

'But, Cousin,' she asked, 'what of the confessions that have been asked of me?'

'They are no longer necessary, Cousin,' replied Robert, 'and what you will sign now cancels everything else.'

What Charles of Valois needed at this time was the multiplication of every possible false accusation against Enguerrand. This one was of that nature, and had more-over the advantage of white-washing, in appearance at least, the King's honour, and above all of getting the Queen to announce her own death. Clearly Monseigneur of Valois was a man of considerable imagination!

'And Blanche,' she asked, 'what is to happen to her? Has anyone thought of Blanche?'

'You need have no anxiety,' said Robert. 'Everything possible will be done for her.'

And Marguerite wrote her name at the bottom of the parchment.

Robert of Artois then rose and leant over her. Upon a signal from him the others had retired to the end of the room. The giant placed his hand on Marguerite's shoulders, close to her neck.

At the contact of his huge hand, Marguerite felt a glowing, assuaging warmth envelop her body. She placed her emaciated hands upon Robert's fingers as if she feared he would withdraw them too quickly.

'Goodbye, Cousin,' he said. 'Goodbye. I wish you quiet repose.'

'Robert,' she asked in a low voice, seeking his eyes, 'the last time you came and wished to take me, did you really desire me?'

No man is completely bad; the Count of Artois at that moment said one of the only kind things that had ever issued from his lips, 'Yes, my beautiful Cousin, I loved you very much.'

He felt her relax under his hands, calm, almost happy. To be loved, to be desired, had been the one important thing in the Queen's life, much more so than crowns and dignities.

It was with a kind of gratitude that she saw her cousin fade before her with the light; so huge was he that there seemed to be a quality of unreality about him, making one think, as he faded into the shadows, of the invincible heroes out of the misty legends of the Round Table.

The white robe of the Dominican and Bersumée's steel helmet passed out before Robert, who drove everyone before him. For one moment he stopped upon the threshold, as if he were subject to an instant's hesitation, as if he still had something more to say. Then the door closed, the room relapsed into darkness and Marguerite, wondering, heard none of the usual sounds of locks. She was no longer to be a prisoner, and this omission, the first in three hundred and fifty days, was like a promise of freedom.

Tomorrow she would be allowed to go down and wander about Châteaud-Gaillard as she pleased; and then, soon, a litter would arrive to carry her away among trees, towns and human beings. 'Will I be able to get up?' she wondered. 'Will I have the strength? Oh, yes, my strength will come back!'

Her arms seemed to be burning, but she would get well, she knew that she would get well. She knew, too, that she would not be able to sleep again that night. But she had so much hope to keep her company till dawn broke!

Suddenly she heard a tiny sound, hardly a sound, the sort of faint rustle in silence that is made by a release of breath by a human being. Someone was in the room.

'Blanche!' she cried. 'Is that you?'

Perhaps the door between the two storeys had also been unlocked. But she could remember no sound of creaking hinge. And why should her cousin have taken so much care to come to her silently? Unless . . . but no, Blanche had not gone suddenly as mad as that. Besides, she had seemed better these last days, since the spring had come.

'Blanche!' repeated Marguerite in an anguished voice.

But silence fell once more, and for a moment Marguerite thought that her fever was conjuring up presences in the darkness. But, a moment later, she again heard the same sound of breathing, nearer, and a light scratching on the floor like that produced by a dog's claws. Someone was breathing beside her. Perhaps it was really a dog. Bersumée's dog, which had followed him in and been forgotten; or rats perhaps, rats with their almost human running to and fro, their rustling, their complicated busyness, their curious habit of working at mysterious tasks throughout the night. On several occasions there had been rats in the tower, and it was in fact Bersumée's dog that had killed them. But you cannot hear rats breathe.

Panic-stricken, she sat up quickly on her pallet; there was a rattle of iron against the stone of the wall. With wide despairing eyes she sought to pierce the darkness around her. It was to the left, it was coming from the left.

'Who's there?' she cried.

There was silence once more. But she knew that she was no longer alone. She, too, was holding her breath now. She was aware of such panic as she had never felt before. In a few moments she was about to die; she was utterly certain of it, and still worse perhaps than the fear of death was the agony of not knowing the guise it would take, what part of her body would be attacked, whose this invisible presence was, closing in upon her along the wall.

A heavy weight suddenly hurled itself upon the bed. Marguerite uttered a cry that Blanche of Burgundy, on the storey above, heard across the night and was never to forget.

The cry was abruptly broken off by the sheet being placed across Marguerite's mouth. Two hands had seized the Queen of France and were twisting the sheet about her throat.

Her head resting against a man's broad chest, her arms flailing the air and all her body twisting in an effort of release, Marguerite's breath came in stifled gasps. The sheet round her neck grew tighter like a collar of burning lead. She was suffocating. She felt her eyes burning; she heard huge bronze bells ringing behind her temples. But the killer had a technique all his own; the bell-ropes suddenly broke in a great cracking of vertebrae and Marguerite was plunged into the shadowy gulf, infinite in space and time.

A few minutes later, in the courtyard of Château-Gaillard, Robert of Artois, who was whiling away the time drinking a goblet of wine and pretending to issue orders, saw his valet Lormet come up to his horse as if to tighten the girths.

'It is done, Monseigneur,' murmured Lormet.

'You have left no trace?' asked Robert in a low voice.

'None, Monseigneur. I put everything back in its place.'

'Not so easy without a light.'

'You know well, Monseigneur, that I can see in the dark.'

Having hoisted himself into the saddle, Artois signed to Bersumée to approach.

'I have not found Madame Marguerite at all well,' he said to him, 'I very much fear, from her condition, that she will not survive the week, perhaps not even tomorrow. Should she die, your orders are to come to Paris as fast as a horse can gallop and go direct to Monseigneur of Valois to give him the news. To Monseigneur of Valois, you understand? And this time try to make no mistake in the address. And no loose talk;

don't think, you're not paid to. And remember that your Monseigneur de Marigny is in prison, and that there might be a vacancy for you on the same gallows.'

Dawn was beginning to break over the forest of Andelys, marking with a faint glow, somewhere between grey and pink, the horizon formed by the trees. Below Château-Gaillard the river glistened faintly.

Descending the hill, Robert of Artois felt the regular movement of his horse's shoulders beneath him, and its warm flanks quivering against his boots. He filled his lungs with deep breaths of the morning air.

'All the same, it's good to be alive,' he murmured.

'Yes, it's good, Monseigneur,' replied Lormet. 'And what's more it's going to be a fine, sunny day.'

5

A Morning of Death

DESPITE THE NARROWNESS OF the window, Marigny could see between the thick bars, let into the stone in the form of a cross, the sumptuous backcloth of the sky in which shone the April stars.

He did not wish to sleep. He hung upon the noises of Paris, as if hearing them gave him assurance of still being alive; but they were few; the cry of the watchman, the bell of a neighbouring convent, the rumbling of country wagons bringing their loads to the vegetable market. This city, whose streets he had widened, whose buildings he had embellished, whose riots he had suppressed, this living city in which one felt the pulse of the kingdom ceaselessly beating and which, because of it, had been for sixteen years at the centre of his thoughts and cares, and for the last fortnight hated by him as one hates a human being.

This feeling had begun upon that morning when Charles of Valois, fearing that Marigny might find accomplices at the

Louvre, of which he had been Captain, had decided to trans-
fer him to the tower of the Temple. On horseback, surrounded
with Sergeants-at-Arms and archers, Marigny had thus
crossed a great part of the capital and had suddenly discovered
that the population who, for so many years, had bowed down
as he passed by, hated him. The insults hurled at him, the
outbursts of joy in the streets as he passed, the raised fists, the
mockery, the laughter, the threats of death, all these had been
for the late Rector of the Kingdom a disillusionment more
serious perhaps than his arrest itself.

When one has governed men for a long time, when one
has thought that one has acted for the best, when one knows
the pains the task has entailed, and then suddenly sees that
one has never been either loved or understood, but merely
submitted to, then one is overwhelmed with bitterness, and
wonders whether one could not have found some better way
of spending one's life.

The following days had been no less terrible. Taken back
to Vincennes, not this time to sit among the dignitaries of
the kingdom, but to appear before a tribunal of barons and
prelates, among whom was his own brother the Archbishop,
Enguerrand de Marigny had had to listen to a lawyer named
Jean d'Asnières read, upon the order of Charles of Valois,
the interminable grounds of indictment; peculation, treason,
embezzlement, secret relations with the enemies of the
kingdom.

Enguerrand had asked permission to speak; it had been
refused. He had demanded the right to single combat; it
also had been refused. It was therefore clear that from now
on he was considered guilty without even being allowed to

defend himself, as if a dead man were brought to judgement.

And when Enguerrand had turned his eyes upon his brother Jean, expecting him at least to raise his voice in his defence, he had met nothing but a detached expression, shifty eyes, and beautiful fingers elegantly toying with the embroidered bands which fell from his mitre upon his shoulders. If even his brother were abandoning him, if even his brother had ranged himself with so much cynicism in the ranks of his enemies, how could he expect from anyone else, even from those who owed their place and their wealth to him, any gesture of justice or gratitude?

Philippe of Poitiers, doubtless chagrined to see that Enguerrand had paid no attention to the warning he had sent him by Bouville, was not present at the session.

Marigny had been brought back from Vincennes amid the shouts of the crowd, who now blamed him at the tops of their voices as responsible for poverty and famine. Then he had been imprisoned in the Temple once more, but this time in irons, and in the same cell that had once been Jacques de Molay's prison.

The ring fixed to the wall was the same to which for seven years the Grand Master of the Order of Templars' chain had been riveted. The damp had not yet obliterated the lines drawn upon the stone by the old knight to mark the passing of the days.

'Seven years! We condemned him to pass seven years here, only to burn him afterwards. And I, who have been here but seven days,' Marigny had thought, 'I can already understand what he must have suffered.'

The statesman, from the pinnacle where he exercises

his power, protected by the whole apparatus of police force and army, feeling as he does that his person is physically unattainable, condemns abstractions when he pronounces sentences of imprisonment or death. They are not men whom he tortures or annihilates; they are oppositions which he is reducing, symbols which he is erasing. Nevertheless, Marigny remembered the disquiet he had felt while the Templars were being burnt on the Island of Jews, and how at that moment he had understood that it was human beings who were involved, that is to say people like himself, and not only principles or errors. On that day, though he had not dared show it, even blaming himself for his weakness, he had felt a certain empathy with the condemned, and had been frightened for himself. 'We have indeed all been accursed for what we did that day.'

And then, a third time, Marigny had been taken to Vincennes, to be present at the most appalling display of baseness. As if all the accusations brought against him were not sufficient, as if there was still in the conscience of the kingdom certain doubts which must at all costs be allayed, they had accused him of extravagant crimes, to establish which an incredible number of false witnesses had been brought forward.

Charles of Valois prided himself upon having discovered in time a monstrous plot of sorcery. Madame de Marigny and her sister, the Dame de Chanteloup, instigated by Enguerrand of course, had cast spells and pierced with needles waxen dolls representing the King, the Count of Valois himself and the Count de Saint-Pol. At least, this was affirmed by people who came from the Rue des Bourdonnais where the business of magic was carried on with the tolerance of the police to whom they served as informers. Accomplices were named: a lame woman, a creature of the devil, and a certain Padiot, who had been caught in some similar affair, were sent to their deaths for it, a fate to which they would in any case have been condemned.

After which it had been announced, to the great horror of the Court, that Marguerite of Burgundy was dead and, as a last piece of evidence against Marigny, the letter she had written from her prison and sent to the King was produced.

'She has been murdered!' Marigny cried.

But the men who were guarding him had suddenly pulled him down, while Jean d'Asnières completed his indictment with this new evidence.

In vain had King Edward II of England intervened with a message, endeavouring to put pressure upon his brother-in-law of France to spare the late Coadjutor of Philip the Fair; in vain had Louis de Marigny thrown himself at his godfather's, The Hutin's, feet, asking for mercy and justice. Louis X, repeating before the Court the words he had uttered to his uncle, had said, indicating Marigny, 'He forfeits my protection.'

And Enguerrand had heard himself condemned to be hanged, his wife imprisoned and all his goods confiscated. While Jeanne de Marigny and the Dame de Chanteloup were arrested and imprisoned in the Temple, Marigny was himself transferred to a third prison, the Châtelet, for Valois had remembered that his enemy had also been an administrator of the Temple. Valois saw accomplices everywhere, and feared right up to the last that vengeance might escape him.

It was, therefore, from a cell in the Châtelet that Marigny, during the night of April 30th, 1315, watched the sky through a narrow window.

He was not afraid of death, at least he compelled himself to accept the inevitable. But the memory of the curse obsessed his mind; before appearing in the presence of God, he needed to have resolved for himself the question of whether he were guilty or innocent.

'Why? Why were we all accused, those named and even those not named, merely because we were present? After all, we acted only for the good of the kingdom, for the majesty of the Church and for the purity of the Faith. So why should heaven have turned so furiously upon each of us?'

When he was but a few hours from his own execution, his mind returned to the various stages of the Templars' case, as if it were in this rather than in any of the other public or private actions of his long life that lay hidden, somewhere or other, the ultimate explanation, the ultimate justification he wished to find before dying. And treading slowly the stair of memory, he suddenly arrived at a threshold where light broke and all became clear.

The curse did not come from God. It emanated from himself and had no other source but in his own actions; and this was true of every man and of every punishment.

'The Templars became strangers to their rule; they ceased to serve Christianity in order to busy themselves with trade and finance; vices crept in among their ranks; their curse lay in that, and it was just that they should be suppressed. But in order to have done with the Templars, in order that he might condemn them on false charges, I made my brother

Archbishop, and he was both ambitious and treacherous. It is therefore not surprising that my brother should have turned against me and has betrayed me when he might perhaps have been able to save me. I should not blame him; it is I who am to blame ... It was certainly a good thing for France to have a French Pope, but because this Pope, in order to get elected, surrounded himself with cardinals who were alchemists and avid, not for virtue, but for the manufacture of gold, he died of the powdered emeralds which the alchemists made him swallow. Because Nogaret tortured too many innocent people in order to extract the confessions he required, thinking them necessary for the public good, his enemies poisoned him in the end ... Because Marguerite of Burgundy was married for political reasons to a prince she did not love she betrayed her marriage, and because she betrayed it she was discovered and imprisoned. Because I burnt the letter which might have released King Louis from his marriage, I condemned Marguerite and condemned myself at the same time ... Because Louis had her assassinated and accused me of the crime, what will happen to him? What will happen to Charles of Valois who is going to have me hanged this morning for invented crimes? What will happen to Clémence of Hungary if she consents to marry a murderer in order to be Queen of France? ... Even when we are punished for the wrong reasons, there is always a real cause for our punishment. Every unjust act, even committed for the sake of a just cause, carries its curse with it.'

When he had discovered these things, Enguerrand de Marigny ceased to hate anyone or to hold others responsible for his fate. He had made his act of contrition, but one valuable in a way different from those made by means of muttered prayers. He felt a great peace, and as if he were at one with God in the acceptance that his destiny should be accomplished in this way.

He remained calm till dawn broke, and had no impression of a descent from the luminous threshold to which his meditations had led him.

At seven o'clock he heard a great tumult beyond the walls. When he saw the Provost of Paris, the Sheriff and the Procurator come in, he got slowly to his feet and waited for his irons to be removed. He took the scarlet cloak which he had been wearing on the day of his arrest, and covered his shoulders with it. He had a strange feeling of strength, and constantly repeated to himself the truth which he had discovered, 'Every unjust act, even committed for a just cause . . .'

He was made to get into a wagon drawn by four horses, and went on his way, escorted by the archers and sergeants-at-arms, by the very men he had commanded, who now were leading him to execution.

To the howling mob closely lining the whole length of the Rue Saint-Denis Marigny, standing upright, replied in the same manner as he would have received their acclamation, 'Good people, pray for me.'

At the corner of the Rue Saint-Denis the procession halted before the convent of the Filles-Dieu. Marigny was made to get out of the wagon and was led into the courtyard of the convent, to the foot of a wooden crucifix placed upon a plinth. 'It is right,' he thought; 'this is what always happens, but I was never present to see it. And how many men have I condemned to death? I have had sixteen years of happiness and riches to reward me for the good I have been able to do, sixteen days of unhappiness and one morning of death to punish me for the harm. God is still merciful.'

At the foot of the crucifix the chaplain to the convent recited above the kneeling Marigny the prayers for the dying. Then the nuns brought the condemned man a glass of wine and three pieces of bread which he slowly ate, appreciating for the last time the taste of this world's food. Beyond the walls the crowd continued to shout for his death. 'The bread they will shortly be eating,' thought Marigny, 'will seem less good to them than that which I have just been given.'

Then the procession set off again by the Faubourg Saint-Martin, and at last, standing upon a mound, the gibbet of Montfaucon came into sight.

It was a huge square construction, erected upon twelve huge blocks of uncut stone forming the foundations of a platform which was itself surmounted by sixteen pillars and covered with a roof. In the interior, the gallows were arranged in a row. The pillars were joined by double beams and iron chains, to which the bodies of the condemned were attached after execution. They were left there to rot at the mercy of the wind and the crows, so as to serve as an example and impress the population with salutary thoughts. On that particular day there were some ten bodies hanging up, some already almost skeletons, others beginning to decompose within their clothes, their faces green or black, appalling discharges oozing from their ears and mouths, and fragments of flesh, torn off by the beaks of birds, hanging down upon their clothes. An appalling stench hung about them.

It was Marigny himself who, a few years earlier, had had this fine, new, solid gibbet built to purify the city's morals. And it was there that he himself was sent to his death. Never had destiny, in one sense, provided a better example of poetic justice than sending the judge to end his life upon the same gibbet as the public malefactors.

When Marigny got out of the wagon, the accompanying priest urged him to confess the crimes for which he had been condemned.

'No, Father,' said Marigny with great dignity.

He denied having cast any spell upon the King, denied having robbed the Treasury, denied all the heads of the charges brought against him, and asserted that the deeds for which he was blamed had all been either commanded or approved by the late King.

'But for the sake of just causes I have committed unjust acts,' he said.

And saying these words he looked at the corpses hanging above him.

The crowd was shouting so loud that he placed his hands over his ears as if he was prevented from thinking. Preceded by the executioner, he walked up the stone ramp which gave on to the platform and, with that authority which had always been his, asked, indicating the gibbet, 'Which one?'

As if from a stage, he glanced for the last time upon the innumerable crowd in which women were screaming hysterically, children hiding their heads in their fathers' cloaks, and men shouting, 'A good job too! He has robbed us enough! And now he's paying for it!' Marigny demanded that his hands should be untied.

'Let no one hold me.'

He himself raised his hair and placed his bull-like head in the noose they held out to him. He took a deep breath, as if to preserve life as long as possible in his lungs, clenched his hands, and the rope raised him slowly into the air.

The crowd, which had been awaiting nothing else, nevertheless uttered a loud cry of astonishment. For several minutes he twisted there, his eyes bulging, his face turning first blue and then violet, his tongue protruding and his arms and legs moving as if he were trying to climb an invisible mast. At last his arms fell to his sides, the convulsions grew less and less and then stopped and his eyes grew sightless.

The crowd fell silent, surprised as always by its own attitude, terrified by its own complicity. The executioners took down the body, dragged it by the feet across the platform and suspended it, in its fine aristocratic clothes, in the place of honour which was its due, upon the front of the gibbet, to let one of the greatest ministers France ever had rot there.

6

The Fall of a Statue

AT MONTFAUCON IN THE darkness, as the chains creaked in
the wind, thieves that night took down the illustrious corpse
and stripped it of its clothes; when dawn broke, Marigny's
body was found lying naked upon the stones.

Monseigneur of Valois, who was told immediately as he
still lay in bed, ordered that it should be dressed and hung up
again. Then he himself dressed and came downstairs. Feeling
peculiarly lively, more so than ever, he went in all pride of his
strength to mingle with the coming and going of the town,
with the trafficking of men, with the power of kings.

He arrived at the Palace and there, accompanied by Canon
Etienne de Mornay, his old Chancellor, whom he had now
made Keeper of the Seals of France, he went to take up
his position at an interior window which opened upon the
Mercers' Hall, so as to feast himself upon a sight for which he
had longed for many years. Beneath him the crowd of merchants and loungers were watching four masons at work upon

a scaffolding. They were taking down the statue of Enguerrand de Marigny. It was well fixed to the wall, not only by
its base, but by the back. Larger than life, it did not seem to
wish to leave its niche or come away from the Palace. Picks
and chisels chipped the stone. White splinters flew about
the masons.

'Monseigneur, I have finished taking an inventory of
Marigny's possessions,' said Etienne de Mornay. 'The total is
pretty large.'

'Then the King will be able to reward those who have
served him well in this matter,' said Valois. 'I insist that in the
first place my lands of Gaillefontaine, which the rascal tricked
me into exchanging to my disadvantage, should be returned
to me. And then my son Philippe is old enough to have his
own establishment outside my house and his own personal
household. This will be a good opportunity; you will tell
the King so. The house in the Rue d'Autriche, or that in the
Rue des Fossés-Saint-Germain, would do very well indeed.
Perhaps that in the Rue d'Autriche would be best. I know, too,
that my nephew wishes to give some reward to Henriet de
Meudon, who opens his baskets of doves and whom he calls
huntsman. Oh, and don't forget that thirty-five thousand
pounds of the revenues of the County of Beaumont are due to
Monseigneur of Artois. I think this is the moment to give him
some of it, if not all.'

'The King will have to make expensive presents to his
new wife,' continued the Chancellor, 'and he seems to have
decided, in his present state of amorousness, upon making
the greatest possible gestures of liberality, though the Treasury is in no state to meet them. Could we not take the

presents for the new Queen from Marigny's possessions?'

'That is well thought of, Mornay. Apportion them in this way to show the King, placing my niece of Hungary at the head of the beneficiaries,' replied Charles of Valois, without taking his eyes off the masons.

'Of course, Monseigneur,' said the Chancellor, 'I ask nothing for myself.'

'And in that you are quite right, for malicious people might say that you wished to get rid of Marigny only so as to profit from his possessions. Make my share a little larger, and I will myself give you what you deserve.'

The back of the statue was now completely freed from the wall; the marble torso was bound with cords and the winches began to turn. Suddenly Valois placed his ringed hand upon the Chancellor's arm.

'Do you know, Mornay, I feel a most extraordinary sensation? I have the impression that I am going to miss Marigny.'

Mornay looked at the King's uncle with surprise. He didn't understand what Valois meant, and Valois himself could not have explained exactly what he felt. Hate creates links as strong as those of love, and when the enemy one has fought for a long time disappears, one feels an emptiness at the heart, the emptiness created by the end of every great passion.

Meanwhile, inside the Palace, Louis X, in his bedroom, was finishing being shaved. A few feet from him stood Dame Eudeline, beautiful, rosy and fresh, holding by the hand a rather skinny and frightened child of ten who did not know that the King before her was her father.

The Hutin had summoned the two Eudelines, mother and daughter. The head linen-maid of the Palace, much moved, and full of hope, waited for her royal lover to speak.

When the barber, having dried The Hutin's chin with a warm towel, had gone out, taking his platter, his unguents and his razors with him, the King of France rose to his feet, shook his long hair about his collar and said, 'It is true, is it not, Eudeline, that my people are pleased that I have hanged Marigny?'

'Certainly they are, Monseigneur Louis ... Sire, I mean to say,' she replied. 'There is a great feeling of happiness throughout the city this morning, and the people are singing in the spring sunshine. One might think that everyone's troubles were over.'

'That is how I wish it to be,' said Louis, interrupting her. 'I promised you to assure this child's future.'

Eudeline went down on her knees, and made the girl do the same, to receive the announcement of benefits which was to fall from the all-powerful lips.

'Sire,' murmured Eudeline, tears in her eyes, 'the child will bless you in her prayers till the end of her days.'

'Well, that is exactly what I have decided,' replied The Hutin, 'that she should pray! I want her to take the veil in the Convent of Saint-Marcel which is reserved for the daughters of nobles, and where she will be better off than anywhere else.'

Stupefaction and disappointment were apparent in the linen-maid's expression. The little Eudeline did not seem to have understood the King's words, nor even that it was her fate which was in question.

'Is that really what you wish for her, Sire? To shut her up in a convent?'

She had risen to her feet.

'It must be so, Eudeline,' Louis whispered in her ear; 'her features are too recognizable. Besides, it will be good for our salvation as for hers that she should atone by a life of piety the fault that we committed in bringing her into the world.[17] As for you . . .'

'Monseigneur Louis, are you proposing to shut me up in a cloister too?' said Eudeline aghast.

How much The Hutin had changed in a short time! She could see in this man who announced his orders so decisively no resemblance to the moody, disquieting adolescent who had made love with her for the first time, nor even to the unhappy prince, shivering with impotence and cold, whom she had warmed one night the previous winter. Only the eyes maintained their shifty look.

Louis hesitated. He was not ready to take every risk. He thought that the future was uncertain, and that he might once more have need of this beautiful, pliant and luxuriant body.

'As for you,' he said, 'I shall put you in charge of the furnishings and linen at Vincennes, to have everything ready for me whenever I come there.'

Eudeline shook her head. This exile from Paris, this sending of her to a secondary residence, seemed to her an offence. Was there dissatisfaction with the way she looked after the linen? In one sense she would have done better to accept the cloister. Her pride would have been less hurt.

'I am your servant and will obey you,' she replied coldly.

As she was leaving the room, she saw the portrait of Clémence of Hungary standing on a table.

'Is that her?' she asked.

'That is the next Queen of France,' he replied.

'Be happy then, Sire,' she said, going out. She had ceased to love him.

'Of course, of course, I am going to be happy,' Louis repeated to himself, walking up and down the room into which the sun streamed.

For the first time since he had become King he felt completely happy and certain of himself. He had had his wife murdered, and his father's Minister hanged; he had exiled his first mistress from the Palace and his natural daughter into a convent. He had cleared the path before him. He could now receive the beautiful Neapolitan princess, at whose side he already saw himself living a long and glorious reign.

He rang for his chamberlain.

'Let Messire de Bouville be summoned,' he said.

At this moment a loud crash was heard somewhere in the Palace from the direction of the Mercers' Gallery.

It was the statue of Enguerrand de Marigny which, taken from its plinth, had been lowered among cries of joy from all those present. The winches had turned too quickly, and the ton of marble had fallen heavily to the ground.

In the front row of the crowd, two men leant over the fallen colossus: Messire Spinello Tolomei and his nephew Guccio. Tolomei was not like Valois; his victory had no tinge of melancholy. His fat stomach had been shaking with fear for two weeks past, and he had slept well this last night for the first time, knowing that Marigny was hanged. He felt that it was a day for a generous action.

'Guccio *mio!*' he said, 'you have helped me well. I look upon you as my descendant exactly as if you were my son.

I wish to recompense you, to associate you still further with my business. What part of it do you wish to have? Have you any particular desires? Tell me, my boy, tell me what would please you.'

He expected that Guccio, as a respectful nephew, would reply, 'Decide yourself, Uncle.'

Guccio looked down his thin nose, lowered his black eyelids and replied, taking his opportunity, 'Uncle Spinello, I would like to have the branch at Neauphle for myself.'

'What!' cried Tolomei in surprise. 'Is that your ambition? A country branch, which functions with only three clerks who are ample for their task? Your ambition does not fly very high!'

'I am rather fond of that branch,' said Guccio, 'and I am sure that it can be expanded.'

'And I am perfectly certain,' said Tolomei, 'that there is a girl in the vicinity, because you seem to me to go to Neauphle more often than business can require. Is she beautiful?'

Before replying, Guccio looked at his uncle and saw that he was smiling.

'She is more beautiful than any other woman in the world, Uncle, and of noble family.'

'Goodness me!' cried Tolomei raising his hands. 'The daughter of a noble family? You will get yourself into great difficulties. The nobility, you must know, are always ready to take our money, but never to let their blood be mingled with ours. Does the family agree to this?'

'It will, Uncle, I know that it will. Her brothers treat me as one of themselves.'

'Are they rich?'

'They have a big manor, with wide lands around it and several villages of serfs that have not yet been freed. All this represents a considerable capital sum. And they are in very close relations with the Count of Dreux, their suzerain lord.'

Dragged by two draught horses, Marigny's statue had left the Mercers' Gallery. The masons were coiling their ropes and the crowd was dispersing.

'And what,' asked Tolomei, 'are these powerful lords, who are so fond of you that they are ready to give you their daughter, called?'

Guccio said the name so low that Tolomei could not hear it.

'Repeat it, I haven't heard it,' he said.

'The Squires of Cressay, Uncle,' said Guccio.

'Cressay ... Cressay ... the Squires of Cressay. Oh, of course, the people who still owe me three hundred pounds! That's your rich family, is it? I begin to understand.'

Guccio raised his head, ready to rebel, and the banker guessed that the matter was really serious.

'*La voglio, la voglio tanto bene!*' said Guccio, mingling the two languages in order to be the more convincing. 'And she loves me too; and to wish us to live without each other is to wish us dead! With the new profits that I shall make at Neauphle I shall be able to repair the manor, which is very fine I assure you, but which requires a certain amount of work upon it, and you will have a castle, Uncle, *un castello* like *un vero signore*.'

'Yes, yes,' said Tolomei, 'but I don't like the country. I had hoped for another alliance for you, with the daughter of our cousins Bardi for instance, which would have extended our business.'

He pondered a moment.

'But it is to love one's dear ones ill to try and make their happiness in spite of them,' he continued. 'Go, my boy! I give you the branch at Neauphle, on condition that you stay half the time at my side in Paris. And marry whom you wish. The Siennese are freemen, and one must choose one's wife according to the dictates of one's heart.'

'*Grazie, zio* Spinello, *grazie tante!*' said Guccio, throwing his arms round the banker's neck, 'and you'll see . . . you'll see . . .'

At that moment fat Bouville, coming from the King's presence, was descending the stairs and crossing the Mercers' Hall. He had that anxious air about him which he assumed for great events, and walked with the firm tread which he adopted when the sovereign had done him the honour of giving him a command.

'Ah, friend Guccio!' he cried, seeing the two Lombards. 'I am in luck to find you here. I was about to send an equerry to look for you.'

'What can I do to serve you, Messire Hugues?' said the young man. 'My uncle and myself are at your service.'

Bouville looked at Guccio in real friendship. They had happy memories in common and, in the presence of the boy, the old Great Chamberlain felt himself grow young again.

'Good news, yes, very good news indeed! I have told the King of your merits and how useful you were to me.'

The young man bowed as a sign of gratitude.

'Well, friend Guccio,' went on Bouville, 'we are going back to Naples!'

Historical Notes

1. At this time there existed two families of Burgundy, ruling over different territorial provinces; on the one hand, the ducal family, whose capital was at Dijon; on the other, the family of the Counts Palatine of Burgundy who, until the reign of Philip the Fair, were subject to the German Holy Roman Empire. Their principal residence was at Dôle.

   Marguerite of Burgundy was the daughter of the Duke and of Agnes of France, daughter of Saint Louis. She had married in 1305 Louis, eldest son of Philip the Fair and of Jeanne, Queen of Navarre.

   Jeanne and Blanche of Burgundy were daughters of the Count Palatine and of Mahaut of Artois. They had married respectively Philippe and Charles, the second and third sons of Philip the Fair.

   When Marguerite and Blanche had been convicted of adultery (as has been recounted in *The Iron King*), Jeanne of Burgundy had been accused only of being an accomplice and had been separately imprisoned in the castle of Dourdan, in far less harsh conditions and for an undetermined period.

2. Guillaume de Nogaret, a Knight of Languedoc, justiciar of Philip the Fair and Secretary-General of the kingdom, celebrated for his military expedition against Pope Boniface VIII, and for having led the judicial and penal action against the Order of the Knights Templar.

To Pope Clement V and the King of France he was joined in the curse pronounced by the Grand Master, He died soon afterwards, following the Pope by a few weeks, and preceding the King by a few months.

3. Since 1309 Robert of Artois had been claiming possession of the County of Artois, which had been given by a royal judgement to his aunt, the Countess Mahaut. He pursued this inheritance suit with rare tenacity for twenty years.

4. In the fourteenth century the principal officers of the Crown were as follows: The Constable of France, Supreme Commander-in-Chief of the Armies; the Chancellor of France, who was responsible for justice, held the seals, dealt with ecclesiastical affairs and what would today be called foreign affairs; the Sovereign Master of the King's Household, who ruled over everyone, whether nobleman or commoner, in the King's immediate service.

The Constable (*Connétable*) had of right a seat on the Inner Council of the King. He had a room at Court and accompanied the King whenever he travelled. Over and above his perquisites in kind, he was paid twenty-five pence *parisi* per day and ten pounds on every feast day in peacetime. In wartime, or when the King was travelling, his payment was doubled. For every day of fighting, when the King was actually with his armies, the Constable received an extra hundred pounds; everything taken in captured enemy castles or fortresses belonged to him, with the exception of gold and prisoners, which belonged to the King. Of the horses taken from the enemy he had first choice after the King. He had judicial powers over all the royal household. If the King were not present in person at the taking of a fortress, it was the Constable's banner that was hoisted upon it. He took part in the Coronation and carried the golden sword before the King. On the field of battle the King himself could not order a charge or an attack without having taken the advice and obtained the agreement of the Constable.

During the reign of Philip the Fair, of his three sons, and during the first year of the reign of Philip VI of Valois, the Constable of France was Gaucher de Châtillon, Count of Porcien, who was to die an octogenarian in 1329.

The Chancellor of France (*Chancelier de France*), assisted by a Vice-Chancellor and by lawyers who were clerics from the Chapelle Royale, was charged with formulating the royal Acts and affixing upon them the royal seal, which was in his keeping. He had his seat in the Inner Council and also in the Assembly of Peers. He was the head of the magistracy, presided over all judicial commissions, and spoke in the King's name at Parliamentary sessions. He was always an ecclesiastic; which explains why, during the last years of Philip the Fair's reign, no one officially bore the title. This came about because the

Archbishop who had been Chancellor in 1307 had refused to seal the order for the Templars' arrest, and Philip the Fair took the seals from his hands and gave them to Nogaret, who was not in holy orders. Nogaret, therefore, did not receive the title appropriate to his functions, and the title of Secretary-General to the kingdom was specially created for him, while the traditional prerogatives of the Chancellor were divided between Nogaret and Enguerrand de Marigny, who was made Coadjutor of the King and Rector-General of the kingdom. On January 1st, 1315, one month after Philip the Fair's death, the post of Chancellor once more received an incumbent in the person of Etienne de Mornay, Canon of Auxerre and Soissons, who had until then been Chancellor to the Count of Valois. He continued in office until Trinity 1316.

The Master of the Household (*Souverain Maître de l'Hôtel de la Maison du Roi*), later called the Grand Master of France, had under his orders the Bursar (*Argentier*) who was responsible for the accounts of the Royal Household, made purchases and kept the inventory of the furniture, hangings and wardrobe. He had a seat upon the Council.

Under them, among the great officers of the Crown, was the Grand Master of the Cross-Bowman (*Grand Maître des Arbalétriers*) who was under the Constable, the Grand Almoner (*Grand Aumônier*) and the Great Chamberlain (*Grand Chambellan*). The principal functions of the last was to care for the arms and clothing of the King, and to remain near him by day and night whenever the Queen was not with him. He had charge of the secret seal, could receive homage in the King's name and administer the oath of allegiance in his presence. He organized the ceremonies at which the King created new knights. He administered the Privy Purse and was present at the Court of Peers. As he was responsible for the royal wardrobe, he had jurisdiction over the mercers and all the various clothing trades. He had under his orders a functionary called the King of the Mercers (*Roi des Merciers*) who checked weights and measures, balances and gauges.

Finally, there were other posts whose titles derived from functions now in desuetude and which were at this date no more than honorific, though they gave access to the King's Council. Such were the posts of Grand Groom of the Chambers (*Grand Chambrier*), Grand Butler (*Grand Bouteiller*), and Grand Pantler (*Grand Panetier*), held respectively at the period we are dealing with by Louis I, Duke of Burgundy, by the Count of Saint-Pol, and by Bouchard de Montmorency.

5. At this period Paris was not yet the seat of an Archbishopric. The Diocese of Paris came under Sens which, from this fact, was politically the most important religious appointment in France. It was, therefore, the Archbishop of Sens whose duty it had been to preside at the Ecclesiastical Tribunal which had condemned the Templars of Paris, and it was to assure their condemnation that Enguerrand de Marigny had nominated his brother Jean for this preferment.

6. The quintain was an exercise on horseback with a lance which consisted in tilting at a body of a manikin attached

to a pivot. It represented a knight in armour, one of whose arms was fitted with a stick. If the player made a false hit, the manikin turned upon its pivot and hit the inexpert horseman.

7. The mysterious power attributed to the Kings of France of being able to cure scrofula by prayer and the laying on of hands was called the Royal Miracle. This power was transmitted from sovereign to sovereign upon the King's deathbed and in the presence only of his confessor (see *The Iron King*).

8. Mercers and the vendors of ornaments, finery and trinkets were privileged to sell their wares in the King's Palace in the Great Gallery called the Mercers' or Merchants' Hall.

9. Saint Louis of Anjou, Bishop of Toulouse, second son of King Charles II of Anjou (the Lame) and of Queen Marie of Hungary, who died in 1299, had renounced his rights to the throne of Naples in order to enter holy orders.

   This Anjou branch, like the Artois branch, was descended from a brother of Louis VIII of France. During its existence it collected two hundred and eight-nine crowns, as well as twelve beatifications.

   Charles of Valois had first married Marguerite of Anjou-Sicily, eleventh of the thirteen children of Charles the Lame and Marie of Hungary. He therefore found himself in the privileged position of being at once the grandson of one saint and the brother-in-law of another.

   The pretensions of the Anjous to the kingdom of Hungary, pretensions that were to triumph, issued from the marriage of Charles the Lame with Marie of Hungary, daughter of Etienne V and grand-daughter of Bela IV, of the Arpadien dynasty – a parallel marriage to that of Isabel of Anjou, sister of Charles the Lame, with Ladislas IV, brother to Marie. Ladislas IV, having died childless in 1290, Queen Marie claimed the throne of Hungary for her eldest son, Charles Martel, who bore the title but did not reign and who died in 1295, while the Hungarian lords preferred to him the King of Bohemia, Wenceslas, another grandson of King Bela IV.

It took another fifteen years of fighting and intrigue between Naples, Buda and the Holy See to make the Hungarian lords accept the son of Charles Martel, Charobert, whose sister Clémence was proposed to Louis X of France as his second wife.

It is to be remarked that Charles of Valois's second wife, Catherine de Courtenay, titular Empress of Constantinople, was also a member of the family of Anjou.

10. The habit of keeping a lighted lamp over one's bed all night lasted throughout the Middle Ages. It was a practice intended to keep away evil spirits.

11. From his marriage with Jeanne of Burgundy, Philippe of Poitiers had only daughters; as for Charles, who became Count of la Marche, his wife Blanche of Burgundy had only produced two children who were born dead. It is important to realize that at this period it had never been established that it was impossible for women to succeed to the throne of France, and for the simple reason that as yet no such case had arisen. During the three centuries of the first Capet dynasty, the Kings of France had always

had a son to whom to hand on their inheritance, and no accident had occurred to interrupt the normal devolution of the Crown, a fact pretty well without parallel in the history of dynasties. But there was nothing in law which excluded women from the succession or incapacitated them from reigning. The notorious Salic Law was drawn up and promulgated only during the years with which we are concerned and in circumstances that will be made clear in a future volume.

12. Jeanne of Burgundy (the Halt), sister of Marguerite of Burgundy (therefore of the ducal branch) and wife of Philippe of Valois, must not be confused with the other Jeanne of Burgundy, wife of Philippe of Poitiers. These two Jeannes, moreover, were both to become, separated by only ten years, Queens of France, one as the wife of Philippe V, and the other as the wife of Philippe VI.

It is to be remarked that, during this period, nearly all the women at the Court of France were called either Jeanne or Marguerite and the men Philippe, Charles or Louis, which does not make the historian's task any the easier and has frequently given rise to confusion.

13. The fighting between the Guelfs, partisans of the Pope, and the Ghibellines, partisans of the Emperor, bathed a whole section of medieval Italy, and particularly Tuscany, in blood.

Dante and the father of Petrarch, both Ghibellines, were exiled from Florence by Charles of Valois.

14. The importance accorded to relics was one of the most marked exterior signs of religion in the Middle Ages. Belief in the virtue of sacred relics degenerated into

universal and widespread superstition, everyone wishing to possess a large relic for their homes, and small ones to take with them on journeys attached to their necks. People had relics in proportion to their wealth. The trade in relics was most prosperous during the eleventh, twelfth and thirteenth centuries, even during the fourteenth. Everyone bought and sold these holy remains; abbots, in order to augment the revenues of their monasteries or acquire the favour of great personages, yielded up the fragments of the sainted bodies in their charge; crusaders returning from Palestine could make a fortune for themselves with the pious detritus collected on their expedition. The Jews had a huge international organization for the sale of relics. The goldsmiths encouraged the trade, because they received orders for shrines and reliquaries which were among the finest objects of the period and reflected the vanity as much as the piety of their possessors.

The most celebrated and most prized relics of the period were naturally pieces of the True Cross, fragments of the wood of the manger, the arrows of St Sebastian, and many stones as well, those from Calvary, the Holy Sepulchre, and the Mount of Olives. In France, for obvious reasons, the most prized were the relics of King Saint Louis, but they never left the circle of the royal family.

15. Roberto Oderisi was the most celebrated of the Giottesque Neapolitan painters, and was the one with the greatest local reputation of his time. His most celebrated works are the Crucifixion in the Church of St Francis of Assisi at Eboli, and particularly the frescoes of the Incoronata

at Naples which until recently were attributed to Giotto himself.

Having first come under the influence of Giotto, whose apprentice he was, he then came under the influence of Simone de Martino and finally became head of the Neapolitan school of the fourteenth century. In 1315 Giotto was wholly employed in painting the frescoes of the life of St Francis on the walls of the Santa Croce at Florence.

16. It was not yet the Palace of the Popes that we know. This was built in the following century.

17. This Eudeline, natural daughter of Louis X, and a nun in the Convent of the Clarisses of the Faubourg Saint-Marcel of Paris, was authorized by a Bull of Pope John XXII, of August 10th, 1330, to become Abbess of Saint-Marcel, or of any other convent of the Clarisses, in spite of her illegitimate birth.

NORTH
KINGDOM of ENGLAN
ENGLISH CHANNEL
Cherbourg
Brittany
Le Mans
Anjou
Poitou
BAY of BISCAY
Saintonge
KIN
Bordeaux
Gascony
Bearn